....

THE $IX TRILLION DOLLAR MAN
DOLLAR MAN

....

Cover and interior design by Emily Dueker

United States Capitol In Washington Dc © Kuosumo. BigStockPhoto.com
American Flag © AlexStar. BigStockPhoto.com
Stirling Castle © Jacqui3. BigStockPhoto.com
MOA Chair Back Abstract 2013 © Emily Dueker.
MOA Railings and Lights Abstract © Emily Dueker.
Duffys 2012 © Emily Dueker.

This is a work of fiction. The events described here are imaginary. The settings and characters are fictitious or used in a fictitious manner and do not represent specific places or living or dead people. Any resemblance is entirely coincidental.

Publisher: Inkwater Press | www.inkwaterpress.com

Paperback
ISBN-13 978-1-62901-023-6 | ISBN-10 1-62901-023-5
Kindle
ISBN-13 978-1-62901-024-3 | ISBN-10 1-62901-024-3

Printed in the U.S.A.
All paper is acid free and meets all ANSI standards for archival quality paper.

1 3 5 7 9 10 8 6 4 2

THE $IX TRILLION DOLLAR MAN

DOLLAR MAN

A STUART-BRUCE BOOK

JIM MOORE

Inkwater Press
Portland, Oregon

CONTENTS

ACKNOWLEDGEMENTS

Many thanks to my friend Dr. Norma Nielson at the University of Calgary for her help during the early days of writing *The Six Trillion Dollar Man*. Norma patiently read the first draft of the book and gave her valuable review that not only evaluated the feasibility of the book but also critiqued the story line. She is a gifted professor and her contributions to this book are truly appreciated. To Gale Crites, who listened to my constant changes in the story line and encouraged me to write them down.

I was fortunate to visit and work in Scotland for 2 years in the 1980s and learned that the Scots are the very best people. They are smart, fun, loyal and hard working. My profound respect and gratitude goes to Scotland, its people and its heritage.

Thanks to all of my family including my brother Virgil; my sister-in-law Becky; my sister Teresa; my brother-in-law Tim; my brother Randy; my sister-in-law Marsha; my cousins Ruby and Pete; my son-in-law Josh; my daughter-in-law Cassie; my grandson Thatcher; and my nieces and nephews. I want to especially thank my father Jim who died a year ago (miss you Dad) who during his 86 years gave his children, grandchildren and extended family his love, his photos and a never ending pursuit of adventure and my mother Della who died in 1994 before I even thought about *The Six Trillion Dollar Man* but always loved and encouraged her children, grandchildren and extended family to pursue their dreams. This book is one of those dreams.

A special thanks go to my best friend for 51 years Gary Creason and his wife Janet (also my best friend for 40 years), Gary's mother Thelma Creason (who is my second mother), Janet's sister Nancy Habluetzel and Walter and Margaret Flückiger, my Swiss friends who live in South Africa. Walter was the first to tell me that I had to write *The Six Trillion Dollar Man* as we hiked in the mountains around Juneau, Alaska. Walter and Margaret even offered to have me stay at their farm (Fans Kraal) in South Africa while I wrote the book. Without my family and friends to pick me up every time I fell, this book would never have been finished. Additionally, I have to mention my mother-in-law Barb Joosten who nagged me (with love) into going to the Idaho Writer's Guild Rendezvous Conference to get help finishing my book.

Through the Idaho Writer's Guild, I met my editor Mary McColl who challenged me to elevate my writing to a far better level than I thought possible and for advising me on the world of book publishing. This book benefitted greatly from Mary's special touch. Additionally, Kathy McIntosh did the final proofread on *The Six Trillion Dollar Man* and proved that there is no substitute for a critical and experienced eye when proofing. Many thanks also to the folks at Inkwater Press for helping me through the maze of publishing options and doing so with much appreciated professionalism.

Probably the most important person in getting *The Six Trillion Dollar Man* published is my wife Kathi. She never wavered in her faith in my talent as a writer, time after time she kept helping me back to the computer to write even when I had too many other things in my mind and was the first to hear my ideas for characters and story line. Thanks to you my love, I couldn't have done it without you.

Jim Moore
Meridian, Idaho
October 1, 2013

PROLOGUE

London, England
August 23, 1305

....

William Wallace's last cry for freedom was still ringing in Robert the Bruce's ears when he bowed to be recognized by King Edward. The king was lying in his huge bed barely able to raise his head to acknowledge Robert the Bruce. His health had been failing for years but the last two months forced the king to his bed. It was obvious to everyone present that the king was dying. Robert could smell the scent of death grow stronger the closer he leaned toward King Edward.

Sir Robert the Bruce wanted to pay proper respects to Edward but after seeing that death was only a few days away, maybe only hours, Robert pushed forward gently but quickly to complete the business of his secret visit. Robert motioned his aide to bring the basket he was holding to Edward's bed. Robert removed the basket's lid, took a silver tray from the basket and placed the tray on the bed next to Edward. Robert's hand then dropped into the basket a second time and he lifted a round-shaped, closed bag from the basket and sat the bag on the silver tray.

The first thing everyone in the royal bedroom noticed was the bag's color. The top was dark brown but their eyes were drawn down toward the bottom of the bag where a shimmering, wet, crimson red color reflected the flickering candlelight. While everyone else was trying to get a clearer view of the bag, Sir Robert untied the thong around the neck of the bag and spread the neck, opening the bag's mouth. He reached into the mouth of the bag with his fingers spread, grabbed an object as he closed his fingers into a fist and pulled by the hair a human head from the bag.

"What is it?" asked the nearsighted archbishop as he leaned closer to the bag — his nose almost touching the head. Then he recognized not what it was, but who it was. He jerked back from the head and the bag quickly and put his hand to his mouth, then crossed his chest, kissed his cross and said, "May God have mercy."

Everyone was revolted by the sight — everyone but the king. Edward opened his eyes slowly at the sound of the priest's prayer. His rheumy eyes were slow to open and slower to focus but finally he saw the severed head dripping blood on the silver tray. Ever so slightly, a faint smile formed on his lips. His enemy William Wallace was dead and the bastard's head was here in his bed-chambers to prove it.

Edward motioned to the Duke of York with his right index finger and the duke placed his ear next to the king's lips, "Have him turn the head around, I want to see his eyes," whispered the king. The king expected to see closed eyes and a face twisted with torture; he wanted the satisfaction of knowing that his death sentence had caused William Wallace the most severe and horrible pain imaginable.

The duke repeated the king's order softly and Robert the Bruce slowly twisted the fist full of William Wallace's hair.

It seemed like the head moved in slow motion, taking too much time to turn toward the king. This rotational movement seemed to click like the hands on a clock that was synchronized to the blink of the king's eyes. The first blink focused on the oblique outline of the nose followed quickly by a second blink that was filled with the dual images of bluish lips at the bottom and a distinctive orbital ridge over one eye at the top. The severed head seemed to stop moving just before the third blink slowly brought the corner of the right eye into view. The white sclera with a sliver of the turquoise blue iris peeked at the king. The head's movement froze at the same time the final blink snapped a full view of the face to the king who studied it with interest for several minutes.

William Wallace had been a handsome man, the kind of man who made many friends with men and, with enviable ease, had no trouble finding attractive women to share his bed. Silently, the king shifted his attention directly to the eyes. What the king saw was not what he expected. No fear, no pain, no begging for mercy, no sign that there was a last prayer of forgiveness.

What the king saw in those mesmerizing eyes was an intense glare of hatred, highlighted with unexpected sparks of defiance. Edward had seen that look before and now the eyes stared back as though they were still alive. The king closed his eyes, hoping that challenging look would not haunt him, but when he opened his eyes, William Wallace's stare conveyed nothing but disrespect and arrogance. In death as in life, William Wallace mocked The King of England and the king would not have it.

That glint of insubordination upset the king so much that he started coughing — a ragged, deep cough that shook every fiber of his body. The spittle on his lips was flecked with blood when the attack stopped and his doctor wiped it away with a blue silk handkerchief. During the uncomfortable minutes of coughing and hacking, Robert lowered the severed head into the pool of blood on the tray. Edward was finally able to breathe normally and again he motioned to the Duke of York who placed his ear next to Edward's face.

"I will not have insolence in my presence, not even from a dead man," said the king, barely audible to the duke. "Command Sir Robert to pull the eyes from the sockets."

The duke reflexively stood straight up and looked at Robert the Bruce, but said nothing. From the corner of his eye, the duke could see the king's finger motioning him to repeat his words as everyone watched the duke with curiosity. Small beads of sweat popped out on his upper lip as the duke began to speak.

His mouth formed the words but no sound came out. He was nervous and scared and did not know if he could continue. What the king wanted was, well, he didn't know what it was, but he was sure that just saying it was an unforgivable sin in itself. He tried to speak again and again no sound came from his mouth. This time the king's whole hand moved, gesturing toward Sir Robert while he said in a hoarse whisper that everyone could hear, "Tell him what I ordered."

The duke forced himself to concentrate on his task. Everyone was staring, including William Wallace's dead but defiant eyes. The duke cleared his throat and began again.

"His majesty will not tolerate insolence, not even from a dead man." He swallowed hard and stumbled as he continued, "His majesty has commanded

… has commanded that you, Sir Robert, … remove the eyes from the sockets of William Wallace's severed head."

Everyone was stunned by the king's horrific order. That is, everyone except Sir Robert and the king. Robert's father had warned him to expect a grotesque, even bizarre request from the king, although this was beyond anything he had imagined.

Robert felt the bile burn as it rose out of his stomach but he willed it back down to its rightful place. He stared hard at the king and the king stared back with a boldness that Robert had not seen for a long time. At that instant, Robert knew that removing the eyes from William Wallace's head was the king's way of reminding him that he had to do what he was told to get the king to sign and seal the document.

Robert's eyes flashed with horror for only a second, but just as quickly the horror was replaced with resolve as he reached for Wallace's left eye. Robert's eyes never left the king's and the king returned his gaze with steady, unwavering, unblinking eyes, which did not move until the first sounds of Robert's fingers tearing at the eyelids. As the fingers worked their way behind the eyeball, the flesh tearing sounds became louder until, abruptly, suction was broken with a sickeningly loud pop. The King watched as the eyeball, with its gray, stringy viscera, uncoiled from the skull with bits of brain still attached. The eyeball stopped moving from its socket and Robert the Bruce had to pull hard to rip the optic nerve from the brain. Then with a jerk, the left eye, optic nerve, brain bits and blood were freed and placed on the silver tray next to the head.

The King looked first at Robert the Bruce who had never stopped looking at the king, then to the right eye. Sir Robert swallowed hard to push the bile back again. He took a deep breath through his nostrils and let it out slowly and lifted his hand to the dead right eye. He worked more quickly this time and the noises of tearing tissue and of a round eyeball being removed from its socket were louder and caused several people in the room to gag. One maid fainted and hit her head on the floor because no one moved to slow her fall.

Everyone was paralyzed. They could not move. They could not think. They could not imagine this was happening in front of them. All of them knew they could not protest this outrage, not now, not ever.

Edward was known throughout Europe for the ruthlessness and savagery he showed his enemies but this would make his lifetime of terror seem like child's play. Everyone knew, from the pope, to the archbishop, to the parish priest, to the commoner, that a person's eyes were the direct link to a person's soul and guided the dead on their journey to heaven. Without his eyes, William Wallace would be sentenced to purgatory for eternity. Not even The King of England should take that God-given right from a man — living or dead. But in his usual unwavering style, Edward risked the wrath of God without the slightest blink of an eye.

Slowly, the 10 people around Edward's bed moved away slightly, not enough to notice, but they wanted to distance themselves from the king before God sought revenge on Edward in their presence. A lifetime of papal-induced fear forced each person to move a few inches away, then another few inches. The king closed his eyes after Wallace's second unsocketed eye was on the silver tray and did not see their retreat, but he sensed it.

To break the spell, Robert the Bruce reached under his cloak and produced a roll of yellow parchment tied with a green and purple ribbon. He untied the ribbon and unrolled the parchment. He turned the document to face the king and moved it down until it touched the top of the king's hand. The king opened his eyes and tried to focus on the document but couldn't, then looked up and focused on Sir Robert. After a moment he knew what the document was and he knew what he had to do. Robert the Bruce and his father had kept their word, now Edward must keep his.

Sir Robert asked the archbishop to bring a quill and ink to the king and the Duke of York to get the king's Royal Seal. As the duke was about to dip the quill in the ink, the king motioned his finger to the duke. The duke moved very close to the king. "Dip it in the blood of the Scotsman, and hand it to me," said the king hatefully.

The Duke of York looked at the king, then at the silver tray with the head and the eyeballs, then back to the king. The king moved his eyes to the tray and back to the duke. The duke reluctantly moved to the tray and looked back at the king. Everyone edged a little farther from the king. God would surely strike Edward dead for the continued desecration of William Wallace's body. The king's eyes commanded the duke to obey his order.

The duke placed the tip of quill in the coagulating blood on the silver tray, twirled the tip to load it with the blood, and handed the quill to the king. A thin thread of Wallace's blood trailed the quill tip and was broken when the king's fingers wrapped around the quill stalk.

The king's hand shook with palsy as he signed his name at the bottom of the document that Robert the Bruce held. The duke removed the quill from the king's fingers, took a candle from the table next to the bed, dripped a pool of wax next to Edward's signature and pressed the Royal Seal into the wax until it cooled.

Sir Robert examined the signature and the seal, carefully rolled the document and retied the green and purple ribbon. He placed it under his cloak. No one in the room other than King Edward and the Duke of York had had a chance to see what was written on the document. The Duke of York had seen only the last sentence at the bottom near the space reserved for the Royal Seal's wax. Those words were now burnt in his memory,

"As long as there is a sovereign England, this bequest shall be honored by all of its future monarchs with no exceptions, until the end of time."

Before being distracted, the duke wondered what bequest could be worth all that he had seen today in the king's bedroom and could last until the end of time. Sir Robert produced a second document from the folds in his cloak. As he untied its red ribbon and unrolled it, Robert asked all who witnessed the signing and sealing of the first document to sign the second document, which he read to them.

On this the 23rd day of August in the year of our Lord 1305, the signers of this testament witnessed Edward, the rightful King of England, sign and the Duke of York press the King's Royal Seal on a yellow parchment document presented to the King by Robert the Bruce the Younger of Scotland.

After the document was signed and sealed, Sir Robert rolled the yellow parchment, tied it with a green and purple ribbon and placed the rolled document in his cloak. None of the signers read the document signed and sealed by King Edward and they do not know what the document contains.

This is sworn before God and the witnesses.

Archbishop Winchelsey, the Duke of York, and four others signed their names since only six of the ten witnesses could write. After he made sure the signatures were dry, Sir Robert rolled the second document up and tied it with its red ribbon and returned it to the pocket in his cloak next to the first document.

He turned to the king, bowed, and backed away from the king's bed. As he left the room, he looked over his shoulder at the silver tray with William Wallace's head.

Sir Robert wanted to take the time to honor the man who had been his friend but time would not permit it. He knew that although William Wallace gave his life for Scotland, it was his severed head and unsocketed eyes that gave Robert's father and his heirs, including Robert, an unprecedented, remarkable, eternal legacy.

What Robert the Bruce never imagined as he walked quickly from the castle was that the parchment bequest signed by King Edward would change the world 700 years later.

....

PART I

Ian, Liddy, and Duncan

....

CHAPTER 1

Castle Hot Springs, Arizona
February 1946

....

As Ian walked across the lawn toward the pool, he heard Jack laughing. Jack liked to laugh and everyone liked to watch and hear him laugh. His all-American, schoolboy good looks always got him attention, but his laugh was what made people like him.

It was spontaneous and genuine, never forced or faked, always genuine. Jack's mother said he got it from her father, Honeyfitz. But where Jack got it did not matter. All that mattered was that everyone including Jack liked it when he laughed.

Ian was glad the war was over and people were having fun and, of course, laughing again. Who would have guessed that he would be at this remote resort? It was like being on a cruise ship only they were in the middle of the American southwest desert. But one thing was the same. Castle Hot Springs was as difficult to get to as a cruise ship in the middle of the ocean.

Jack Kennedy invited Ian to Castle Hot Springs when they were both in the hospital in Hawaii in 1944. Jack said that his family sent him to Castle Hot Springs before the war to recover from a serious bout of influenza he got during his first year at Harvard and now again after he returned from the Pacific war theater. The warm days, cool nights, lots of exercise, no stress and, of course, the healing hot springs water were the right prescription to treat what ailed Jack. The injured back Jack got when his PT boat was cut in half by the Japanese destroyer in the Straits of Tortuga required a very big dose of Castle Hot Springs.

Jack and Ian met once before the war at a birthday party for the then 11-year-old Princess Elizabeth. The 19-year-old Jack accompanied his mother, Rose, and the 16-year-old Ian joined his family at his first Royal reception. It wasn't until they were in the hospital in Honolulu seven years later that they remembered being at the same party in Edinburgh.

Castle Hot Springs' owners gave a barbecue tonight as a going-away party for Jack, who had to go back to Boston after six weeks in the desert. Ian was planning to stay for a couple of additional weeks, maybe take the horse trails through the hills and along the streams around the resort. There were some new guests coming in tomorrow from the airport in Phoenix and Ian was fascinated by the diversity of people who came to Castle Hot Springs to rest and relax. Barbara Stanwyck has been here for a couple of weeks. Clark Gable had come to the resort to hide from the press during January when it was rumored that he was dating another starlet from the MGM fringe benefit program.

Not everyone was rich and not everyone was famous. Some came from Chicago or Rochester or Detroit to get away from the dreary winter weather. Others came to hike and ride through the desert. Some came to play horseshoes or tennis, swim or tan in the sun. But everyone had one thing in common: they were interesting and fun and they liked to have parties. Dancing parties, dinner parties, come-as-you-are parties, barbecues, swimming parties, let's-ride-out-and-see-the-sunset parties. Ian had not spent much time in America but he loved the attitude and freedom he found everywhere he went. The whole country was unspoiled by the war. Everything was undamaged and properly put together, not blown apart, torn and wrecked like England and the rest of Europe.

The party finally wound down at 4:00 a.m. Ian was not drunk and had not hooked up with one of the young women at the party. He decided to climb to the top of ridge behind the resort and watch the sun come up over the mountains to the east. He found a spot protected from the wind by an overhang in the rocks, sort of a cave but shallower. He rested his eyes and the next thing he saw was bright sunlight.

His watch showed it was 11:00. Ian stood, looked at the mountains and saw an eagle gliding toward a cliff to the north. He started back for the resort to tell Jack goodbye but when he walked into the dining room, he found that

Jack had left for the airport in Phoenix 30 minutes earlier. Ian promised himself he would write Jack a note and wish him the best.

Energized from a long swim in the sparkling pool, Ian was toweling off when he noticed the resort's bus pulling up in front of the main building. Only one person was in the bus with the driver. The converted school bus was painted a light blue color with *Castle Hot Springs Resort* in red letters on the side. What caught his attention was that the one and only passenger was seated in one of the last rows, looking out the rear window. The person was not looking at the cactus and mountains; he or she appeared to be watching for someone or something following the bus. Ian had done enough intelligence work for MI6 in Shanghai, Hong Kong and Manila to know when a person was checking to see if someone was following. Strange, why would someone be checking out the rear of the bus out here in the middle of the desert? He dismissed the thought the moment he saw who emerged from the bus.

He watched as a woman, a young woman, stepped down from the bus, looked around, and took off her hat. He was too far away to tell much about her except her slim figure and her hair. It was shoulder length and blonde. A clean blonde, not too yellow, a pure color that was healthy looking. Definitely not dyed or tinted, just natural blonde hair.

Ian watched her walk into the lobby and disappear from view. Nice walk, confident but feminine. He liked what he saw. He wondered if she was married or engaged or committed to some lucky guy. He hadn't let his imagination get this carried away since, well let's see … since that quick romance in Honolulu with the nurse. Nothing lasting since his first serious love affair with Felicity McWilliams in Aberdeen in 1939.

He walked into the bar at 5:00 and looked for the group that was with Jack every evening. He did not see any of them. Either too early or too late, he guessed too early since everyone was still napping after the late party last night. Ian ordered a beer and sat listening to the guitar players, Marion Coil and Ralph Faulkner the bill card stated, strumming a lonely song, what Americans called country and western music. He liked the sound but thought that the lyrics were pretty shallow. Then again, that is what he thought about a lot of Americans, he liked what he saw but thought they were somewhat shallow. That was a bit crass and unfair considering all that America had done for the

U.K. and the rest of the Allies during the war. Shamus definitely would not approve of these cynical thoughts. Shamus always went to great lengths to state how much he admired Americans for their spirit, ingenuity and loyalty. Much like the Scots themselves.

Ian was sitting at a table facing the strumming musicians and did not see her come into the room until she was at the bar. She was wearing a black sweater and tan slacks. Both fit her perfectly, not too tight, not too loose. She ordered a cocktail and turned to scan the room. Since he was the only other guest in the bar, she was left with little choice but to look at Ian and nod a greeting.

Ian got up, went to the bar, extended his hand and introduced himself to her. "Good evening, I am Ian Stuart-Bruce. I saw you arrive this afternoon. Did you catch a ride from the Phoenix airport?"

"Yes, I did," she answered, meeting his eyes. They stared for a long time, each admiring what they saw in the other, each very pleased with what they saw.

"My name is Liddy Adams," she said with a smile. "I took a plane from San Diego to Phoenix. Is your name Stuart hyphen Bruce?"

"Yes. Yes, it is. I hope it doesn't sound too pretentious?" Ian said and quickly changed the subject, by asking, "So you live in San Diego? I have never been there, but I hear that the harbor is one of the best in the world," Ian said while returning the smile.

"I'm actually from a town north of San Diego called San Clemente. It is really a village. Your accent tells me you're not from Central Arizona, maybe some other part of the state?" Liddy asked with a tinge of mischief.

Ian laughed. "Yes, a remote section of Arizona called Scotland. It's a wee bit north and east of here."

She deserved that response and now it was her turn to laugh, "Of course, I should have known. Scotland has been in the papers ever since Arizona annexed all of it and hid it in the Grand Canyon. It must have come as a shock to the Scottish people that they were now part of Arizona," she said with twinkling eyes.

"Enough, enough, I give. If my ancestors heard this conversation, they would consider it blasphemy."

The bartender served her a martini. The singer started with a familiar song that Ian could not place. Liddy looked at the man playing the guitar and they both enjoyed the music for a moment.

Ian tried not to stare but she was stunning. Great eyes, dazzling smile, a small band of freckles on her nose and, of course, the blonde hair. She turned to him and he quickly looked at the singer, pretending to listen intently to the song.

What she saw was a tall, striking man who had brown hair, a strong jaw, a quick smile with straight teeth, complete with a slight overlap of the two front ones, and deep blue eyes that actually sparkled when he smiled. His skin was tanned and had a glow confirming that he had been in the sun a lot. He had a high forehead and a straight nose. Not only handsome, but also something more. Maybe it was the way he held his head or walked or made eye contact when he talked. She couldn't pinpoint the precise reason but she knew that he was someone very special.

Liddy turned back to Ian and said as she looked around the room, "I was told that there were 30 or 40 other guests here at the resort and I haven't seen anyone but you."

Ian responded with an inviting smile, "There was a party last night that lasted until the wee hours and I think they are all taking naps." Liddy could hear an accent, like English or Irish or something; she didn't know for sure.

"A special occasion or the normal resort activities?" Liddy inquired as she absently twisted the narrow straw from her drink.

"Actually, it was sort of a farewell party for a friend of mine," said Ian with a warm voice. "Was it a good party?" Liddy continued as she thought, *What is that accent?*

"You bet. The best. Lots of laughing, drinking and dancing. The recipe for a great party." Ian smiled some more, chuckling to himself as he talked.

"Did you have a good time?" Liddy asked, trying to keep things going.

"Yes, but I wanted to see the sunrise over the mountains this morning so I hiked to the top of ridge and promptly fell asleep. In fact, I didn't get back to the resort in time to say goodbye to Jack. Hope he has a safe trip back to Boston," Ian said with genuine disappointment.

"Is Jack a close friend, I mean, someone you have known a long time?" Liddy asked with interest.

"Not really, it seems like we have been friends a long time but I met Jack in one of your naval hospitals before the War ended. We ended up on the same ward. He was recovering from a back injury and I was being treated for a wound in my left leg. We started talking one day and found that we knew the same people in London and that we both loved sailing," Ian continued casually, trying not to name drop. "It turns out we were at the same mandatory Royal party in 1938 and probably met, but both of us were young and only remembered that the party was a bore."

Ian almost stopped talking. Why was he telling her all of this, they had just met? She was a good listener and she seemed to be genuinely interested in what he was saying. Was he starved for attention or was he trying to attract a very beautiful lady? He didn't care why and he continued by saying, "Jack's father was sent to England by your government in 1938 and he remained there until he returned to Boston in 1940." Ian took a sip of his beer.

Liddy looked puzzled for a second and then the light of recognition showed in her eyes as she put everything together and she said with astonishment, "You're talking about the Boston Kennedys – Ambassador Kennedy and his family. You know Jack Kennedy."

Well, well, he did have friends in high places. This could be a very interesting man to get to know.

Ian did not acknowledge her amazement but went on by saying matter-of-factly, "I really enjoyed talking with Jack and hearing the stories about his brothers and sisters. I can't imagine having eight siblings. I was an only child and didn't even have any first cousins."

"Me, too," said Liddy. "I am an only child, too. I always dreamed of having sisters to play with. I made up a make-believe sister when I was 6 or 7. I did have some first cousins but they were so much older that we have never been close. My dad's family was from northwest Missouri and mother's family from northern California near Napa. I guess the closest I came to having a sister was at the sorority house at school in Palo Alto."

"Palo Alto?" asked Ian.

"Actually, Stanford University, south of San Francisco," responded Liddy. "Haven't you heard of it? Surely, we make the papers in London, once in a while," she teased.

"Of course, I didn't associate the town with the college. And, yes, we do hear about American universities in England. But that sort of news is usually buried somewhere at the back of the paper, near the classifieds," he threw back to her.

There's that smile again. Wow, it took his breath away. He glanced up and saw that the bar was filling up with people and he realized that he had not heard any of them come in. How could that have happened? There must be 25 or 30 people and they were talking up a storm and yet he didn't hear them.

He looked at Liddy and saw that she was surprised, too. Had they become so wrapped up in themselves that they shut out everything else?

Ian snapped out of his dream-like cocoon and asked, "Umm, would you like to have dinner with me?" All of a sudden, Ian wanted to be alone with Liddy.

"Sure, I would like that, but I need to freshen up a little. Can we meet in the dining room in 20 or 30 minutes?"

"That would be great. Do you like red wine or white?" asked Ian with newfound enthusiasm.

She turned to him and said, "White would be nice. A nice, dry white wine would be perfect."

They both smiled and left the bar. Ian was pulling his clothes off before he got to his room. He wanted to take a shower, shave and put on that new cashmere sweater he bought at Bullock's in Los Angeles. He stopped and looked in the mirror. Was he nervous about being with Liddy? My God, they had met only an hour ago. He couldn't be nervous. Ian Stuart-Bruce did not get nervous over women and especially not an American woman he had just met. He had dined with some of the most sophisticated women in England, Europe and Hong Kong and he had not been nervous. Nervous was not one of the things Ian did on a regular basis. He couldn't remember the last time he was this nervous. Oh yeah, now he remembered, it was when the doctor wanted to do that prostate exam. Now that really made him nervous.

world were taking the first steps to healing the underlying grief set aside for so long and this would be a long journey for the millions of survivors.

With a blink of his eyes Ian was back in the dining room with Liddy. His private war and remembrance had lasted only seconds but he felt like he had slipped away for a long time. Seeing Liddy brought again the reality that he was alone. All alone. No one he was close to. Only Uncle Shamus in Scotland but everyone else was gone.

He twirled his glass, took a drink and said very quietly, "My apologies, I rarely let myself think about my parents but today would have been their 30th wedding anniversary."

Liddy did not want this evening to become maudlin so she motioned to the waiter. "Could we have menus, please?" She then held up her glass to Ian and said, "To my first dinner at Castle Hot Springs." Ian met her glass with his and with the second ping of crystal he was back from his distant memories as quickly as he had gone.

Ian was embarrassed at sharing an emotional place he did not visit often. He did not know how to start the conversation again. What he did recognize and appreciate was both the speed and cool finesse that Liddy used when she took charge. She did not make it obvious that Ian had drifted away and she ordered the menus to fill the void.

Ian's tone showed his appreciation when he said, "You're right, let's have a great dinner." With a cheerier tone he changed the subject. "Now, what do you want to do while you are here?"

"Well, let's see, I want to swim, lie in the sun, read a book, hike and go horseback riding. Oh, and the driver told me that there are abandoned mines in the mountains to the north. So I want to explore. What do you recommend?"

"I haven't been exploring in the mountains, but I think we can borrow a jeep and get a picnic lunch from the lodge. That is, if you want company?"

"Of course I want company. Are there others you want to have join us?"

"Why don't we ask? Let's order and I will introduce you to a few of them while we wait for dinner to be served."

The waiter took their order and Ian walked Liddy into the main dining room. He made the introductions to Joyce, Ray, Paula, Don, Jean and Richard.

All of them were friendly, young, good-looking and laughing. Ian could tell they were curious where he had found such a beautiful woman in such a short time. But for tonight, Ian was keeping Liddy to himself.

The dinner was simple but delicious — salad, grilled chicken, green beans, new potatoes, homemade bread and of course, the chilled, crisp wine. With coffee, they had baked apples with a cinnamon sauce that had a touch of brandy.

"Do you smoke? " Ian asked, "I can get you cigarettes, if you would like?"

"I have smoked since my freshman year at Stanford, but wanted to stop for months. I couldn't seem to muster the willpower. How about you, do you smoke?"

"No, not really, a pipe or cigar once in a while. I tried cigarettes when I was stationed in Australia, but they always left such a bad taste in my mouth that I had to stop. But I don't mind if you have one with dinner."

Liddy said with finality, "No, this is the excuse I needed to stop — fresh air and new surroundings. No, I think I will throw the carton in my suitcase away. I think I smoked for social reasons rather than because I enjoyed it. First the sorority and then the people I worked with. You know how it is." What she didn't say was that she smoked because Juan Emilio smoked but now that she had walked away from him there really was no reason to smoke. Getting rid of two bad habits at the same time, how very efficient. Aunt Bess would be proud of her resourcefulness.

"If you are sure?" responded Ian. "Can I show you to your room? I'll wager you are tired after riding in that dust-filled bus today."

"Thank you but I think I want to wander the grounds a little before I go to my room, do you mind?"

Ian smiled, causing the corners of his eyes to crinkle. "I know a guide who would be able to show you the secrets of Castle Hot Springs."

"Do you now?" stretching out the now as Liddy said, teasing him, "And who might that be and can I trust this guide to show me the sights when it is dark?"

"Oh, he comes from an impeccable heritage, is trusted by the members of England's Royal Family, and he has discovered secrets at the Springs that not even the owners and the staff know about," Ian threw back. His smile was beaming and inviting.

"All right, but let me go to the ladies' room first. I drank half a bottle of wine."

"Let's meet on the front porch," Ian said.

"Okay, give me five minutes. And I think they call it the veranda here in the South," she tossed over her shoulder drawing out veranda with a singsong Scarlett O'Hara southern drawl.

They had been walking for 15 minutes without really saying anything. Ian pointed out buildings, tennis courts, pool and stables. But nothing like the discussion during dinner. The spell had been broken and neither one of them seemed to know how to put it back together so they lapsed into silence. The sounds of the night and their footsteps crunching on the gravel kept them from sharing their thoughts.

Ian caught Liddy looking around, again, like she had on the bus that afternoon. As if she did not trust her surroundings and wanted to make sure that she was not being followed. Nothing overt, but he had the feeling that she might be hiding from someone or something. What was bothering her?

As they headed back toward the resort's main building, Ian said quietly, "I had a wonderful time talking with you this evening. I want to see you again, if that is all right with you."

Liddy did not answer immediately; she walked on with her head down. She turned to look at Ian. "Yes," she said slowly, "yes, I would like that. Maybe we can go up in the hills and explore them together. Does 9 o'clock tomorrow morning sound about right?" she asked with a warm smile.

Ian's face burst into a smile and he said, "Yes, ma'am. That will get you a front row seat on the Castle Hot Springs' tour package number 12."

Liddy laughed and gave Ian a light peck on the cheek as they parted in the lobby. Ian could not remember walking back to his room because he thought of nothing but Liddy's smile. Ian thought about how Jack described the boyfriends his sister Kick had and how those poor boys were always smitten. Now he was the one smitten and he liked it. Being smitten was nice, very nice.

CHAPTER 2

Castle Hot Springs, Arizona
February 1946

....

L iddy slept until 7:30 the next morning.

She got out of bed and peeked through the narrow slit in the curtain to see if any new vehicles had arrived or were coming down the gravel road. No sign of any additional cars, trucks or buses. That was a relief. She let down her guard a little. She had been very careful about her plans to come here to Castle Hot Springs, making the reservations through an agency in Los Angeles so that there was no local trail to follow in San Diego. But she was still concerned. Juan Emilio's family was very powerful and there were people working for them everywhere. For the time being she believed that she was not followed on her journey from San Diego to Phoenix and on to this resort. After a few more days she would be able to convince herself that Juan Emilio had not followed her.

She showered and went to the dining room for breakfast. She did not see Ian, but said "Hi" to one of the couples she met last night. Don and Paula were their names, she thought. She looked out beyond the veranda toward the stables and saw Ian loading a picnic basket and a backpack in the jeep.

Ian saw her walking down from the main lodge, wearing khaki slacks, white blouse and rugged looking shoes. She was carrying a jacket and a hat.

"Right on time. Are you ready? "Ian smiled at her. "I need to stop at the garage and get a can of petrol. I brought water in canteens and some sandwiches for lunch."

She was anxious to go. "Let's get going. You want me to drive?" She asked without even thinking whether he would mind, it seemed very natural.

15

"Sure, if you want." Ian was somewhat surprised but tried not to show it. "I will drive when we get in the rough stuff farther up in the mountains if you want me to. Anyway, I need to study the maps to make sure we don't get lost."

They drove for an hour up ridges, down washes, along streams and past old mining camps. The sun was glorious, warm without burning. The sky was so clear that Liddy felt she could almost reach out and touch the mountains she knew were at least 50 miles away. At the same time she kept her eyes moving from the narrow dirt road in front of her to the rear view mirror. She wanted to drive so she could scan the surrounding area, particularly the road behind them, to assure herself that no one was following them.

She watched Ian; he was funny. Studying the map and pretending not to notice her. She liked the way he seemed to be bashful like a boy but at the same time have the confidence of a very worldly and experienced man. His legs were long, muscular and covered with pale brown hair. He was wearing shorts like the British Army officers wore and they cut his legs at mid thigh. Very sexy. She could see a scar on his left thigh that must have been the wound he talked about last night.

As she scanned the mirror for the umpteenth time, she thought of how different Juan Emilio's legs were from Ian's. Juan had wiry black hair on his legs. The hairs were stiff and poked her like little needles. Ugh, how could she have loved that man? *What a monster. I am so glad to be free of him.* She knew the trick was to stay free of him. He would not take her leaving easily or graciously. No, he would be like one of the bulls at the fights in Tijuana he liked to attend. Full of fury — attacking anything and anyone that tried to stop him. That is what frightened her, his uncontrolled temper and utter lack of reason when his temper flared. *Enough about Juan Emilio. I am with Ian and I am going to have a great time.*

They stopped for a water break and Ian spread the map on the hood of the jeep. "See here," he said pointing with his finger, "This is where we are going, Minnehaha Flats."

"You're making that name up. It doesn't say Minnehaha, does it?" Liddy laughed.

"Look. It's printed here on the map." Ian continued to point and watched her as she read the map. The print was small and hard to read and Liddy got very close to him as she looked at the map. He could smell the perfume again. What was that scent? Not peach. Gardenia, maybe?

"Sure enough," Liddy chirped, "I guess the next thing you will show me is where Emerald City is hidden behind Big Rock Candy Mountain."

The rest of their day was glorious and they talked about everything from desert animals and plants, to fashion magazines, to restaurants in San Francisco, to tennis, and great writers. It was the kind of escape each of them needed, be it for different reasons. They got to know each other.

As Ian drove the jeep back to Castle Hot Springs — it was only fair since she had driven all morning — Liddy rested her head on his shoulder. It felt natural because she was relaxed and he was contented.

They found that they did not even need to talk all the time to be comfortable together. So the drive back was quiet, nice but quiet. The sunset set new records for majesty and sheer beauty. Neither one of them had expected the desert to be so astounding in its beauty, almost too much to take in at one time.

They were inseparable over the next 10 days. They swam, they rode horses, they read together, they had great dinners and went with a group on an overnight trail ride. It was all so new and so very, very good.

Two days later they scheduled another jeep trip to the mountains and packed a picnic lunch, with a thermos of strong coffee and a bottle of the same Pouilly Fuisse they had at their first dinner. They met near the barn and Ian had an extra can of gas — petrol to Ian — blankets, and rain slickers.

"The folks here think we could have some rain this afternoon so they want us to take some extra gear," said Ian, unconvinced, "but I cannot imagine that this desert can produce more than a few drops of rain at a time."

"To be on the safe side, we should make sure we don't get caught in any creek beds during our drive," Liddy said as she scanned the sky and the hills around the resort. "Maybe we should not venture out today."

Ian responded, "Nonsense! I come from an area in Scotland that gets rain almost every day and we never delay anything for rain or for that matter, snow either."

"Okay, but let's grab a tarp to put over the jeep in case it does rain more than a few drops," said Liddy with concern in her voice.

Ian grabbed a tarp from the barn and put it in the jeep. To his surprise, Liddy was already in the driver's seat and the engine was idling.

"Hope you don't mind me driving again," Liddy said lightly, "Maybe you can look at the maps again because we haven't been here before. What is it called — Kirkland Junction?"

Ian already had the map out and was tracing his finger along a squiggly line that was the trail they would follow to the base of the Bradshaw Mountains about 15 miles away. They had to cross several washes along the trail but as he looked out across the landscape, everything was as dry as a bone.

Liddy drove with concentration, watching the mirror closely. Ian knew that she was worried about someone following her or them. *Wonder what she is running from? Must be something serious or she would not check the mirror every two minutes.* He did not want to get too nosy but he liked her. No, it was more than like, but he did not want to offend her by pushing into her life too far, too fast. He thought to himself, *Let her talk about it when she wants to. Be patient.*

They stopped to stretch their legs and for a nature call. When he walked back to the jeep, Liddy had her eyes to the binoculars looking to the south back toward the resort.

"What are you looking at?" he said as he walked up behind her. "It is a very pretty vista."

"Yes it is. Very pretty indeed," she said in a preoccupied voice. "I was trying to see the resort from here but I guess we are too far away."

Ian studied her for a moment. Her skin was tanning an even brown with rose-colored highlights from the hours in the sun. She was even more beautiful than when he first saw her twelve days ago. Then, as now, it was not her physical beauty that captivated him. It was the way she stood and the way she walked and the way she listened and the way she talked and ...

His thoughts were interrupted by the jeep's starter grinding. She was ready to go and in the driver's seat again. Oh well, why fight it? She was a good driver and he could watch her more closely than if he were driving.

Ian marveled how they could ride for a long time without talking, enjoying the scenery, the adventure, and being together. It was a very comforting solid feeling. As if they had known each other for a long time and trusted each other without having to talk constantly. These were rare feelings for him but they were very, very good.

They got to the base of the Bradshaw Mountains and decided to stop for lunch at a large rock where they could park the jeep and lay out the blanket for the picnic. The chicken salad sandwiches, coleslaw, chips and wine were delicious. The deep-dish apple pie and coffee finished the meal perfectly.

They put their jackets under their heads to rest for a moment and fell asleep. The party last night at the pool lasted until about 1:00 a.m. and they both arose about 7:00.

CHAPTER 3

Yavapai County, Arizona
February 1946

....

The first raindrops were fat and cold and splashed on Ian's face with a force that startled him. Before he could get up, the downpour fell in earnest. Liddy got up quickly and the two of them grabbed rain slickers and tarp, and stowed the picnic supplies under the jeep for protection.

As they were pushing the picnic basket under the jeep, Ian heard the distinct ricochet of a bullet somewhere near his right foot. A split-second later, the crack of the rifle shot came from across the dry creek where he, Liddy, and the jeep were located. He grabbed Liddy's hand and they ran to a small cave-like depression in the rocks about 50 feet away. The second bullet hit the rocks to the immediate left of Ian as he ran.

Ian had spotted the cave when they first got out of the jeep for their picnic. The entrance was hidden from across the creek but deep enough for both of them to crawl into. Ian moved the dried wood to one side and managed to sit up inside. He knew he was okay. Now he looked at Liddy to make sure she was not harmed by the bullets or by the frantic run to the cave.

Ian asked quickly, "Are you all right?"

As he studied Liddy he noted that her face was stark white and there was a look of terror in her eyes. She nodded, but pulled her knees up to her chest and wrapped her arms tightly around them. She looked like she had seen a ghost or something worse than a ghost.

"What is it? Are you afraid of the rain or the rifle?" asked Ian as he stuck his head out the cave entrance.

The third bullet hit the outside of the cave, close above Ian's head. A shower of broken rock stung his face and arms before he could pull back into the cave. He looked at Liddy. She was a very frightened lady. He asked quietly, "Are you afraid of the rain?"

She shook her head "no."

"Then you must be afraid of the rifle shots," said Ian slowly, giving her a chance to settle a bit.

She looked at him finally and nodded but still would not, or could not, say anything.

Ian watched her closely as she sat hunched over with her arms around her knees. Her eyes were wild with fright and frantically searching for something outside the cave. What is she so frightened of? He studied her some more and the fright was still there but now she actually seemed embarrassed. No, not embarrassed but more like ashamed. She hung her head sort of between her knees. That's it, she is ashamed. But why? Is she ashamed of the fact she is frightened?

Her gaze darted around the entrance to the cave but all she saw were sheets of rain. Ian moved closer to her to put his arm around her shoulders. She leaned into his chest and started crying loudly. Not even the noise of the torrential rain could drown out her weeping. Finally, Liddy raised her head off Ian's chest and wiped the tears from her face. Ian handed her a red bandana. She dried her eyes, blew her nose, and sat up straight, getting control of herself again. Ian was puzzled by her behavior. Yes, the bullets were frightening but not enough to cause the kind of reaction he saw from her. What is she really afraid of? He wanted to ask but decided that it was better to wait until she was ready to tell him.

The rain seemed less intense than when they first got into the cave. Ian thought maybe the storm was moving on. Now that there was less noise from the storm, he heard another sound — a roaring, splashing sound like ocean surf. He looked at Liddy and said, "Are you okay?"

She nodded but still said nothing.

"I am going to see what is making that noise," said Ian with concern. "I will only be gone a few minutes. He grabbed a slicker and put it over his head as he ducked through the cave's entrance. Keeping the jeep between him and the opposite side of the little canyon, he walked toward it and searched the area where he had heard the rifle shots but found no signs of the shooter. He cautiously put the slicker up above the back of the jeep to draw any fire. Nothing. No bullets ricocheting off the rocks. No rifle shots. Nothing. He waited a few minutes and tried the slicker above the back of the jeep again. Nothing.

With extreme caution, Ian peeked around the right side of the jeep and scanned the rocks on the other side upstream for a 100 yards or so, including the top of the ridge, which was about 50 to 75 feet above his location. He repeated his move on the left side of the jeep. The area downstream was wider and there were fewer big rocks in this area. The opposite ridge dropped quickly so that it was level with his location about 25 feet downstream. Then, to be on the safe side, he looked behind him and up the steep wall of the canyon. Seeing nothing, he started to relax a bit but he kept his eyes moving constantly through all the points on the compass and up and down the canyon walls.

Very quickly, he reached into the jeep and tilted up the passenger seat to grab the long package wrapped in a light brown tarp. Then he reached under the jeep to get the picnic basket. He scooted back to the rear of the jeep, waited for more than two minutes, then as the rain was diminishing, ran back to the cave. He pushed the picnic basket toward Liddy and set the long package near the rear of the cave. He then spread the slicker out on the cave's floor and sat on it.

"In the few seconds I was near the jeep, I saw that the dry creek is now a raging river pounding its way from the mountains down toward the river near Castle Hot Springs. I think it's called the Hassayampa River. I read about it in a brochure at the lodge," Ian said, trying to sound calm and casual as he unrolled the long package. He held the rifle in his hands and inspected it. He released the magazine that fell into his left hand. Again, he inspected it and slapped it back in place. He pulled a second magazine from the end of the stock, inspected it, and pushed it back into its holder in the stock. Then he chambered a round and made sure the safety was on.

Liddy watched all of this carefully then said, "Why do you have a rifle?"

"The folks back at the resort asked me if I wanted one and I thought it was a good idea. Turns out it was a very good idea," said Ian quietly.

"Do you know how to use it?" asked Liddy.

"Yes, I started hunting when I was about 7 years old and got my own rifle when I was 11." Ian spoke as he checked the rifle's sights and the balance, then leaned it against the rear wall of the cave. "Then there was the shooting competition at Sandhurst and special shooting skills training with the British Army. Do you know how to shoot?"

"More with pistols and skeet shooting while at Stanford. Only a couple of times with long barrel rifles," said Liddy with a note of pride. "I was on the women's shooting team my junior and senior years and competed at the college level, mostly at meets on the West Coast but once at an exhibition in Sun Valley, Idaho. I was told that Sonja Henie was there filming *Sun Valley Serenade* but I did not see her."

This was more talking than she had done since they got shot at earlier. She seemed to be her old self and Ian was relieved to see she was in control again. Nonetheless, Ian was puzzled that she was so afraid of the rifle shots when she was on a shooting team at university. He said only, "Good to know. Your shooting skill will probably come in handy if we have any more trouble."

They were both quiet for a moment, and then Liddy looked in the picnic basket and saw that there was still one sandwich, two apples and some pie left, along with the bottle of wine.

"Are you hungry?" she asked quietly.

"No, not right now," answered Ian, wrinkling his nose a bit. "I am still a bit worked up about all the noise outside from both man and river."

"Me, too," she said as she closed the lid on the basket.

Liddy looked out the cave and saw that there was sunlight streaming down through the clouds. She was restless and fidgeted some, straightening her clothes and patting her hair. "Can we go outside?" Liddy asked hopefully, "I need to go to the bathroom."

Ian reached for the rifle and said, "Let me check for any activity outside and for a spot for you behind a rock." Ian stepped out of the cave, trotted to the rear of the jeep and looked first upstream and up on the ridge, then downstream and behind him. When he was satisfied that there was no one near he called for Liddy to come out of the cave.

She shielded her eyes from the bright sun as she came out of the cave. She glanced around carefully and walked quickly to where Ian stood behind the jeep. He motioned with his right hand to look upstream, then downstream and then behind them. Liddy could see water still flowing furiously downstream, carrying dead plants, a couple of trees, and large rocks rolling and crashing into the little canyon walls. She was surprised by the ferocity of the moving water. It was moving faster than she would be able to run. The water was chocolate brown with its sediment and dirt. She was very glad to be on higher ground and not caught in the newly-formed river. Intellectually she knew that it would go away in a few hours or maybe a couple of days but that did not reduce the emotional impact of the attacking force that she saw.

"Over here," Ian called while pointing to a rock eight or nine feet in diameter about 30 feet downstream from the jeep. "I think this will offer enough privacy for you." He turned and walked back to the jeep, keeping the rifle at the ready supported by his left arm. A few minutes later Liddy joined him and they both walked to the edge of the rock to watch the torrent of water rushing past.

Ian thought to himself, *We sure can't drive back across the creek when it is like this so I guess we are stuck here until the water subsides.* He let his gaze drift upstream trying to see if the water was slowing any. He turned and walked around the jeep checking to make sure it had survived the storm without any damage. *I wonder if it will start.* He sat in the driver's seat, pulled the choke out halfway, and depressed the starter button with his foot. After grinding for about 10 seconds, the engine coughed once and roared to life. *Well, that is one less thing to worry about. Now for something to eat.*

"I'm hungry. Can we share the sandwich and apples?" he asked, watching Liddy to make sure she was okay.

"Yes. I'm starving. Let me get the picnic basket from the cave and we can eat out here. The cave is really not very big, is it?" Liddy answered with new spirit in her voice, "I think there is half a pie, too, maybe enough for dessert now and a treat before we sleep." She smiled at Ian as if the whole rifle-shot incident had not taken place.

They ate in silence while watching the river continue at a steady pace. There must have been more rain up in the mountains.

Liddy bit into one of the apple slices. "It smells so fresh and alive after the rain. Strange, I didn't think that the desert would be so intriguing. Even the instant river fits with the mystique of the desert."

Ian nodded his head as he finished his half sandwich, then said, "That was great. I am starting to feel better."

He was determined to let Liddy talk as much as she wanted, hopefully getting back to what she was so afraid of. Ian started putting away the leftovers and trash from the picnic dinner. They put the picnic basket in the cave but came out to enjoy the sun as they sat on the big rock overlooking the river.

"Wonder if they had as much rain at the resort as we did here?" Ian said quietly, almost talking to himself. Louder, he said to Liddy, "We had better get the blankets, tarps and jackets together, I think it will get cold tonight."

"Okay," Liddy answered as she got up and went to the jeep. "Here are the extra tarp, the blankets and jackets. Good news. They are all dry. Lucky we put them under the jeep before …" Her voice trailed off to silence.

Ian watched her carefully but said nothing. She was starting to panic again. She rubbed her arms with her hands, shook her head, and started saying very softly, "No, no, no. Please no." She continued, as her wide eyes searched across the river. "I knew he would find me. I knew it."

Ian could barely hear Liddy and in a quiet and soothing voice he said, "What did you say?" He wanted to hold her and protect her but knew that if he touched her she might not say anything else so he waited until she spoke a wee bit louder.

"I said, 'I knew he would find me. I knew it.'" She turned to face Ian, looked up at him with clear eyes. Liddy was no longer frightened but Ian could see she was having difficulty saying more.

Ian asked tentatively, "Who would find you?"

Liddy then looked over at the rocks and ridge across the canyon, then turned back to Ian and said, "Juan Emilio." Tears welled up in her eyes and rolled down her cheeks.

"Juan Emilio?" Ian probed, "Who is Juan Emilio, Liddy?"

Liddy stood dead still and Ian could not see her breathe but he could see a vein in her forehead throb with each heartbeat. She ran her fingertips through her beautiful blonde hair but kept eye contact with Ian.

Ian thought that her eyes and body language said that she was no longer afraid as she decided what words to speak while she searched his eyes. With great effort she started very slowly, speaking each word as though they were not attached.

"Ian, I do not want to get you involved in my personal problems," said Liddy with determination growing with each word, "But I believe that you are involved by being with me today. So I will do my best to explain. I don't know how much I should tell." Ian grabbed the front seat lower cushions from the jeep and took them over next to a rock so they could sit and lean their backs against the rock.

"Thank you," she said and settled into the makeshift chair and watched as Ian did the same.

She took a big breath, let it out slowly, and began, "I was engaged until about a month before I came to Castle Hot Springs. I broke it off because he was too angry at the world and when his anger surfaced I got scared." She went on with a clear voice, "He was very generous and kind when he wanted to be. Basically, when he was good he was very, very good and when he was bad he was very, very bad. He had two completely different personalities."

She stopped, looked around again, then turned her eyes to Ian and continued, "I fell in love with him when he was good. He tried to please me in every way he could, but about one month ago I saw his bad side and it terrified me. Although he lived on the beach close to the Hotel Del Coronado on San Diego's Coronado Island, he often visited his family in Ensenada about 25 miles south of Tijuana. I would take the ferry to Coronado Island and he would pick me up at the pier and about every other weekend we would head south to Ensenada. Other weekends we would stay at his home at the beach."

"His name is Juan Emilio Fuentes. He is 28 years old and his family is from a long line of wealthy shipping and importing barons. The Fuentes family is one of the leading families in Mexico with business interests in Mexico, the U.S., and throughout Central and South America. Juan Emilio works for his uncle in the family business although I never understood what he did. He never talked about the family business except to report his travels."

She stopped and reached for the bottle of wine in the picnic basket, took out a Mason jar, and poured herself some wine. She held out the bottle to Ian and he shook his head.

"We dated for about a year before he asked me to marry him and I accepted. That was about eight months ago. He bought me a ruby engagement ring and started talking about a wedding in May or June of next year. Everything was fine until we went to Ensenada one weekend to attend his cousin's wedding. There were about 400 people at the wedding and reception, a really great party with lots of singing, dancing and drinking. Then Juan Emilio, who drank only a couple of glasses of champagne, got upset when a friend of the family asked me to dance. I did not know the proper protocol for an engaged lady in Mexico. I later learned that dancing with someone your intended husband did not approve of was more than a social faux pas. It was grounds for a fight."

Liddy rubbed the base of her left ring finger and Ian noticed the faint line where a ring had been. Her action was unconscious and did not stop her explanation.

"Juan Emilio asked the young man, I never knew his name, to meet him out in the front yard so they 'could talk.' They left the reception with five or six of Juan Emilio's cousins and friends close behind. About five minutes later Juan Emilio came back to the reception, sat next to me and said, 'Never, never do that again. You embarrassed my family and dishonored me. You are a disgrace and we are leaving right now. Get your wrap and your purse and follow me quietly to the car. Do you understand these simple instructions?' The hate and malice in his voice shook me to the core and I knew at that moment that I would not marry him. I was so repulsed by him I didn't even want to ride with him back to San Diego."

"As we drove through Tijuana, I asked him what he had done to the man who asked me to dance. He turned to me slowly, pulled the car over to the side of the road, then he grabbed me by the arm and shook me. He shook me so hard my teeth rattled. With real hate and rage in his eyes and his voice he said, 'I made sure he will never dishonor my family again.'" She paused to take a deep breath as Ian continued to watch her face. The fear was replaced with resolve as she continued, "I asked Juan Emilio again exactly what he did to that man. He pulled back onto the road and said with pride in his voice,

'I broke both his arms and both of his legs and left him in the road. He will never bother you again.'" I didn't know what to say so I kept quiet until we crossed the border. Then I started talking about all the beautiful dresses worn by the ladies at the wedding. I told him that one of my sorority sisters, Madeline, wanted me to come to San Francisco for a few days so we could shop at I. Magnin and some of the boutiques. The dresses at the wedding reminded me that I needed to update my wardrobe. I would go up on Thursday afternoon and come back Monday evening if he didn't mind. He wasn't the least interested in what I said. He simply grunted his assent."

Liddy looked at Ian to see his reaction and his face showed concern. Liddy was satisfied that Ian was not going to make any rash comments or threaten Juan Emilio, so she continued. "I did not go to San Francisco but to L.A. I had another sorority sister who lived in Pasadena with her grandparents. Ruth listened to my story, then helped me disappear. I never went back to San Diego until last week. I had to arrange to sell my furniture and ship my personal items to my aunt in San Clemente. I have not seen or talked to Juan Emilio but I knew he was looking for me. He tore up San Diego searching and then he hit San Francisco. Madeline was in Palo Alto at her parents' home and she never heard from Juan Emilio."

She stopped, looked at Ian again making sure he was all right with her confession, then pressed forward to the most important part, "When I caught the plane in San Diego, I am pretty sure I saw one of Juan Emilio's cousins at the restaurant and he probably saw me. So when I got off the plane in Phoenix, I started checking to see if someone was following me. Twice after I got on the bus at the Phoenix airport, I saw the same blue convertible tailing us. I thought we had lost them when we pulled off the highway at that little train station in Morristown. So I watched carefully for the next hour until we pulled into the resort and I have been checking every chance I've had. I thought that I had escaped Juan Emilio until today when they started shooting at us."

She turned away so she did not have to look at Ian's eyes. She was done with her story. She felt a huge weight had been lifted from her shoulders but now she had to deal with Ian. Before she could say anything else, Ian said quietly in a comforting but determined voice, "Liddy look at me." She turned her head to meet his eyes.

"Three things – first, thank you for trusting me with what I am sure is a very difficult period in your life. Second, I observed your wariness from the time the bus arrived with you sitting in the last row of seats watching out the back and at other times like when you had the binoculars scanning the area toward the resort. You are careful and you should give yourself a pat on the back for your perception about what Juan Emilio was capable of doing. Third, I will make sure that Juan Emilio does not bother you again. His family is not the only one with friends in high places. Don't ask me what I am going to do and how I will accomplish this promise to you. Please accept it as a given. Do not tell anyone that I am interceding on your behalf to get Juan Emilio to leave you alone. I do have a personal request. I want you to go back to having fun on your vacation here in Arizona." Ian's eyes became happy and he was relaxing, so Liddy did too.

"Now let's get into the cave and get some sleep. Let's hope that when we wake in the morning the river will be at a level at which the jeep can ford it so we can make our way back to the resort." Ian got up and took the seat cushions back to the jeep. "Can you imagine what they are saying about us back at the resort? 'Why, Miss Liddy, you are like that brazen vixen Scarlett O'Hara and every time I think of her I get the vapors. I feel the vapors coming on now. Oh my!'"

Liddy looked at Ian and then started laughing. It was funny to hear Ian's Scottish brogue trying to imitate a southern accent. She felt much better because she was able to relax a bit and laugh. Maybe there was truth in the adage that laughter is the best medicine.

She slept soundly, only waking once when she heard a coyote yelping in the distance. The trip back to the resort was without incident and they showed up at lunch all cleaned up like shiny pennies when the rest of the group came to their table and wanted to know what had happened on the jeep journey. Liddy gave most of the story with Ian throwing in a comment or two but Liddy was enjoying the attention.

Later that day, Ian drove to Wickenburg in the resort's Ford station wagon to make a phone call to San Francisco. Ian was assured that there would be no more problems for Liddy or Ian from Juan Emilio Fuentes of Ensenada, Baja Norte, Mexico and Coronado Island, San Diego, California.

Two days later Liddy received a telegram at the resort, a rare event because it was about 30 miles to the Western Union office in Wickenburg. The telegram was brief and announced that Juan Emilio Fuentes had been appointed by his uncle, managing director of a copper mine in the mountains in Bolivia and he was expected to be there modernizing the operations for the next five years.

Liddy never heard from Juan Emilio again.

CHAPTER 4

Castle Hot Springs, Arizona
February 1946

....

On her thirteenth evening at "The Springs," as everyone called the resort, Liddy was walking with Ian and holding his hand. She stopped, turned to him and looked in his eyes.

"Are you ever going to kiss me?" Liddy said softly, "Don't you know that girls liked to be kissed by boys who give them a lot of attention?"

Ian did not say anything, he simply looked into her eyes for a moment. Then he placed his hands on both sides of her face and kissed her on the lips. A strong, firm but sensuous kiss. Ian was not the kind of guy who had to be told to do something twice, particularly when it came to kissing a very beautiful woman. A very beautiful woman he was falling in love with.

After they kissed, they held each other. She rested her head on his chest and he rested his cheek on the top of her head.

"I'm in love with you, you know," whispered Ian. "I can't believe this is happening to me, so quickly."

Liddy pushed back and looked into Ian's blue eyes. "Ian Stuart-Bruce, I am in love with you, too, and I know this is the love I have been looking for since I was 16. I have grown to trust you in a mere 10 or 12 days and I do not have to look any further. You are the one and only man for me."

"Liddy, I have been around the world, even before the war, and have known other women, but this is the first time I have been afraid. Not even when I slept with a woman the first time was I as afraid as I am at this moment. I am afraid that I will not be able to control my love for you. And my passion too. You see, I now know that I have never really been in love with any of the others. Now, I am in love with you and I am afraid that I will not be good enough. I want to be a good husband, good friend and, yes, a good lover."

Liddy put her finger to his lips to shush him. "You are a good friend now and I know you will be a very good husband and ..." she patted Ian's butt and smiled at him. "Yes, you will be a good, no, you will be a great lover. Women can tell about these things."

He smiled back with a genuine joy that he had known only a few times in his life. He grabbed her arms and gave her another long kiss. This time the kiss was filled with a yearning to have more than a teenage romance with Liddy. He was a man and she was a woman and they loved each other, so what else was important?

"Ian, I hate to sound old-fashioned, but I don't want to sleep with you until we are married and you haven't even asked me to marry you yet." Liddy pushed Ian back from her. "I want to, too, but not now. I'm sorry."

Ian was trying to calm down but he had gotten pretty worked up. He wanted to make love to Liddy in the worst way and getting himself to relax now was difficult. He did not know whether to be angry, sad or depressed. He took a big breath and let it out slowly.

"Okay, if that is what you want, then that is what you will get," he said with determination. He took her hands in his, looked at them, then looked in her eyes. "Will you marry me? Will you marry me tomorrow? I do not want to wait. I want to get married tomorrow," Ian said with genuine sincerity.

Liddy looked at him. Her eyes started to tear up. She usually did not cry because of an emotional moment. But this was different. The man she loved asked her to marry him and the happiness she felt made her lightheaded and tingly all over.

"Yes, you fool. Yes, yes, yes. I will marry you. I will marry you today, tomorrow, whenever you want..." she said as she laughed out loud and kissed him again. "But how will we get married tomorrow here in the middle of the desert?"

Ian smiled broadly and said, "My dear, your husband-to-be is a very resourceful man. Let me worry about where we will get married tomorrow and how we will get there. Your only responsibility is to get a wedding dress. I will take care of everything else. Now, let's go to the bar and get a bottle of champagne to celebrate before we say good night."

The cork soared across the bar and bounced on their table. Joyce, Ray, Paula, Don, Jean and Richard looked up and saw Ian pouring the champagne. Richard motioned Ian and Liddy over to their table and said, "What are you celebrating? Getting married or something?"

Ian held his glass up and said, "Matter of fact, Liddy agreed to marry me about 30 minutes ago. There will be a wedding tomorrow. Do you all want to come along?"

The ladies started clapping and hugging Liddy and the men jumped up and gave Liddy a peck on her cheek, shook Ian's hand and slapped his back.

"Everyone, get a glass of champagne, let's have a toast to Liddy and Ian," said Ray to everyone in the bar. "Don is buying." He pointed to Don as he nodded to the bartender.

After the toast, Liddy started talking with Joyce, Paula and Jean. "Where can I get a wedding gown by tomorrow?" she asked with a worried smile.

The ladies looked at each other. They'd been given the ultimate fashion challenge here at Castle Hot Springs that was closer to the dusty, dirty gold mines of Prescott and Jerome than to the boutiques in Hollywood, department stores in Los Angeles and shops in Phoenix.

"I know," Joyce said with interest, "I know where you can get a wedding gown by tomorrow."

"Where?" said the group in unison.

"At my mother's house. She is storing my wedding gown. Ray and I got married last year and I would love to have you wear my gown at your wedding and I think you are about my size, size 4, right?"

"That's right, a size 4, but I think you are a little taller than I am," Liddy said. They both stood up and Paula said, "Yep, Joyce is about two inches taller, but the rest is almost identical."

"Terrific, what size shoe do you wear?"

"Size 8½."

"Great. I wear a 9, so we will put some paper in the toes of the shoes. I am sure they will work."

"Is there a veil with your gown?" asked Liddy cautiously.

"Sure, it's kind of long though, about 10 feet of lace." Joyce took obvious pride in her veil.

While the ladies took care of the wedding dress, the gentlemen were talking about where to have the wedding.

Don said, "Well, Ian, you have a choice, you can go to Mexico or you can go to Nevada if you want to get married tomorrow. Those are the only places I can think of with no waiting period to get a marriage license."

"Nevada gets my vote," said Richard. "You know how things can be in Mexico, sometimes you can get what you want, sometimes you can't. Remember how much Dad paid to get his car out of Mexico last summer? Wasn't it $500? And he has a 1000-acre farm in Hermosillo."

"You're right," said Ray, "and now that I think of it, why don't we call Don Laughlin and see if he can arrange for a wedding at his place on the river? That would be really great. Isn't Don the justice of the peace in that county?"

"I'm sure he is," replied Richard, "he can conduct the ceremony. This is going to be terrific. Does this sound okay with you, Ian?"

"As long as I can marry Liddy tomorrow."

Ray said, "Let's see if we can get Don Laughlin on the phone. I'll call, you all stay here."

As Ray got up, his wife, Joyce stood up and said, "Ray, I need to call my mother in Sedona and see if she can get my wedding dress ready for Liddy."

Ray said, "I'm calling Don Laughlin to see if he can conduct the ceremony at his place on the Colorado River."

Paula said, "That would be great. Maybe we can have the wedding on the terrace overlooking the river. Wouldn't that be perfect?"

Richard asked, "How are we going to get from Castle Hot Springs, to Sedona and on to Laughlin, Nevada, all in a few hours?"

"Richard, call Dad and ask him if we can borrow the Stagger-Wing. It has seats for eight and that would be ideal for the trip tomorrow," said Ray.

"Okay, we need to make three calls. Joyce, you go first, call your mother; then Richard will call Dad in Phoenix; and then I will call Nevada."

After the calls were made, the rest of the plans were firmed up and everyone needed to be packed and ready to go after breakfast by 7:30 the next morning. The plane was going to be in Wickenburg at 9:00 and they needed to get to Sedona before 10:00 to get the dress. They planned to be in Laughlin by 1:00 or 2:00 and the wedding was set for sundown tomorrow on the terrace overlooking the Colorado River.

Ian and Liddy were so excited they could barely sleep that night but fell asleep about 2:00 a.m., each in their own room. All of this was like a dream, but very romantic. They were going to be married and the rest of their lives was going to be perfect.

Ian had been most excited about the second call he asked Richard to make to his dad in Phoenix. They made arrangements for a jeweler to send an engagement ring and wedding band on the plane. Richard was shocked when Ian had written him a check from Bank of America in San Francisco for $5,000 to pay for the rings. You could buy a very nice house for $5000. Ian wanted a very high quality diamond that was at least three carats and he was willing to pay for the best. Ian also gave Richard a check for $1000 to cover the cost of flying the plane from Phoenix to Wickenburg to Sedona to Nevada and back. Richard wanted to cover the cost as a wedding present but Ian wouldn't hear of it.

When Richard told the rest of their group, they all wondered where Ian was able to get his hands on that kind of money. Did his family have money? No one knew, since Ian had never discussed what business he was in or his family background. All they knew was that he was from Scotland and he was Jack Kennedy's war buddy.

* * * *

The next morning, Ian and Liddy, along with Ray, Joyce, Don, Paula, Richard, and Jean piled into Ray's 1939 Buick sedan for the trip to the Wickenburg airport to pick up the Beech Stagger-Wing. The Buick's straight-eight engine burbled as it was loaded with people and bags. Ray had the Buick modified so it could travel on the back roads with ease and when they hit Highway 60 Ray pushed the big sedan to 100 mph. When they got to the airport, the plane was there and in the co-pilot's bus seat was a brown paper bag. Richard looked inside the brown bag, saw that it contained a small box and handed the whole bag to Ian.

Ian walked to where Liddy was standing with the ladies. He took her hand and guided her to the tail of the plane. He opened the bag and removed the black velvet box. He opened the box and took out the engagement ring. He knelt in front of Liddy, took her left hand and looked into her eyes.

"Will you marry me and be my wife?" Ian said with such eloquence and gallantry that Liddy couldn't help herself. Her eyes glistened with tears and she thought she was going to cry. But she bit the inside of her cheek, looked at Ian and gathered herself. "Yes, it would be an honor to marry you and be your wife." She started crying in earnest. Ian stood and she threw her arms around his neck and for the first time she really saw the ring.

It was huge. A diamond that was at least 1-inch long, marquise cut with a triangular emerald on each side. It dazzled in the sun and now she was crying again.

"Where did you get this ring? It's gorgeous," said Liddy with astonishment. "How did you know that diamonds and emeralds were my favorite? Oh, Ian, I do love you and I do want to marry you." They kissed this time with more passion than they had last night.

"Careful. We'll stay here in Wickenburg and find the closest preacher to marry us right now," said Ian as he caught his breath.

Liddy pushed him away slowly but firmly. "No you don't, mister. You promised me a wedding with a gown, on a terrace overlooking the Colorado River and you are not going to weasel out of it for a few minutes of unbridled passion. Not from this girl." Liddy turned to Ray. "When do we get this show on the road? I have a man who wants me in the worst way but I won't let him until after the wedding, so we had better get moving or we will have to tie him up to keep him away from me." Liddy laughed with the group.

Ray and Don flew the plane while everyone else was talking in the passenger cabin. The Beechcraft Stagger-Wing was one of the most luxurious private aircrafts in the skies. Only 500 had been built from 1936 through 1940 and already they were collectors' items. The Stagger-Wing was also very expensive but worth every penny. The cabin had soft leather seats, the carpets were plush and the engine was very powerful. This particular Stagger-Wing had been modified and could easily carry eight people with their luggage and take off from airports above 8,000 feet without fear of any air-density problems. Partially because of its powerful engine and partially because it was a biplane. A staggered wing biplane, where the upper wing was attached to the top of the fuselage and the lower wing attached to the bottom about two feet forward of the top wing, was wonderfully aerodynamic, a treat to fly.

Ray and Richard's father owned 1/3 interest in the specially built, extended fuselage Beech Stagger-Wing with another 1/3 owned by real estate developer Del Webb and another 1/3 owned by department store owner and Phoenix City Councilman Barry Goldwater. The plane was christened *The Glendale Glider* honoring the farming community west of Phoenix where Ray and Richard grew up. They were lucky it was in Phoenix when they called; it was usually flying to California, Mexico, Texas or Colorado. The plane cost a lot of money and had to fly a lot of hours to pay for itself. Their father told them that they had to have it back in Phoenix the day after tomorrow because Councilman Goldwater had an appointment in Washington to meet with President Truman. And we couldn't have him late for his appointment back East, could we?

The Glendale Glider landed in Sedona and Ian and Liddy could not believe how beautiful the mountains were. Everywhere you looked the views became more incredible.

"Ian, I can't believe I'm looking at all of this," said Liddy with a whisper. "I must be in a dream. I never knew that Arizona had so much to see."

"Liddy, stop gawking at those rocks and try on this wedding dress," said Jean, "We will never get it fitted to you if you don't come inside."

"But everything is so very beautiful, I want to take it all in," said Liddy distractedly.

Jean clapped her hands in front of Liddy's face. "Can you tear yourself away long enough to remember that you are marrying Ian today?" And Liddy snapped back from being mesmerized by the sites around Sedona.

Joyce's mother and sister had driven in from Page Springs where they lived and were at the airport to meet them. All the ladies commandeered the airport manager's office to finish fitting the wedding gown and veil. In less than an hour, the ladies were ready to go and the dress was safely on board the plane.

After taking off from Sedona, the plane went due north along Oak Creek on its way to the Grand Canyon, passing west of the San Francisco Peaks in Flagstaff. Everyone on board was treated to a view of the Canyon from below the rim. Everywhere you looked there was more spectacular scenery and both the south and north rims were covered with a deep blanket of fresh snow, making the reds redder, the browns browner and the yellows more vibrant. Even the slate gray-brownish color of the river was more pronounced when you look straight down on it from 4500 feet above the water.

They finally came to the dark blue of Lake Mead and followed it for about 45 minutes before turning to the southern tip of Nevada. They landed at a dirt strip across the Colorado River from Laughlin and took a rope ferry barge across to Don Laughlin's bar and casino, Riverside.

The ladies took over Don's ample office and the men started drinking Jack Daniel's and Coca-Cola. At 5 o'clock, Ian went to the terrace with Don Laughlin to get ready for the ceremony.

The day had passed too quickly but now everything was perfect. The sunset was glorious, the temperature about 65 degrees, with no wind and a pleasant fragrance in the air. Then Ian saw Liddy as she came out on the terrace.

The wedding dress was designed and made by Priscilla's of Boston 10 months ago when Joyce and Ray got married. Now Liddy wore it on her wedding day. It was ivory satin with tiny pearls on the bodice and around the hem. Liddy's face was covered by the veil, which spilled off the back of her head to a 10-foot train. It couldn't have been more perfect if they had married at Westminster Abbey in London.

But the dress paled when compared to Liddy. Even through the veil, she was radiant. The days in the sun had tanned her face to a healthy glow and her hair was piled on top of her head with ringlets around the top like a crown. That was it, Ian thought, she did look like a queen. Ian knew that there was not a member of any royal family in Europe who looked more regal than Liddy did at that moment on the terrace of this new Nevada casino on the Colorado River. He knew at that moment that their marriage would be something very special and that their children would have her beauty, common sense, and good disposition and his courage, humor and fierce loyalty.

Suddenly, watching her walk toward him, he could not wait to have children with Liddy and watch them grow. Was it supposed to happen this way? Start thinking about their unborn children on their wedding day?

The ceremony lasted 15 minutes and Ian kissed Liddy long enough to have all their friends howling like coyotes by the time their kiss ended. As Ray took pictures after the ceremony, Ian noticed the bouquet Liddy was holding. A large white flower in the middle was surrounded by a cascade of red slender flowers. He learned later that the white flower was from the saguaro cactus and the red flowers from the ocotillo cactus. They were the perfect color and texture to complement both Liddy and the dress. It was all perfect.

Their wedding day was February 28, 1946, a Thursday. Ian was 25 years old and Liddy, 23.

CHAPTER 5

San Francisco, California
March 1946

....

Ian sent a telegram to his Uncle Shamus in Aberdeen, Scotland, announcing that he had married Liddy Adams of San Clemente, California, and that they were very much in love. Ian said that he would stay at the Mark Hopkins Hotel only until he and Liddy found a house. Ian asked Shamus to come to San Francisco to meet Liddy and enjoy America, where the war had not destroyed everything.

In his response Shamus congratulated the newlyweds and invited them to Scotland for their honeymoon. Shamus also reminded Ian that he is required to assume control of the family business in seven years. Shamus continued by asking if Ian had told his new wife about his family responsibilities.

Damn Shamus, he is as subtle as a sledge hammer. The family business issue was not something I really wanted to worry Liddy about, particularly during the first days of their marriage. But taking Shamus's advice, Ian explained to Liddy that his Uncle Shamus had run the family business since his father joined the British Secret Service in 1939. Actually, Shamus Stuart-Bruce was Ian's great uncle, his grandfather's much-younger brother. Ian assured a quizzical Liddy that the family business issue was under control and not to worry about it.

What caught Liddy's attention during the family business talk was that Ian was very serious and that he never actually said what kind of business the Stuart-Bruce family operated. An interesting omission, but Liddy did not dwell on it because she knew Ian would tell her when he was ready.

They found a house in Pacific Heights, close to a park. Liddy was originally concerned about the price but Ian assured her that the family business could afford the house and the cost of redecorating it. There was the family business thing again. It didn't really worry Liddy but she wondered why Ian didn't tell her more about his family's business.

Ian bought Liddy a Ford convertible for a wedding present and she busied herself getting the house painted and papered and meeting with the drapery and furniture people. She loved every minute of it and she loved Ian with all her heart. She couldn't have been happier.

Liddy spent several weeks searching for the right wedding present to get Ian but everything seemed too small or too impersonal or just not right. Finally she settled on a Philippe Patek pocket watch that chimed a Scottish ditty on the hour. Although the watch was splendid, what made the watch a wedding gift was the message Liddy had engraved inside its gold cover –

My Darling Ian,
From Castle Hot Springs to Minnehaha Flats to Laughlin and our wonderful wedding Thank you for capturing my heart and never forget I love you with all my soul.

Ian read the inscription and smiled, then looked into Liddy's eyes. "I will never forget and I love you with all my soul, too." Ian said with a quiet but firm voice. "You have made me happier than I thought I could ever be and I will keep this watch close to my heart to remind me that I have the most precious thing a man can ever have – a woman who loves him and wants to spend the rest of her life with him."

Everything was perfect. Most days Liddy had to pinch herself to make sure that it was all real. Ian, their wedding, the ring, the house, their lovemaking and the laughter, always the laughter; it was so much better than she expected. What else could any woman want or need to be happy?

* * * *

Liddy was stunned. She was pregnant. It was not what she expected when she went to the doctor for a routine check-up. But the doctor said that there was no doubt she was about three months pregnant. She wanted to call Ian but he was in Vallejo at the U.S. Navy shipyards for the day and would not be back until later in the evening.

Liddy was still not comfortable driving her Ford convertible on the steep hills in San Francisco so she took the bus to the baby store on Gerry. She had often walked past the store and looked at the cute little outfits and adorable baby room furniture. Now she wanted a closer look. She looked at the furniture, the infant clothes and the maternity clothes. She stayed a couple of hours and the clerk kept asking her if she needed help. "No. No, I'm only looking," she kept replying without looking at the clerk. Finally, she got hungry and left to get sandwich.

She changed her mind and went to Chinatown. She found a little restaurant and asked for some won-ton soup. She was tired and the soup hit the spot. She left the restaurant and walked toward the cable car stop. She noticed a little shop down a half flight of steps. The window had a sign, "Fortunes Read 25 cents." Liddy walked down the steps and eased her head into the small shop.

It was really tiny, barely room for a small round table and two chairs. She said hello and an ancient Oriental lady came out from behind a screen. "Welcome, please sit down." Liddy pulled the chair out and sat.

The lady said that she would read Liddy's future and she did not have to pay unless she liked the reading. Liddy thought this was fair and relaxed a little. The lady motioned for Liddy's hands and asked Liddy to close her eyes. The old woman held Liddy's hands in her warm but arthritis-gnarled fingers.

"You are going to have a baby in six or seven months." Liddy was so surprised that she automatically said yes she was pregnant. The old lady studied Liddy's palm more closely and quietly told Liddy that her baby was a boy and was a special gift from God. She continued with more. Now the lady looked in Liddy's eyes and studied them for a long time. Then she said very quietly, "Your baby's ancestors are very noble people. Your baby, like your baby's father and grandfather, is the continuation of a secret legacy that dates back centuries. But there is a darkness surrounding your baby's future that I cannot see through now."

Liddy wanted to laugh but she stopped herself. This fortuneteller knew she was pregnant when no one else but her doctor knew. Now this mystic was making outrageous statements about her unborn baby and she wanted to toss them out but something in the old woman's steady gaze made Liddy pay very close attention to what was said.

The old woman warned her to take very good care of herself while the baby was inside. "Make sure that you drink very pure water until the baby stops nursing. Pure water will keep bad spirits away from the baby. You must come back to see me two to three weeks before the baby is born and I will give you more about the baby's future. Now is too soon, I cannot see the baby's future." Liddy promised she would return in five months but she never did go back to the tiny fortuneteller's shop on the edge of Chinatown.

Ian was delirious with joy about having a baby. He and Liddy couldn't stop talking about the things he wanted to do to get ready for the baby. But in the excitement of that day Liddy decided not to tell Ian about the fortuneteller. In fact, she never did share the fortuneteller's future with Ian. She did not know why but something told her not to mention it.

But she drank only bottled water from a spring in the Sierra foothills near Angel's Camp. She found it at a shop on Sutter Street and the owner was always curious why she came into the city to buy the water. The pure water was not the only thing Liddy remembered from the ancient Oriental woman's incredible predictions and Liddy was somewhat anxious about what she was told by the old woman, "You will have a special child." But no matter how much anxiety she felt, Liddy did not tell Ian about the fortuneteller.

Liddy could not get the woman's words out of her head, particularly about the baby's ancestors and the darkness. She did not think any famous people resided in her family tree, maybe a distant connection to both Presidents Adams so she started asking Ian a lot of questions about the Stuart-Bruce family. Ian was surprised by her sudden interest in his family's background and frankly he was curious where this interest came from but eventually he shrugged it off as part of the "being pregnant" mystery that comes with every new baby, particularly the first one.

She started talking to members of the San Francisco Genealogical Society and she found that their library was lacking specific references prior to 1500. So Liddy started writing and calling Uncle Shamus to get more information and track the Stuart-Bruce family lineage. She became obsessed with the task of unraveling old records. She had Ian put up a floor-to-ceiling bulletin board that was 10 feet long in the living room so she could try to piece together all the branches of the family tree. She asked for a second room-sized bulletin board, then a third one.

Ian thought the living room looked like one of General Eisenhower's war rooms shown in the newsreels during the war. Amazing that Liddy had enough energy to research his family and still take care of herself, the unborn baby and the house. But she did. She said that it made the time go faster and that she did not worry about the baby as much as she did during her first months.

Every Friday evening Ian would get an hour-long update on that week's successes and failures in tracking the Stuart-Bruces back in time. Ian even got interested as Liddy started digging up more and more contact with the Royal Family in the late 1400s. Ian loved to watch Liddy talk about all the discoveries she had made. Her eyes sparkled and her cheeks grew rosy as she explained some of the outrageous relationships that surfaced under her archeological inquisition.

Fathers had children with daughters, and brothers and sisters recorded as parents of others, even one case where a great-grandfather had an affair with his great-granddaughter that resulted in twins. The old man was 88 and the girl-mother was 13. Liddy was really enjoying this search, so Ian always encouraged her to continue, but with a loving request to rest for the baby's sake.

Shamus was as impressed as Ian with Liddy's genealogical pursuits. She uncovered family tree branches that had remained hidden for centuries. Some of them would have been best undisturbed. But on the whole, Shamus was very pleased with Liddy and her love for Ian was unmistakably genuine. Maybe he would outfit a library for her at the castle when they moved to Scotland. Maybe he should start now to entice her to Scotland. He decided to see what her interests were after the baby was born. If she were still interested in the Stuart-Bruce heritage, there would be time for a library.

CHAPTER 6

Carmel, California
January 1947

....

"Liddy, I want to go to Pebble Beach this week to play golf. We can stay for a few days and come back by Sunday." Ian peeked over the newspaper he was reading. Liddy turned and looked at him with a puzzled look.

"Ian, we cannot go running around everywhere so close to when the baby is due. You know that." Liddy used her newly-acquired maternal voice as she finished the scrambled eggs.

"But it is still six or seven weeks before the baby is due and I don't want to stay cooped up in the house for the next two or three months. We can drive down there this morning and I can be on the course by late afternoon and get in at least nine holes." Ian's voice had a pleading tone to it.

"Well, I do feel fine and the baby has been kicking some but no real problems and I would like to get in a relaxing few days at the beach before the baby comes." Liddy seemed to click through a mental checklist of reasons to go versus why not. Finally, her face brightened and she said, "Okay, let's pack and get on the road. Where are we going to stay while we're there?"

"I'll make a couple of calls and get Stan to let us use his house. It is right across the road from the beach." Ian got up to go to the phone in hall.

Liddy could hear him talking and when he came back into the breakfast nook, he said, "All arranged. Finish fixing breakfast so we can leave before 9:00."

He watched Liddy for a moment. As always Ian could not believe he was married to Liddy and she was going to have their baby. She was absolutely radiant. Other than a few bouts of morning sickness in the first two or three months, she looked and acted happier than ever. Ian was glad that the pregnancy had gone so well. He wanted a lot of kids, maybe five or six. Slow down, one at a time, he couldn't overwhelm Liddy. She had said maybe two, then no more, but he knew he would get her to go along with more children once she had the first one. She was a natural and he knew she would be a great mother to their children, no matter how many there were.

With the car packed, they drove south through Pacific Beach to Half Moon Bay and on to Pescadero where they stopped for a bathroom break and bought some fresh fruit at a stand by the road. On to Santa Cruz and down the coast past Fort Ord and into Monterey. Another bathroom stop and fill-up the gas tank, then a few miles to Carmel itself.

They drove down the hill from Carmel Village and pulled into the drive of a pleasant looking beach house with a large front porch looking over the bay. Ian helped Liddy into the house and they toured all the rooms together. Large living room at the front of the house with huge windows looking out to the beach and water beyond. The living room was large enough for a dining table with eight chairs, a wonderful room that had a large rock fireplace and comfortable furniture. The kitchen was next back but open to the dining and living room and it had all the latest appliances and room for a work island table in the middle. Three very roomy bedrooms, each with its own bath, and a separate powder room for guests. There was even a separate laundry room with one of those new automatic washing machine and a matching electric dryer. All in all, a wonderful place.

"Whose house is this again? It is gorgeous." Liddy poked her head into room after room. "Ian, can you hear me? Whose house is this? I don't think I heard you say." Liddy walked back into the kitchen.

Ian was closing the door to the refrigerator and turned to her with a bottle of champagne. He removed the wire around the cork, twisted the bottle around the cork in that funny way he opened champagne bottles. A loud pop followed by a little foam from the bottle before Ian poured a small amount in a glass and a much more generous amount in the second glass. Ian picked up both glasses, handed the one with a swallow of champagne to Liddy and kept the other.

"This house, my dear, is yours," he said with a grin as he touched his glass to hers and got the same ping he heard on their first dinner date at Castle Hot

Springs. "This is a place where we will bring our baby and have wonderful beach adventures."

Liddy looked at Ian, then around the house, then back to Ian. She could not say anything. She was so surprised she did not know how to react. Finally, she looked at the bubbles streaming up the side of the glass, tipped it to her lips and drank a small sip. "Everything you do continues to remind me that when I agreed to marry you at Castle Hot Springs, it was the best thing I have ever done," Liddy said with warmth in her voice. "I love you more today than I could ever imagine possible. It is so extravagant, a beach house. Can we afford it?"

Ian looked at her and shook his head slightly, drank his champagne in one gulp and said quietly, "I have told you many times, money is not a problem in my family and yes, we can afford it. In fact, the title to this property is in a file folder on the dining room table." Ian put his arm around Liddy's ample waist and walked her into the Big Room where he opened a file and handed her a few pages.

Liddy looked at them for a moment, then looked at Ian, somewhat confused. "These papers say that the house is mine and mine only, your name is not on the title."

"I wanted you to have something and someplace that is all yours where you knew you could come whenever you wanted," Ian explained. "Taxes, insurance and maintenance are paid for by an escrow trust account my office set up so that there will never be any reason to worry about any of the mundane details of home ownership."

"Thank you, Ian," Liddy said, teary-eyed, "How did you know I was feeling a bit insecure and needed to have something real to call my own. You are a thoughtful man and your wisdom is one of your best traits. Promise you will help me raise our children and pass on that wisdom to them."

"You know I will without even asking," Ian said as he put his arms around Liddy, "For the record, yes, I will help you raise our children and hope that they can have a bit of my humor along with the wisdom. I want them to get your common sense, honor and love of America. Enough promises, let's go sit on the swing and enjoy the view from YOUR front porch."

Ian wanted to make another trip to the beach house before the baby was born and they drove to Carmel the third weekend in January. Liddy was a little nervous, being so far from her doctor and the hospital in San Francisco, but Ian said that they could get back to the city in a couple of hours if she felt any signs of labor.

It was beautiful there and Liddy contacted two of her sorority sisters who lived in Monterey and she enjoyed the afternoons talking with them. They wanted her to join one of the bridge groups but Liddy had never really enjoyed playing cards. Ian kept busy playing golf and tennis and, of course, sailing. Their weekends seemed so short but each one of them renewed her spirits.

Every weekend but this one. Something was nagging at her and she couldn't pinpoint it.

Liddy woke at 2:30 a.m. and knew she was in labor. She had read all the books and listened to Kathleen talk about when she had had her baby Ellen last summer. She knew it was time to go to the hospital. Then she remembered, they were in Carmel. What hospital? She started to panic.

She shook Ian but he was sleeping very soundly, he always did at the beach house. She turned on the bedside lamp and pinched him hard on the soft underside of his upper arm.

Ian jumped awake. "What is it?" he snapped. "You don't have to pinch me. I'm too tired to make love, so go back to sleep." He rolled over and pulled the quilt over his head.

"Ian, listen to me. I think I'm in labor. I think I am having the baby right now," Liddy yelled at him.

Ian jumped from the bed and rushed to her side of the bed. "Are you sure?" He said anxiously. "We need to get to the hospital. Let me get your suitcase." He started for the door. "Oh my God, we're at the beach. What hospital should we go to? Now it was Ian who was panicking.

Calmly, Liddy said, "There is the clinic in Carmel Village, we can be there in five minutes."

They rushed to the clinic and Liddy was in labor for six hours. The baby, a boy as the old woman predicted, was born at 9:15 a.m., on January 18th, a Saturday. They named him Duncan Logan Stuart-Bruce. Liddy nursed the baby less than an hour after delivery and mother and son were soon asleep.

Ian adored Liddy even more now that she had given him Duncan. Ian filled the room with flowers and bought every piece of baby furniture and baby clothing at two stores in Monterey. Liddy stayed in the clinic 10 days and on January 28th Ian drove her and the baby to their home in Pacific Heights.

Ian became more attached to Duncan every day and could barely stand to go to work because he wanted to be with Liddy and Duncan all the time. Liddy enjoyed being a mother more than she ever imagined she would. She loved holding Duncan and nursing him. It was an extremely intense and sensual experience, something she did not expect when Duncan first started nursing.

She took Duncan everywhere with her — to the market, to the hairdresser, and shopping downtown at the department stores.

Ian and Liddy both really enjoyed the long weekends at the beach house in Carmel and Duncan loved to go down by the ocean. He watched the sea gulls gliding and killdeers running up and down the sand. He liked to watch bright red, blue and yellow kites flying over the ocean.

On Duncan's first birthday, Ian stayed home from work and helped Liddy make a cake and prepare everything for the party. Two neighbors came over and Ian's secretary from the office brought party hats. Duncan didn't really understand all the fuss that his mom and dad went to but he did like the chocolate cake and vanilla ice cream.

Duncan always resembled Ian but he started to look more and more like his dad every month. His eyes were the same shade of blue and his hair was brown and shiny like Ian's. They sent photographs of Duncan to Uncle Shamus in Scotland and in each return letter Shamus stated how much he thought that Duncan looked like Ian.

They made a very attractive happy family. Sort of the all-American family. Liddy kept her hair the same length as when she was married. Ian became more tanned with his every other Saturday morning round of golf at Pebble Beach and Saturday afternoon sailing in and around Monterey Bay. Sunday afternoons were Liddy's time off and she spent it with her sorority sisters in Monterey or going to the ballet or opera in San Francisco.

Ian would take Duncan to Fisherman's Wharf or to tidal pools at Bolinas north of Sausalito. Duncan loved to see the crabs as they moved sideways on the rocks above the tidal pools. They would spend hours poking a stick into holes to make crabs move or to make sea anemones shrivel up and disappear. Ian liked spending time with his son and Duncan loved his father's attention.

Even as early as two years old, Duncan started acting like Ian. The facial expressions and body language were identical and Duncan was so cute when he wrinkled his forehead when he did not understand something. By three, Duncan was becoming Ian in almost every way except he did not speak with a Scottish brogue. This both pleased and concerned Ian — he was pleased Duncan was talking like an American but it made him realize that Duncan was not getting any exposure to Scotland and her demanding ways.

Time enough for all that. Let's have fun, thought Ian, tossing aside the thoughts of his all too soon looming responsibility in Scotland.

"Duncan, let's go to Chinatown today. I want to find you a Chinese finger lock," Ian said excitedly.

"Can we drive with the car top down?" said Duncan with big eyes. "I like to go fast with the top down."

CHAPTER 7

San Francisco, California
March 1951

....

By the time Duncan turned 4 he changed from their gorgeous baby to their gregarious little boy. He was inquisitive, talkative, full of energy, liked reading and being read to, and loved games. Board games, card games, hangman games, connect-the-dot games, any game that would challenge him. In short, he was a joy to both Liddy and Ian.

About two years earlier when Duncan was 2, Liddy and Ian decided to try for another child but nothing seemed to work. All the remedies from the books did not work and none of the doctors were able to come up with a solid reason for not conceiving. At least the trying part was fun.

In April, Liddy and Ian went to visit a fertility expert at Stanford Medical Center since she knew the medical center well when she did volunteer work on and off during her time at Stanford. Both of them had complete work-ups and they were called to Dr. Epstein's office to discuss the results and plan a positive course of action to get pregnant.

Dr. Epstein was a serious young man who had the most intense black eyes Liddy had every seen. But his manner and speech were friendly and created an atmosphere of confidence. He was well respected and some considered him a world expert in gynecological and fertility medicine.

"We have performed all the standard and a few new tests on both of you and we have found the cause of the infertility. This is not good news and I do not know an easy way to say this," the doctor said quietly.

"Mrs. Stuart-Bruce — Liddy, you have cervical cancer. I am afraid it is more advanced than expected and we must operate very soon to have any hope of containing the spread from your cervix to other areas, particularly your ovaries, bladder, and pancreas." He stopped to give all this a chance to sink in on both Liddy and Ian.

Liddy stared directly at the doctor but did not see him and Ian turned to stare at Liddy. Tears welled up in his eyes and he looked to the floor to keep from actually crying out loud. He got that tight feeling in his stomach, like when he heard of his mother's death and, again, when his father died.

Liddy turned to Ian and said quietly but firmly, "I want to have the operation tomorrow morning unless you object, Ian."

Ian looked up at her, but couldn't speak and only nodded his head in a yes.

She stood and asked the doctor, "What time should I be at the hospital for surgery tomorrow morning?"

Dr. Epstein was surprised that they made the decision so quickly but answered, "Check into the hospital by 9:00 this evening and we will prep you for surgery tonight. I will schedule surgery for 7:30 tomorrow morning. The operation should take about two to three hours and you will be in intensive care recovery for 10 or 12 days." He continued, "I must warn both of you that this is a very serious operation and the outcome is not always certain."

Liddy spoke sharply, "What are my chances without the surgery?"

Dr. Epstein eyes showed instant appreciation for a woman who could analyze the facts this quickly without emotion. "No chance at all," he said firmly.

"Then I will be back here at 9:00. Thank you for helping us." She picked up her coat and purse and reached for Ian.

Ian stood but couldn't bring himself to shake the doctor's hand. He followed Liddy to the car. Once inside, they just sat there. They both sat in the car. They didn't talk, they couldn't. They both had their private thoughts.

"I want to go home and read Duncan a story before his bed time. Then I want you to hold me until I leave for the hospital. That's all I think I can handle right now," said Liddy in a tight, controlled voice, "I can't talk about this right now. Please understand."

Ian was staring at the center of the steering wheel. The Plymouth Clipper ship logo charged forward in the sea as it stared back at him. He could only nod his head to acknowledge Liddy. He knew that if he tried to talk he would lose control and right now neither of them needed that.

He reached over to turn the ignition and said softly, almost a whisper, "I will drop you at the house and pick up hamburgers at Hank's for dinner. Is that all right?"

"Yes, that would be nice. Maybe you could get Duncan a chili dog, you know how he loves them." Liddy added with a little lighter voice, "I'll make chocolate shakes. I bought ice cream yesterday. Would you like that?"

"Sounds great." Ian tried to be more cheerful.

To break the silence in the car, Ian turned on the radio and listened to an all news station in Oakland. He liked the emcee of the talk show and tonight's subject was the McCarthy hearings in Washington. The drivel from the radio kept both of them from thinking morbid thoughts too long and when they pulled in front of the house, Ian leaned over and gave Liddy a kiss on her cheek.

"Never, never, never forget for one second how much I love you no matter what," said Ian with a clear, strong voice. "Now go in and give your son a hug and get him ready for the feast. Tell him his father is going to slay the hot dog dragon for dinner tonight." He smiled.

She couldn't resist. She smiled a little. Then she opened the car's door and turned to Ian and said, "My hero, the hot dog dragon slayer," and smiled broadly.

There it is again. The smile that still takes my breath away. WOW.

Please, Oh God, please take care of her for Duncan's sake.

CHAPTER 8

Carmel, California
May 1951

....

Liddy stayed at the beach house with Duncan while she recovered from surgery. Duncan became her caretaker and helper. The surgery plus radiation treatment weakened her so much she could hardly get out of a chair without help. Slowly her strength returned and she was able to move around the beach house and take short walks on the beach. Duncan, always sensitive to his mother's needs, barely left her side but each day Liddy convinced Duncan to play with the other children on the beach and ride their bicycles to Carmel Village to get groceries and supplies. Duncan acted much older than his 4 years and Liddy was always amazed at his ability to deal with this whole ordeal like an adult.

Ian continued to work at the shipyard in San Francisco for three to four days each week and joined Liddy and Duncan for long weekends in Carmel. He wanted to stop working to take care of Liddy but she would not let him and she wanted to maintain the old routine as much as possible. On his weekend visits, Ian would sail with Duncan, golf with friends, cook tasty breakfasts and dinners. Lunch was usually sandwiches while he was out of the house. Each evening after Duncan went to bed, Ian would read to Liddy. She loved to hear his voice. The soft Scottish brogue topped off with the cultured, high-toned English accent added something special to each book he read to her. She particularly liked Ian to read books about Scotland and her favorite was a biography about a Scottish nobleman named William Wallace.

Liddy felt her strength coming back more and more each month and she settled into a steady productive program of exercise to increase her strength.

At the end of July she had an appointment with Dr. Epstein to check her progress. She knew that the surgery and radiation did not stop the cancer even before the tests were completed. Ian waited in Dr. Epstein's office while Liddy finished dressing. Dr. Epstein sat quietly at his desk, scanning the various reports, looked up at Liddy and said, "I am sorry but the cancer is back and appears to be spreading. We do not have any other treatments available. We are making breakthroughs almost daily but I am afraid there is nothing we can recommend. I cannot tell you how badly I feel that we cannot help you." He stopped talking and let his words settle on Liddy and Ian.

Ian could not contain his emotions and silently cried. Liddy twisted the handkerchief in her lap for a couple of minutes, looked up at Dr. Epstein and asked, "How long before I will have to go to a hospital?"

"You have about two or three months before the pain will become so intense that you will have to be hospitalized." Dr. Epstein glanced at the reports again. "After you are hospitalized, you will most likely see the cancer progress very quickly and in one to two weeks you will go into a coma until your body cannot overcome the effects of the cancer any longer. At the end, you will not feel any pain and you will not be conscious."

"Will there be any restrictions for the next two months? Can I maintain a fairly normal life?" Liddy asked quickly. "Can I travel to visit family and friends and go to the beach house?"

"Yes, I will give you a prescription for pain medicine and other drugs that will delay the effects of the cancer as long as possible." Dr. Epstein nodded his head. "And I will give you a list of the best cancer treatment centers in the country so that you can be treated while you travel. Do you expect to travel far from California?"

Liddy turned to Ian, who was wiping his eyes, "Maybe. Thank you, Doctor, for your kind words and concern. You and your staff and everyone here at Stanford have done a wonderful job of caring for me and watching over Ian and Duncan while I was in the hospital. We will call your office with our travel plans in the next day or so." Liddy stood, nodded to Ian and left Dr. Epstein's office.

For a second time, the drive back to their house was made tolerable by the radio to break the silence. That evening after Duncan was asleep, Liddy sat in her favorite chair on the sun porch looking at the groomed backyard. Ian brought two glasses of wine and sat on the sofa and looked at Liddy. He was afraid to talk, afraid he would break down and cry again. So he sat very still, mechanically raising the wine glass to his lips and taking small sips of the wine.

Finally he got control of himself and said quietly, "What do you want me to do?"

Liddy sipped her wine and looked at him thoughtfully and said firmly, "Promise to love and care for Duncan. You are the only one he will have after I am gone. Promise."

Ian looked down at the wine in the glass, and then up at Liddy with clear eyes and a steady voice, "I promise. I will love and care for Duncan. And I will make sure he always has great memories of his mother."

Liddy looked out at the yard again and nodded her head and said with a satisfied tone, "Thank you that is all I can ask."

They sat and did not talk. Did not hold hands. Did not look at each other. They simply sat together sorting out their thoughts. It was one of the things that Ian would truly miss, being with her like this was a comfort and he got a great sense of well-being during times like this.

Liddy was thinking about what Dr. Epstein said earlier about being able to travel. After about 15 or 20 minutes, she turned to Ian and said, "I have never really asked how much money your family has but I know that you have quite a bit. People like the Crockers, Huntingtons, Kaisers, Hearsts, Harrimans and Gianinnis at Bank of America don't do business with people unless they have some really substantial financial holdings. I am not asking you to tell me where the money is held or exactly how much your family has. What I am asking is if there is enough money for us to travel for the next two months and travel extensively and travel in style with lots of supporting care. I want to take Duncan to Hollywood, the Grand Canyon, Niagara Falls, Lake Tahoe, Seattle, Victoria, to my hometown in San Clemente and I want to take him to New York and Washington then down to New Orleans, Charleston and Miami. Then off to Scotland to spend time with your Uncle Shamus. I want Duncan to know Shamus and know that he will also care for and love Duncan and you. Can we do all of those things?"

Ian was not only surprised but also very pleased by Liddy's request. "Sure we can," he said. "You bet," as he became more enthusiastic. "I didn't think you would want to leave San Francisco and the beach house but the answer is a definite yes. When do you want to leave?"

"As soon as we can put together all the arrangements. Two or three days if we can afford it. Travel like this on a short notice is so expensive," Liddy said with a worried voice.

"I ask only one thing — do not worry about the money and how much we are spending for this trip. No matter what we spend, I assure you the Stuart-Bruce family can afford it. No matter what the cost. So promise not to worry and not to ask how we are paying for this. With one phone call, I can get the money from the trust fund my father left when he died."

"Good. I promise not to worry," said Liddy as she stood, pulled Ian up so she could hug him and give him a kiss. "I can't wait to tell Duncan in the morning."

Ian looked into Liddy's eyes, "I love you. I will always love you and I will love and care for Duncan."

Ian changed his focus to the backyard and Liddy could see the wheels moving in his mind as he said, "I am going to plan the adventure of a lifetime and I will have Duncan help me. Let me write down all the places you want to go to so I can start working on the plans."

The next morning at breakfast, they told Duncan. He literally jumped up and down. "Wow, we are going to see the Grand Canyon and Niagara Falls and the tallest building in the world and we are going to fly over the ocean and visit a castle!" said Duncan without stopping, "Dad, I can't wait. Let's pack right now."

Very quickly in the planning process Ian discovered that trying to schedule all the places with airlines and trains was almost impossible. The fix, Ian realized, was to buy their own plane, hire a crew and then go where they wanted, when they wanted.

Duncan was so excited about having his own plane, Ian and Liddy christened the Lockheed Constellation plane "Duncan's Delight." He wanted to sit up front with the pilot and co-pilot when they were flying.

And fly they did. First to Portland, then Seattle and Victoria to see Mount Hood, Mount Rainier and the gardens near Victoria. Riding the ferries across Puget Sound and Strait of Juan de Fuca were one of Duncan's favorites. They stayed in the best hotels and had private cars and drivers take them to all the places they wanted to see. They spent an afternoon on Vashon Island at the summer home of a shipyard owner Ian knew. All of this was very expensive, Liddy knew, but she promised not to worry so she didn't. She focused on making sure that Duncan and Ian had every chance to strengthen their love for each other. And every day she could see that Ian shared his thoughts with Duncan and that Duncan's love and trust for Ian grew stronger. This gave Liddy a sense of well-being because she knew that Ian would do anything for Duncan's care and welfare.

They flew south to Southern California and went to San Clemente so Liddy could show Duncan where she grew up and went to school. She sold her parents home after they died in a car wreck the week before she graduated from Stanford. Duncan wanted to know about his grandparents and Liddy told him funny stories about how her mother really hated having snails eat her flowers.

Back north to Beverly Hills and Santa Monica. Duncan loved the Ferris wheel at the pier and visiting the movie studios in Hollywood. They stayed at the Beverly Hills Hotel and swam in the pool when they were not sightseeing.

One evening when Liddy, Ian, and Duncan were having dinner in the hotel's Polo Lounge, Duncan overheard the couple at the next table talking about their horses. Duncan asked Liddy if they could go riding the next day and she said she didn't know if the hotel had stables or horses. Duncan said he would go ask and was getting ready to run to the front desk when the very handsome man said, "Excuse me. We really weren't eavesdropping but we could not help but overhear your son ask if he could go riding. Can we invite you all to join us when we ride in the hills above Pacific Palisades tomorrow?"

Ian and Liddy looked at each other, then at Duncan, who said, "Can we?"

Ian stood, walked around the table, extended his hand and said, "I am Ian Stuart-Bruce." Pointing to Liddy and Duncan, he said, "This is my wife Liddy and our son Duncan. And your invitation is very kind but we couldn't impose."

"No imposition, Mr. Stuart-Bruce. Nancy and I like to have company on our rides. Oh, sorry, my name is Ron Reagan and this is my wife Nancy," he explained as he shook hands with Ian and nodded to Liddy.

"You're both movie stars, Ronald Reagan and Nancy Davis!" said Liddy with astonishment. "I guess I did not expect to meet any movie stars while we were eating dinner. That's foolish, you have to eat too, so why not here in this beautiful restaurant?"

"We love it here," said Nancy with a smile. "We probably come for dinner at least once a week."

Looking at Mr. Reagan, Duncan asked with enthusiasm, "Do you play cowboys in the movies?"

"Sometimes," said Ron directly to Duncan, "Sometimes I play good guys and sometimes I play bad guys. What is your favorite movie, Duncan?"

"Well, let's see," said Duncan thinking hard, "I think my favorite movie is Zorro but I like Pinocchio, too."

"Pinocchio is my favorite, too, Duncan," said Nancy. "How long before you leave Los Angeles?" she asked.

"Three days before we leave for the Grand Canyon and Sedona," said Duncan. "Me and my dad planned the whole trip."

"My dad and I," corrected Liddy, "My dad and I planned the whole trip."

"Yes, ma'am," said Duncan with a bit of his lower lip showing. "My dad and I planned the whole trip."

"Duncan," said Nancy Reagan, "I went to school on a ranch not far from Sedona and my parents live in Phoenix in the winter. We visit them two or three times a season."

"Wow, you went to school in the desert," exclaimed Duncan. "I can't wait to see the desert. My Mom and Dad met in the desert at … at something Hot Springs. I forget the first name."

"Castle Hot Springs," said Nancy. "I know where it is but I haven't been there. Well, I look forward to talking more tomorrow on our ride together." She glanced at Duncan's folks.

Ian looked at Liddy who nodded, then back to Nancy and Ron. "Well, if you are sure that it is no trouble, we would love to ride with you," Ian said with a tone of appreciation. They made plans to meet the next morning at the stables a few miles from the hotel and Ron and Nancy left the restaurant.

"That was very nice of them," said Liddy with a bit of surprise in her voice. "Who would have thought that movie stars would be so friendly?"

"They are more than friendly. They are very special," Ian said as he watched the Reagans leave the restaurant. "They will do something remarkable with their life together. Something truly remarkable."

CHAPTER 9

Washington, D.C.
July 1951

....

Everywhere they went was an adventure for Duncan and for all of them as a family. The Grand Canyon was more spectacular than he could have imagined and Liddy was constantly in fear that Duncan was too close to the edge at the viewpoints they visited. Hoover Dam was so big that Duncan kept asking about the size and Ian kept reading from the guidebook the height and width and capacity, all numbers too large to really fully understand, especially for a 4-year-old boy.

Liddy and Ian were having a grand time enjoying the sights and the travel across the U.S. but they truly marveled at how much Duncan could remember about each place on their tour. Ian was convinced that he made the right decision after their three-day excursion through Yellowstone and Grand Teton National Parks. What a beautiful place and the wildlife was so plentiful and diverse. Duncan really liked watching the buffalo, elk and trumpeter swans. The highlight was a float trip down the Snake River, south of Jackson, Wyoming. After leaving Wyoming, the Black Hills of South Dakota and Mount Rushmore were pleasant surprises. Such a beautiful monument to America's most famous presidents.

Ian noticed that Liddy was tiring sooner each day, so he encouraged everyone to slow down. Liddy would not hear of it. They made their way east across the Rockies, the Mississippi River and on to Niagara Falls for two days and then down to Washington, D.C.

Ian had only been to Washington briefly once when he was boy so he wanted Duncan to see all the sites — Smithsonian and its many museum buildings, the Mint where money is made, National Archives to see the Declaration of Independence and the Constitution and Arlington Cemetery across the Potomac River. Duncan was most impressed with the Washington National Zoo and the monkeys.

Ian called his old friend Jack Kennedy and found that Jack had a speaking engagement in Boston and a dinner at the family compound in Hyannis Port. They promised to get together in California later in the year when Jack had a West Coast speaking tour planned.

One morning Ian woke Duncan without waking Liddy and they slipped out of the suite at the Hay Adams Hotel to walk across Lafayette Park to Pennsylvania Avenue. Ian wanted to walk around the White House so Duncan could see it from all sides.

The White House was undergoing a significant renovation and President and Mrs. Truman resided in Blair House across the street from the White House while construction crews finished their work. As Ian and Duncan rounded the corner and were pointing at birds in a tree, a group of men walked toward them. These men were walking with purpose and several of them seemed to be almost running. As they approached Ian and Duncan, the man in the center of the group stopped, then walked over and asked, "What do you see in the tree?" in a clipped mid-western, almost southern, accent.

Duncan turned and said with authority, "a red bird."

"A red bird, now. Show me where it is." His gaze followed Duncan's pointed finger. "I want to see a red bird."

"There it is," said Duncan, pointing to the large evergreen tree, "At the top. See it?"

"Yes, I do see it. You have good eyes and you are right, it is a red bird," said the man. "Do you know another name for a red bird?"

Duncan thought for a moment, "No, I don't see many red birds in California."

"So you are from California. That is a long way from here." The man looked at Ian to make sure Ian approved of the conversation. "What is your name, young man?"

Duncan looked the man straight in the eyes and said clearly, "Duncan. What is your name?"

The man leaned over and offered his hand to Duncan and said, "My name is Harry." The man shook hands with Duncan and then offered his hand to Ian, saying "Harry Truman."

Ian responded with mild amazement about the informality of the moment, "My name is Ian Stuart-Bruce. Duncan is my son."

"What a good-looking boy. I'll bet he's a handful," said Harry with a smile. He turned back to Duncan and said, "Another name for a red bird is cardinal. Can you remember that name, Duncan?"

"Yes, sir, I will," said Duncan, carefully repeating, "cardinal."

"Do you know who lives in that house?" asked Harry as he pointed to the White House.

"Yes sir, my dad told me that the president lives there," said Duncan, hesitating a bit.

"That's right Duncan," said Harry with a laugh in his voice, "Do you know who the president is?"

Duncan frowned and thought for a minute and said, "Yes sir. He is the man who lives in that house."

Harry laughed out loud. "Good answer. Accurate without giving away any new information." Harry continued with respect, "Most of the time I wish that the members of my cabinet and staff could do what you did, give accurate answers without giving away any new information." Harry looked seriously at the group of men a few feet away. They all looked down at the sidewalk and some cleared their throats with embarrassed looks on their faces.

Harry asked, "Mr. Stuart-Bruce, do I detect an accent?

"Yes, sir. I was born and raised in Scotland but settled with my wife Liddy in San Francisco after the war," answered Ian cheerfully.

"Your family name seems familiar to me. Where would I have heard it before?" Harry studied Ian's face.

"Well, my father fought with the French resistance in the war and my uncle is known in Edinburgh and London. For a brief time in 1945, my uncle accompanied Winston Churchill on his travels."

"That's it. I met your uncle in Potsdam in the summer of 1945. His name is.... don't tell me. I will think of it." Harry held up his hand to stop Ian from saying the name. "I'll remember his name. Give me a minute."

"Shamus. Shamus Stuart-Bruce." Harry beamed as he remembered the name. "How is he?"

"Shamus is doing very well," said Ian with a resigned respect. "Uncle Shamus always does very well."

"Be sure to give Shamus my regards." Turning to Duncan he continued, "Young man, I need to finish my walk. I have several important meetings today." Harry reached to shake Duncan's hand, then Ian's. "It was an honor to meet you and your father today."

"Thank you, sir," said Duncan. With a grown-up tone to his voice, he added, "But the honor was all ours. Thank you for teaching me the new red bird name, 'cardinal.'"

Harry turned back to look at Duncan then to Ian. "You are a lucky man, Mr. Stuart-Bruce," said President Truman with a father-to-son tone. "Duncan must bring you and your wife a great deal of joy. He would if he were my son."

Ian took Duncan's hand and walked back to the hotel.

When they got to the suite, Liddy was in the bathroom and she called to Ian through the door. He went in to see what she wanted and he stopped as he closed the door. He knew this day would come but never wanted to admit it would be this soon. Liddy was very pale, lying on the tile floor, covered with a towel.

"Liddy, what is it? My god, what is it?" Ian spoke in as low of a voice as he could considering the panic he felt. He went to her and lifted her head. Her eyes were closed and she was barely conscious.

"Ian, get me to a hospital," Liddy whispered. "Please don't let Duncan see me like this."

Ian never understood why people installed telephones in bathrooms until now. He dialed the hotel operator and asked them to call an ambulance. He also asked that they send the concierge George up to watch Duncan while he took his wife to the hospital.

"I will tell my son that the concierge asked to have breakfast with him." Ian hoped she would pass the message along. "And please have the ambulance hurry."

The doctors at Georgetown Medical Center were able to stabilize Liddy in about three days. Ian did not want to leave the hospital but he had to watch over Duncan. After 72 hours of juggling the demands of being with Liddy and taking care of Duncan, he knew he needed someone he could trust to take care of Duncan while he was with Liddy.

The connection had static characteristic to long distance calls but a bit more pronounced. "Shamus," said Ian into the receiver, "I need your help." He knew his voice sounded strained but he was doing his best to maintain control.

"Yes, Ian," said Shamus quietly but with caution. "Anything. Anything at all."

"Can you drop whatever you are doing and catch the next plane to Washington?" asked Ian with a quiet voice that told Shamus something serious was taking place. "I need you here to take care of Duncan while Liddy is in the hospital."

"Hospital? Washington?" said Shamus with a worried and puzzled tone. "What is wrong? Is Liddy ill?"

"Liddy was diagnosed with cancer a few months ago and the treatments were not successful. I don't really want to go into all the details now on the phone but you should plan to spend a few weeks with us here in America." Ian spoke quickly, hoping to dodge any more questions. "Call me at the Hay Adams Hotel when you have an arrival time. I will have a car waiting at the airport for you."

"Yes, of course," said Shamus with confidence, "I will catch the next flight to Washington. Is there anything I can do from here?"

"No, but please hurry," said Ian with genuine concern. "We need you here."

"It may take a day to get there but I probably will see you tomorrow afternoon." Trying for a cheerier note, Shamus added, "I can't wait to spend time with Duncan."

"Thanks, Shamus," said Ian firmly. "You will never know how much this means."

Ian rang off and Shamus immediately called British Airways to book the first flight out to Toronto, Boston, New York or Washington. He had to get to America, as soon as possible, to take care of Ian, Liddy and, of course, Duncan.

Duncan had never met Shamus Stuart-Bruce. He had seen photographs and his father read letters they received and once talked on the phone for about

30 seconds. But he had never actually met Uncle Shamus. The more correct title would be his great-great Uncle Shamus since Shamus was Duncan's great-grandfather's brother. Liddy tried to explain all this to Duncan but it was too complicated for a 4-year old boy who did not spend much time with relatives and had no grandparents or aunts or uncles or cousins. It was a distant concept that Duncan could not put together yet.

So the first impression Duncan had of Uncle Shamus was that he was a big old man with a very deep voice but bright blue eyes that smiled. Duncan watched his dad carefully and saw that his dad liked Uncle Shamus and Uncle Shamus liked his dad. They whispered about things but Duncan knew they were talking about his mom in the hospital. Duncan took his bird book over to a chair close to his dad and looked at the pictures while he listened. After about five minutes, Uncle Shamus said with that deep voice, "Duncan boy, what is that book you have there? Bring it over here and show me what is in the book."

Duncan looked at Ian, sort of asking permission, and Ian nodded. Duncan walked over to Uncle Shamus's chair and stood in front with the bird book.

Shamus looked a Duncan with eyes that were the same vibrant blue color of his dad's eyes and Duncan knew was the same color as his own eyes.

"This is a book my mother and father bought me at the Smithsonian Museum," said Duncan tentatively. Gaining a bit of confidence, he continued. "And I was looking at pictures of red birds. Did you know that red birds are also called cardinals? My friend Harry taught me the word cardinal a few days ago."

Shamus looked up at Ian questioningly and Ian interrupted Duncan. "Duncan, you know his proper name is not Harry and that he is an elder and a very important man so we do not use first names, do we? So what is your friend's proper name?"

Duncan did not like to be interrupted, even by his dad, so he frowned slightly before replying directly to Uncle Shamus. "My friend's proper name is President Truman, but he told me to call him Harry."

This time Shamus sat back in his chair looking first at Ian, then to Duncan and back to Ian.

"We met President Truman and some of his staff on a walk around the White House a couple of days ago. So now Duncan thinks he can forget the manners his mother and I taught him about addressing elders with the proper names."

Shamus waved his hand in dismissal, looked at Duncan and said with a twinkle, "I met President Truman a few years ago in Germany. I was impressed with his easy-going manner and straightforward talk. America is lucky to have him as president."

Duncan looked at Ian as he said proudly, "I know. President Truman said he knew you and to tell you hi when we saw you."

"That is so like him. Friendly, genuine and always wishing everyone the best," Shamus said with respect. "Hope he and his family are doing well. Now, show me a picture of a — what did you say the other name for a red bird was?"

"Cardinal." Duncan almost shouted as both Shamus and Ian laughed.

Ian watched Shamus slowly gain Duncan's confidence and trust and after 10 minutes he knew he would never worry about them together. It would be a contest to see who could talk the most. Ian hoped that Shamus would teach Duncan to listen with the same fervor as he talked.

After dinner Ian wanted to go the hospital and explained to Duncan that it was his responsibility to entertain Shamus while Ian was gone but bedtime was still 8:30. So when Ian left for the hospital, Shamus was reading a Superman comic book to Duncan while Duncan sat on his lap in the big chair next to fireplace in the suite at the Hay Adams Hotel.

The next morning while Ian was brushing his teeth, Duncan came into the bathroom and asked. "How was Mom last night? Was she okay? When can I see her?" asked Duncan in rapid-fire succession before Ian could even get his toothbrush from his mouth.

"Whoa. Slow down. Mom is doing great," said Ian with a foaming toothpaste smile; "In fact the doctors asked me check with you about taking Mom home to California. Would that be okay with you?"

"Sure, that would be great. When do we leave?"

"How about tomorrow?" said Ian as he looked at Shamus. "Will you come with us to California, Uncle Shamus?"

"Yeah, can you come to our house, Uncle Shamus?" asked Duncan as he ran toward his new best friend. "We can show you the beach house, too."

"Of course, I will come to California with you," Shamus said with enthusiasm as he put his hand on Duncan's shoulders.

CHAPTER 10

Carmel, California
February 1952

....

Liddy died on February 28, 1952, a Thursday, their sixth wedding anniversary. Duncan turned 5 years old a month earlier and had to grow up too much in the last year. He was still a little boy but now he was a little boy without a mother. Although everyone saw sadness in Duncan's eyes, they also saw an unmistakable resilience to Duncan's young frame as he stood with his father and Uncle Shamus at the graveyard in front of his mother's coffin.

Duncan stood alone as Shamus walked with Ian to the casket before it was closed and removed the diamond and emerald wedding ring from Liddy's finger.

"You must keep this in a safe place for Duncan. When he is older, you will be able to tell him the whole story of how you and Liddy met and the ring will be very important to him. Promise me you will keep the ring for Duncan." Shamus spoke solemnly.

Ian could only nod his head and hold the ring on the little finger of his right hand as he turned to join Duncan.

The clergyman continued the graveside service as the coffin was closed and, although he did not fully understand what was going on, Duncan leaned into his father's chest and cried, tears flowing down his cheeks. Duncan knew his mother had died but he wasn't sure exactly what this meant. He knew he was sad but at the same time he knew he had to take care of his dad now, like he took care of his mother after she had the operation and came to the beach house to recuperate.

Surprisingly, the next month passed quickly while Shamus, Ian and Duncan stayed at the beach house. Ian spent time sailing alone out and around Carmel, Monterey and Big Sur. Shamus worried about Ian becoming too melancholy but the time alone on the sailboat seemed to help Ian come to grips with Liddy's death. In the meantime, Shamus got to know Duncan better during walks on the beach, riding bicycles and playing games in the big room overlooking the beach.

Each night after Duncan was asleep, Shamus and Ian sat in front of the fireplace and talked about Scotland, Ian's dad and Ian's grandfather, Shamus's brother. Shamus shared stories about each person that Ian had never heard before. He was anxious to learn more about his family since he had not lived in Scotland since 1941, and paid only a few short visits during the war.

One evening Shamus seemed more distant than usual. Ian sensed that Shamus wanted to talk about future plans, so Ian opened the discussion by saying, "Shamus, after you leave and go back to Scotland, I am going to close the house in the city and live here with Duncan."

Shamus listened as Ian continued, "I have checked into schools here in Carmel and made tentative plans to enroll Duncan at the Justin School. I have also talked with Father Bennett at St. Paul's Episcopal Church in Monterey about Duncan and he has assured me that both Duncan and I are always welcome." What Ian did not share with Shamus was that he was joining the church for Duncan's sake. Ian was deeply uncomfortable with the church. Somewhere along the way he lost his faith, mainly because he blamed God for letting Liddy die. He was bitter. He felt that God betrayed Liddy and him both.

Shamus lit his pipe, took a couple of puffs, got up and poured some more brandy in his glass, then turned to Ian. "I hoped you would move to Scotland and bring Duncan to our home in Aberdeen so we could patch together a family for him. I understand your wanting to stay close to where you and Liddy and Duncan had so many good memories, but after spending time with Duncan, I am sure he would thrive in Aberdeen at the castle."

Shamus sat back down in his chair, puffed some more on his pipe and continued. "You must remember also that I am now 42 years old and not getting any younger and I am ready to retire from running the family business. I had to take over running everything in 1939 when your father decided to serve the

Crown as an intelligence officer and ran off to literally the four corners of the earth. Then your mother died and your father took that crazy assignment in France in 1943. I was left with no choice but to continue as Managing Director until you take over. And that date is coming up soon. You will be 32 years old in a few months. You will become Managing Director and you are expected to live at the castle and run the family's businesses from Aberdeen as it has been done for more than six hundred years."

Ian sat listening but staring in the glowing embers in the fireplace. He knew what Shamus was telling him was true and that he had to fulfill the family tradition and run the businesses as his father had before he left for the war. But not right now. Ian could not leave Liddy yet.

"Shamus, you have set aside all your duties, responsibilities and obligations to be with Duncan and me for the last few months. My love and respect for you has grown and I know that Duncan loves you and enjoys his time with you but I cannot leave this place. Not yet," said Ian with soft voice. "I do not want to quarrel with you about this."

Both men sat listening to the wood spit and pop as it burned and warmed the room, warding off the ocean's chill that settled each night. They did not talk for 15 or 20 minutes then Shamus took another sip of the brandy and said, "Ian, I will make a deal with you. You stay here in Carmel with Duncan for a year and then you bring Duncan to Scotland for a visit. A long visit, not just a week or two, but at least two months."

Shamus looked directly at Ian and continued, "And after the two months, we will have another talk. But keep in mind that you will be within a few weeks of your 32nd birthday and that is when you are required to take over the family business."

Ian looked up and smiled a bit, then said, "You are a wise and patient man and I accept your deal. Duncan and I will miss you but we need to stay here for the time being."

Shamus got up, put his hand on Ian's shoulder, and said, "I will leave for Scotland on Saturday. Will you and Duncan take me to the airport in San Francisco?" He then walked to his room.

CHAPTER 11

Aberdeen, Scotland
June 1953

....

Ian and Duncan were getting settled at the castle where they arrived after a long train ride from Southampton, London and Edinburgh. Ian decided to make their trip to Scotland a journey by taking a train from San Francisco to Chicago and then New York. The train trip across the country was about three days long and, fortunately, Duncan spent his time in the company of 8-year-old twin boys accompanying their grandparents from Sacramento to Rochester, New York. The three boys basically terrorized the rest of the passengers with their games and pranks. Duncan even got caught trying to tie a man's shoelaces together. Ian made him stay in their compartment for four hours as punishment. The boys ran foot races up and down the aisles and their enthusiasm and energy got the rest of the passengers to start cheering them along until the conductor announced that the bar car was open.

After only a two-day stopover in New York, they boarded the *RMS Queen Elizabeth* for the five-day run to Southampton. Duncan found a group of boys to play with on the voyage across the Atlantic and combined with scheduled activities by the Cunard staff, Duncan barely spent any time with Ian after they left New York. Duncan had a great time in London visiting the museums, the Tower of London, and many shops. Duncan was most interested in maps and atlases and Ian and Duncan spent two afternoons pulling old tubes with dusty maps out of racks at rare manuscript shops. Finally, they boarded a train for Edinburgh and Aberdeen. Duncan was happy when they arrived at Uncle Shamus's home and he had his own room again.

71

Duncan was absolutely fascinated with everything about the Stuart-Bruce clan except the part about men wearing skirts, or kilts, as they were called in Scotland. He wandered through the castle in Aberdeen and studied the old paintings of all the men and women lining the halls of the castle. The biggest painting was of a man named Robert the Bruce who was the head of the family a long time ago. Duncan couldn't remember the number of years but it was a number bigger than he could count.

Uncle Shamus was the same loving, funny man and Duncan spent a great deal of time with his uncle as they walked the hills behind the castle, fished the streams for salmon and trout, and rode horses down on the seacoast. Shamus explained new things; Duncan rarely had to be told twice about anything he learned. The shaggy-haired Scottish cattle caused Duncan to laugh out loud until he got up close to them and saw how big they were. Shamus introduced Duncan to a lot of people and, again, Duncan's great memory almost never forgot a face or a name.

After about three weeks of learning about Scotland and its people, Duncan was concerned because he had seen very little of his father. Ian and Shamus both explained that Ian would be in Glasgow and Edinburgh looking at family businesses to become familiar with them again. Much had changed since 1940 and Ian was anxious to learn what new things they were working on.

A project that caught Ian's attention involved their Clyde River ship salvage operation that was very busy with all the war ships scuttled or sunk in and around almost every port in Europe, Asia, North Africa, the Middle East and a few in South America. Much of the work was to remove the sunken craft from navigation lanes. In most cases, the salvage company had to raise ships and tow them to deeper water where they were sunk again so that they would not be a hazard to other vessels.

This routine salvage work was rarely interesting because most of the ships had already been stripped of anything valuable including machinery, engines, navigation and communications equipment, and interior fixtures. There was scrap metal value for the hull but the cost of getting the hull to a scrap yard could easily exceed any intrinsic value from the metal.

All salvage companies kept secret what they found in each ship they decommissioned. At times things were found that had incredible value. Sometimes art objects were found — like the ten Ming vases found on the ship outside Rotterdam — turns out the vases were worth about $25,000 each. That gave the salvage company a big-enough windfall that they were able to finance two additional salvage jobs that year. Such finds didn't occur often, but often enough to keep everyone interested. But the secrets from the salvage companies were just that … secret, and although you could find many rumors and tales in the offices, bars and pubs around the shipyards, the rumors were as hard to hold onto as the fog on the docks.

Ian sat in the salvage company office outside Glasgow and listened to the report presented by the Captain and First Mate of the *Sassy Lassy,* a newer barge-like salvage ship currently positioned about 10 miles from Aberdeen harbor. The doors to the office were closed and the blinds pulled down to the windowsills. This was one of those secrets that must be kept quiet, very quiet.

"So we took the ship's log from that German tanker we salvaged last year in Calais, translated it starting with the most recent entries and going back," said Captain Watts quietly. "We found the log in a false panel under the deck of the bridge. Only Fergie and me know what the log has in it."

"The last date entered in the log was April 22, 1945. The ship was refueling in Bremen and apparently was abandoned there by the crew. This was close to the end and the crew was probably made up of mostly civilians and prisoners-of-war. Who knows what happened? Our guess is that the tanker's captain was ordered to meetings somewhere in Bremen and never returned and after a couple of days the crew left." Captain Watts continued, "It is not important now because all we wanted was the log and when we found it, we started looking back to see if there was anything interesting recorded. And there was. Look at the entry on December 24, 1944."

Everyone gathered around the table and looked at the open page of the log, which had an entry halfway down the page showing, "24 December 44 0525."

Captain Watts said that after translating the German the entry read, "Transferred 25,000 liters of fuel to U-4977. Refueling took 5 hours 15 minutes. The crew of U-4977 seemed unusually happy not because of the Christmas holiday tomorrow, we did not believe it was cause for concern until one crew member said that they would be having their New Year a little late with Latin ladies enjoying the wines of Argentina in two weeks. That was the reason everyone on U-4977 was so happy and looking forward to this particular cruise."

"Two things caught our attention about this entry. One is the amount of fuel transferred — 25,000 liters is about 10,000 liters more than a normal fuel transfer to a German U-boat. Why so much more fuel? The second was the cruise to Argentina. Why to Argentina?" said the captain with emphasis on Argentina.

This information tied into reports they got of a submarine discovered off of Storm Island. The submarine sat on a shelf about 10 miles east of Aberdeen and down 300 feet. As a group, the salvage team and Ian decided to make a dive to look at the submarine and determine if it was salvageable and if it contained anything worth salvaging. The captain had already contacted British archives in London and found there was no record of a U-4977, other than a brief entry at the shipyard in Bremen where most of the German U-boats were built. The records from the Wermacht's Kriegsmarine office were taken by the Soviets when they occupied Berlin in 1945 so getting more detailed records seemed remote at this time.

British and Allied naval records showed that the submarine was not one of theirs. Early research reports indicated that the submarine might be one of the cargo submarines used by the Nazis to transport the gold, silver, platinum and art treasures from the German treasury to South America. The German naval records thus far did not show what was on board the lost U-boat but discreet inquiries had been made to examine ship manifest records captured in Berlin by the Soviet army in May 1945.

Ian got very interested in the submarine salvage project, which was kept very quiet. Until more information was known, no one wanted to attract the attention of international salvage firms and the pirates that gathered around them.

Shamus monitored progress and made sure that Ian had as much control of the project as he wanted. As Shamus suspected, the more control of the project Ian got, the more Ian wanted. Finally, the day before Ian and Duncan were to return to California, Shamus suggested that Ian take firm control of the entire project and oversee the salvage of the U-boat. Ian agreed and postponed leaving with Duncan to return to Carmel.

Using the family's far-reaching connections, Shamus was able to secure the use of a special deep-sea vessel developed in France that could easily reach a depth of 300 feet. Ian went to Marseilles to learn how to use the Sea Rover, as it was called by the crew.

The Sea Rover was a remarkable, revolutionary machine capable of performing many of the simple and complex tasks necessary during salvage operations. Under the guise of a British Petroleum oil exploration project, the salvage ship and the Sea Rover began more thorough inspections of the U-boat. Hundreds of still photos were taken and the movie cameras never stopped.

The first thing Ian noticed was the eight-foot hole in the sub's sail. Ian threaded the Sea Rover's remote controlled movie camera through the hole into the hull. After several days of uneventful exploration of the engine rooms, control room, galley and crew quarters, the Sea Rover found a hatch leading to a previously unexplored mezzanine level, sort of halfway between levels 1 and level 2.

The compartments on this mezzanine level were barely six feet tall. Each of the five compartments was about 12 feet wide by 24 feet long. Each compartment had only one hatch, no other way in or out.

The first compartment entered was at the aft end of the sub and contained thousands of bars of gold, each with the Nazi eagle and swastika crest on it. Some stacks went to the top of the overhead from the deck floor. The second compartment hatch was easier to find and inside it was loaded to capacity with silver bars. The third compartment's hatch was amidships and was secured with a lock that had a large body and thick hasp.

Ian continued to the fourth hatch and found it had a lock identical to the one on the third hatch. The fifth hatch opened easily and contained bars marked with the Nazi crest but he did not recognize two letters — capital "P" and small "t" — Pt. Then he remembered the chemical symbol for platinum.

Ian guided the Sea Rover back to the third compartment and got a close-up picture of the lock. Ian activated the rotary-cutter wheel attachment and the spinning blade became visible on the lower right side of the video screen as it reached toward the lock. Ian activated an arm and it became visible in the lower left-hand corner of the video screen. The clasping fingers of the arm held the lock steady as the rotary wheel made its way through the hasp. The job took about 30 minutes and then Ian was able to slip the lock out of the latch.

The hatch opened easily but the only thing Ian found in the compartment were small metal boxes the size of ammunition boxes — hundreds of ammo boxes. He tried to open one of the boxes and it wouldn't budge. He tried several others and all seemed to be welded shut.

He was afraid to use the cutter because there could be live ammo inside that could cause an explosion. He moved about 25 of the boxes and found a new layer underneath.

The first box in the new layer opened easily and what he found inside took his breath away. Diamonds. Hundreds of diamonds. No, thousands of diamonds in one box. Ian guessed that the diamonds were one to two carats in size.

If all the boxes in this compartment and the still-locked compartment next to it contained diamonds, my god, it would be a fortune! When combined with the gold, silver and platinum, it would be the most valuable salvage job ever.

Now that he knew what the prize was, he worked more quickly to open more boxes. Each contained diamonds. He opened six more boxes with the same result. He was so excited he could hardly contain himself.

He had to restrain himself so he could keep all that he had found to himself. Not even the crew could know about the contents of the submarine. He must get back to Aberdeen to talk all this over with Shamus. Together they would figure out the best way to salvage the treasure and how to keep it secret at the same time.

As quickly as possible, he maneuvered the Sea Rover to the locked hatch on the last compartment. He made fast work of cutting off the lock and was inside the compartment within 30 minutes. Again, he made his way past the ammo boxes filled with ammunition and then to the layer of boxes filled with diamonds. He opened the first box from the "hidden" layer and instead of diamonds this time he found square, colored stones. These new stones looked like emeralds due to the square cut but he could not be sure with only a black-and-white image.

The next box was full of round cut colored stones. Ian thought they were rubies because they were translucent and looked the size of the diamonds, about one-two carats in size. The next box was full of what Ian thought were sapphires since although they were round cut they were more opaque and again they were about one-two carats in size.

He checked 10 boxes and found four with emeralds, three with rubies and three with sapphires. There must have been at least 100 boxes.

What a fantastic find! Ian thought all the greatest jewels from Europe were in the submarine.

He had been working the Sea Rover for seven straight hours and his eyes, arms, hands and neck were tired and sore. He was exhausted both physically and mentally. But at the same time, he had never felt so alive. What a phenomenal treasure! He could not wait to tell Shamus.

He wanted to leave the ship immediately and take the trawler back to Aberdeen. It would take a couple of hours to get to the harbor and he could relax a little on the short voyage. He needed to organize his thoughts so he could tell Shamus everything with enough detail to convince Shamus that the submarine contained a terrific treasure. But he wanted to spend time with Duncan. He looked at his watch. 6:00 p.m. Would he get back to the castle before Duncan went to bed? He would call as soon as he got to the harbor and let Duncan know that he would be back tonight.

He called and talked with John, Shamus's valet/butler/bodyguard and now Duncan's de facto nanny. John said he would wait dinner until Ian got there. Ian asked if Shamus was going to have dinner with them. John stated that Shamus was having dinner in town with a friend and would not be back at the castle until late.

Ian frowned. He would have to wait until tomorrow to talk with Shamus. Oh, well, more time with Duncan. Maybe he would read to him about pirates for the bedtime story. All of a sudden, he had a fierce longing for Duncan, almost a physical need to be with him. Ian missed Duncan so much at that moment that he started tearing up. All of this would go away the second he had Duncan in his arms. Very discreetly he wiped the tears from his eyes and sighted the harbor's quay in the distance.

Duncan laughed at his dad's stories over dinner. Stories about the sailors on the ship slipping and sliding on the deck after a rainstorm. And he laughed even more when Ian told him about the horrible food and how everyone tried to sneak to the side of the ship when the cook, a Greek man named Theo, was not looking and throw it overboard. And how Theo would pout for hours when he caught someone trying to toss his gourmet delights to the fishes.

Ian remembered the first time he saw the look on Duncan's face and knew he had a sense of humor and enjoyed Ian's stories and jokes. Duncan was about 3 years old when Ian knew that Duncan was not only his baby boy but also a thinking, reasoning and, yes, funny human being. Ian realized he could share his thoughts, dreams and his funny stories with Duncan so that Duncan could learn and laugh. That is the moment that Ian knew he was not only a father but also a dad and a friend to his son. Ian also remembered that Liddy was so happy when Ian finally figured out that Duncan was more than a baby.

Ian listened to Duncan tell him about the horses and fishing and soccer and secret rooms in the castle. Duncan was so very bright and when he talked like this, Ian could see Liddy. He had pangs of sadness but would look at Duncan and know that Liddy had given Duncan life and there was no greater gift she could have given him than Duncan.

Although Ian did not allow it often, tonight he wanted Duncan to sleep with him. He wanted to know that Duncan was all right. He wanted to hear Duncan breathing and know that his son was safe and he wanted Liddy close tonight and Duncan was the best way to bring her back.

Duncan stayed awake for an hour listening to Ian read *Treasure Island*. Then he nodded off and was sound asleep. Ian covered his son, turned out the light and looked out the window. The moon was shining through the haze and Ian did something he had not done since Liddy's death.

He prayed. He asked God to care for Duncan if anything ever happened to him. He said a prayer for God to keep Liddy's memory alive for both Duncan and him

For the first time in a very long time, Ian was at peace with himself. And now he was at peace with God because he trusted God to take care of Duncan.

CHAPTER 12

Aberdeen, Scotland
June 1953

....

Ian woke to Duncan's voice. He was reading *Treasure Island*, out loud and he was good at it. He did not stumble over any words and his voice had a natural cadence that drew the listener to the story. Ian lay very still because he wanted to listen to Duncan for as long as he could.

Duncan stopped reading and looked at his dad. "How long have you been awake?" asked Duncan, suspicion in his tone.

Ian opened one eye, then the other and smiled at Duncan. "Long enough to know that you are reading a book that I could not read until I was 12 and that most adults would have trouble reading out loud. Where did you learn to read so well?"

"Mostly from Mom and school, but Uncle Shamus has me read to him for one hour every day. He says he cannot read very well because his eyes are not as good as they used to be, but I think he is tricking me into reading. What do you think? Would Uncle Shamus do something like that?"

"I think you know the answer to your own question," said Ian with respect. "Your Uncle Shamus has a way of convincing people to do the things they do not like to do and do those things well. Enough of this. Go in and take a bath before we begin the day. I will shave while you're in the tub, then I'm going downstairs to get some coffee. We'll have breakfast when you get to the kitchen. Okay?"

"Do I have to take a bath? They're boring." Duncan pretended to pout.

"I know but we don't want you to become a troll just because you didn't bathe." Ian laughed. "Now get moving."

"Yes, sir," said Duncan with a big smile on his face.

Duncan liked to watch his dad shave and paid particular attention to how he put the shaving cream on his face. But he could not imagine having a razor scrape across his face. It must hurt but his dad's face did not show any pain. Wonder how he shaved without it hurting?

Always observing and always with questions, Duncan said casually, "Will I get hair on my chest and under my arms and," Duncan hesitated a bit, "and around my willie like you have?"

Ian wiped a big spot on the steamed mirror so he could look at Duncan in the mirror's reflection. He and Duncan had only had a couple of talks about "man things" and Ian was always a bit cautious. "Yes, you will. But usually the hair starts growing when you are 11 or 12 or 13 years old. It happens at different ages for different boys, some sooner and some later. I did not grow any hair until I was thirteen and a half and it first showed up around my penis."

Duncan watched him carefully as he talked then looked down at his groin to check for hair around his willie.

"Duncan," Ian continued, "You know that a willie is really called a penis. You learned that when you were 4 years old. Why do you call your penis a willie now?"

Duncan looked away from his dad's image in the mirror and then Ian thought Duncan was blushing slightly.

"Some of the boys I met in town started talking about their willies and how big their willies are. They wanted me to show them my willie and I ran away and came back here to the castle," said Duncan quickly.

Ian studied Duncan as he sat there in the bathtub, so vulnerable, so innocent, so much to learn. Ian wiped the shaving cream off his face and turned to look directly at Duncan. "Please listen to me Duncan. Thank you for sharing all this with me. Every boy gets teased about things like you told me. Every boy. It is sort of like seeing which boy can run faster or jump higher or kick a ball farther. Do you feel threatened if someone wants to run a race against you to see who is faster?"

Duncan was listening to every word and said quietly, "No, but the other thing is different."

Ian stepped over to the bathtub and sat on the edge, "I agree it is different but you should say No to those boys who try to tease you and then walk away. Not with fear or anger but with the knowledge that you made the decision that was right for you. Just like if you did not want to try to jump a fence when you do not want to or do not feel like it. It is your decision and you have a right to make that decision for yourself."

Duncan looked puzzled so Ian continued, "Duncan, would you steal a book from the library even if the other boys teased you and threatened you if you did not steal a book?"

Duncan looked into his dad's eyes and said firmly, "No."

"Then you do not have to show anyone your willie or penis if you do not want to because you know what is right and wrong for you," said Ian carefully. Duncan looked at the faucets in the bathtub, then back at Ian.

"Do you understand that it is your decision and no one else's?" Ian said firmly. "My dad taught me that lesson but I was a couple of years older than you are now but I have never forgotten it and I hope you will never forget it either."

"You are not to be ashamed of your body because it is what God has given you and it will serve you well for your entire life." Ian studied Duncan's face to make sure he understood what they were discussing then continued. "If you ever want to talk about anything involving your body and how it is growing to make you a man, come and talk to me. I will never criticize you for asking and I will always give you the best answer I can. Are you comfortable with our discussion?" Duncan nodded and Ian said, "Let's call this talk done and go down to have some breakfast. I am hungry, how about you?" Again a nod from Duncan but now he had a more satisfied look on his face, like his world got a bit less complicated.

Ian got up from the edge of the bathtub and turned once more to Duncan, "And if I am not here when you want to talk, ask Uncle Shamus. You can trust him as you trust me." Ian left Duncan in the tub and told him to be downstairs in 15 minutes.

As he walked downstairs, Ian thought proudly, I had my first facts-of-life talk with my son. Wonder who is growing up more today? Duncan or I?

81

Ian poured coffee from a silver pot on the sideboard in the morning room. He asked Mrs. Kelley, the cook, if John was about. She said he went to the garage to get Mortimer to wash Mr. Shamus's Daimler. He would be right back.

Ian was looking out the window when John entered. Ian asked if Shamus was up and about. John said he did not know. Ian turned to look at John. John always knew exactly what Shamus was doing, so how come he did not know if Shamus was up yet? Curious.

"John, have you lost interest in Shamus's well-being?" asked Ian in a sharp tone.

"Of course not, but by mutual agreement, there are times that Shamus can take care of himself and, naturally, I honor his requests," said John in an equally sharp tone.

"Oh, come now John, I have never known you not to know what Shamus is doing."

"That is because Shamus did not want you to know," touted John.

"Then, when would you not know what he is doing?" Ian persisted.

"When Shamus is with a guest," John said in a quiet but firm voice that left no doubt he was bored with this conversation.

"A guest, you say now. What kind of guest would Shamus be with at 7:00 in the morning?" Ian asked with exasperation.

John looked at Ian and said nothing. Ian slowly grasped what was being said or more specifically, what was not being said.

"Are you telling me that Shamus had a lady guest upstairs all night?" said Ian with mock shock. "That old bugger. I would never have guessed. Not here at the castle? Well, I'll be," said Ian shaking his head. "Thank you John, that is all I need right now."

Ian smiled a knowing smile and said to himself, "Good for him."

Ian went to the kitchen to order breakfast for Duncan and him and found not Mrs. Kelly with her ample housedress and her red hair, but, instead, a trim brunette woman dressed in tailored slacks and a form-fitting sweater. She turned and Duncan could not believe his eyes.

"How are you Ian?" she said with a slight accent. "It has been too long."

"Isabella, what are you doing here? I thought you were at the Lake Como villa. My god, you're still as beautiful as I remembered."

She walked to him, gave him a hug, and looked him up and down. "You do look like your father. I remember him when he was your age," said Isabella, "but I think you are even more handsome than your father, if that is possible?"

"What are you doing here in Aberdeen?" asked Ian wanting to know more about her visit.

"Shamus invited me to visit, so I took him up on it," said Isabella lightly. "I wanted to see you and meet your son. Where is he?"

"You are not going to change the subject until you answer me. When did you get in?" asked Ian firmly.

"Yesterday afternoon. Shamus picked me up at the airport and we had dinner at that lovely restaurant on the river. You know the one?" Isabella said, trying to change the subject.

"No you don't, you can't change the subject." Ian persisted, "Did you stay at the castle last night?"

"Of course, I did. Do you think Shamus would have me stay at a hotel?" said Isabella indignantly.

Ian looked at her as she poured a cup of coffee. Then it hit him. She was Shamus's guest!

Ian decided not to press the issue at this moment. Shamus would be furious if Ian embarrassed Isabella.

"How is your family? I was so sorry to hear about Federico's death last year. Sorry I was not able to attend the funeral. I hope you understand?" Ian said with genuine sympathy.

"It is very kind of you to say those things. I know you had a great deal of difficulty with your wife's death and I also know that attending a funeral would not have been a healthy way to heal your wounds. Your thoughts now mean a great deal to me. Thank you," said Isabella with respect.

Ian wanted to stop talking about death so he did change the subject.

"I am going upstairs to find Duncan. I will be back in a few minutes. Please excuse me," said Ian as he walked out of the room. "How long are you going to be here? I want to catch up on all your family news."

Ian went upstairs to Shamus's sitting room and bedroom and found him in his dressing room putting on a jacket.

"Shamus, why didn't you tell me that you had a thing going with Isabella?" Ian asked with an accusatory tone. "I saw her downstairs and she practically admitted spending the night with you here at the castle. Is it true?"

Shamus looked at Ian in the mirror, adjusted the collar on the jacket and said very quietly, "What Isabella and I are doing is of no concern of yours and I expect you to honor our privacy. She has her own rooms here in the castle and I do not want Duncan to know anything about this and neither does Isabella. And this is not a request. Do you understand?"

Ian stood staring at Shamus and before he could say anything else, Shamus smiled and said, "Good morning, Ian. How was your trip back to Aberdeen? We all missed you. I look forward to talking with you at length after I see to my guest and make sure that Duncan has a good breakfast. Care to join me in the morning room for coffee and breakfast with Duncan and our guest?"

Ian looked resigned and said with a tinge of sarcasm, "Sure, if it is a request not an order, sir." Ian changed his tone as he continued, "Shamus, I am not judging you or Isabella, but you know how close I was to her, Federico and their children. I am surprised. Now that I think about it I am pleased. Still surprised but pleased. There is a certain symmetry to you and Isabella being together. Please accept my apologies for coming across with a pseudo-Victorian attitude. I did not intend to invade your privacy and especially not Isabella's. Can we drop it for now?"

"Apology accepted and, yes, we can drop it," said Shamus with sincerity. Then he changed the subject again. "How is Duncan? Ian, he is a true joy. He is smarter than either you or I, probably smarter than both of us put together."

"Thanks, you're right, he is smart. This morning he was reading *Treasure Island* like a Shakespearean orator. He truly amazed me." Ian beamed with pride. "And thanks for pretending to need to rest your eyes and get him to read to you. For the record, he saw right through you. He knows you do it to get him to read, not because you need help. Clever kid to figure that out at 6."

"Tell me about the salvage operation," asked Shamus. "What have you found?"

"You are not going to believe what I found but I want to give you the details with the whole story, let's meet in your study at 10:00, that is unless you have some woman hidden here in the castle that will distract your attention," Ian teased.

"As a matter of fact, I do have a woman here at the castle and she asked if she could take Duncan into Aberdeen to shop with her," said Shamus in a no-nonsense tone. "Now, let's have breakfast and stop this fencing contest."

Duncan met Isabella at breakfast and agreed to accompany her on her shopping trip to Aberdeen after Shamus pointed out that escorting a lady on a shopping trip was usually reserved for young men who were at least 11 or 12 years old. Shamus had hooked Duncan as quickly as he had the salmon in the stream next to the castle.

The main thing was that Duncan felt very important. Signora Isabella, as Uncle Shamus had asked him to address her, was a friendly but exotic woman whom Duncan instantly liked but was a little afraid of. He had never met anyone from Italy and he found her accent sometimes difficult to understand. But he had an important assignment from Uncle Shamus and he would not disappoint him. So his best manners and proper speech were used at all times with Signora Isabella.

They left at 9:45 with John driving the Daimler and Duncan acting as a tour guide pointing out all the sites along the route. Isabella was intrigued and charmed at the same time. Shamus was right, Duncan was a very special child and she must learn as much about him as she could.

CHAPTER 13

Aberdeen, Scotland
June 1953

....

S hamus and Ian took a silver coffeepot into the study and closed the doors. They sat next to the fire and talked small talk about Duncan for 10 minutes and then Shamus said, "Well, what is under the surface of the ocean off Storm Island?"

"The submarine U-4977. It was a cargo submarine designed to carry the German treasury from Berlin to South America. It was one of three super-cargo submarines commissioned by the Kriegsmarine under secret orders from Hitler. We got some of the German Navy records from files kept after the war by the Russians in Moscow and they confirmed the U-4977 sailed from Bremerhaven just before Christmas Day, 1944, and that it was bound for Montevideo, Uruguay. But sometime on December 28, the U-4977 was caught on the surface off Storm Island by a British Coast Guard patrol boat. They fired at the U-4977 but reported that the submarine had escaped underwater before they could confirm damage. The patrol boat captain did not make a big deal of the sighting and firing on the sub since they saw at least one sub a week and fired on two or three each month.

What actually happened is that the shell caught the sub on the sail and the sub sank in minutes, not longer than 15 or 20 minutes. Probably before a message could be sent to Kriegsmarine headquarters. No one knew where the sub went down until your salvage team found it three months ago," explained Ian.

"Are you sure?" asked Shamus with intense interest. "Are you sure, the German naval records show no location for the missing U-4977?"

"I am pretty sure. The Kriegsmarine sent Hitler a coded message in early January 1945 stating that the U-4977 did not arrive in Montevideo on January 7 and the last message from the sub was in the North Sea at noon on December 28. U-4977 was reported missing in action and presumed sunken somewhere in the North Sea. Hitler ordered a massive search for the U-4977 but there was a terrible storm in the North Sea between Scotland and the European mainland in late January and the search turned up nothing. The last entry in the naval records shows that letters to relatives of the crew of the U-4977 were sent out the first week of February, 1945."

"So what is in the sub?" said Shamus with increasing interest.

"Shamus, you are not going to believe it. I found five compartments on the sub, three were unlocked, one with gold, maybe five tons, 10,000 pounds; one with silver, maybe 10 tons; and one with platinum, maybe 2000 to 3000 pounds. There were also two locked compartments." Ian added with an air of suspense, "and it took me about an hour to open the first one.

"The compartment was filled with ammo boxes and they were rusted shut, at least the first layer. But further digging showed a lower layer of ammo boxes that were not rusted. I opened the first box and ... are you ready? ... It was full of diamonds. Thousands of diamonds. One to two carat stones based on my estimate. It looks like there are at least 500 boxes full of diamonds. I only opened 10 to 15 but they were selected from the hidden layer at random."

Shamus stood, looked at Ian, went to the coffeepot, refilled his cup and held the pot out to Ian. Ian walked over and Shamus refilled Ian's also.

"The second locked compartment was easier to open. Inside I found rusted ammo boxes on the top layer but the second "hidden" layer was filled with unrusted ammo boxes. I opened the first one and saw thousands of emeralds. Really beautiful stones. Then a box of rubies, then sapphires. I opened 10 boxes, four with emeralds, three with rubies and three with sapphires. Absolutely incredible!"

Shamus looked at Ian for a moment, and then asked, "Who else knows about the contents of the compartments and boxes?"

"No one," Ian responded immediately. "That's the reason I came back last night, to discuss all of this with you and determine what we should do. This could be the largest salvage operation in history and I wanted to make sure that we could remove the contents of the sub without any problems."

"No one saw you looking at the pictures of the sub?" asked Shamus with a doubtful tone. "Are you sure that no one looked over your shoulder?"

"The monitor is surrounded with a shroud like the radar sets used during the war, to keep out excess light that would wash out the images. Sending me to Marseilles to learn how to use the Sea Rover your friend Dr. Levy invented was what made the difference. The crew on the salvage barge did not know anything about the Sea Rover or the camera equipment and left it all to me. I had my face against the shroud opening all the time the Sea Rover was operational. I was very careful," said Ian confidently.

"How long do you think it will take to bring the contents of the compartments to the surface?" Shamus asked while trying to decide what to do with all that gold, silver, platinum and gemstones.

"The removal will be pretty straightforward but the Sea Rover can only carry two bullion bars at a time, so I would guess about six to eight weeks of very steady work. And keep in mind that the Sea Rover is a prototype and probably will have to be rebuilt at least once during the salvage operations. Maybe Dr. Levy and his team can start building a second and third Sea Rover to back up the first one?" Ian asked. "I wouldn't want to be out there by Storm Island when the winter weather starts kicking up the sea. It can be treacherous."

"I will call Guy later today and give him a report about your success with the Sea Rover, at least in general terms, and find out about additional Sea Rovers. That's a great idea." Shamus was thinking about how to keep this project quiet. They could not attract attention, not even the slightest.

"Ian," said Shamus, "We must keep this absolutely confidential between you and me. We cannot have any of this information leak to the press, the government or other salvage firms. We need a cover story and oil exploration is not enough. There is too much at stake for us to risk even a hint of interest by the government. You know how those busybodies at Whitehall are, always looking for some kind of reason to investigate what is happening in Scotland. For some reason, they think we are going to take over the Empire from the Royal Family. Little do they know we already did that 700 years ago."

Ian looked at Shamus, "What are you talking about? Does this have something to do with our bloody family heritage and the famous duty we have to carry on the family business?"

Shamus went to his desk, opened the bottom drawer on the left side, removed the drawer and turned it upside down. He slid the bottom of the drawer to reveal a hidden compartment on the underside of the drawer. From it he took a key, a very old looking key. With the key in hand, he strode across the room to the floor-to-ceiling bookcase. He inserted the key into a hole behind a book that had the ironical title of *The Keyhole Mystery,* and the bookcase opened into the study.

Shamus motioned to Ian to follow him into the room behind the bookcase. Ian was surprised and curious. He had never known that this room was in the study. It was about 10 feet square with a low ceiling. There was a table in the center, an armoire against one wall, and two chairs against the opposite wall. Shamus closed the bookcase and pulled one chair to the table and asked Ian to pull the second up.

Shamus opened the armoire and removed a newer looking strongbox. Shamus pulled a chain around his neck over his head and opened the strongbox with the attached key. Inside the strongbox were three envelopes, two of them bulky and bulging, one flat. Shamus removed the envelopes and set the strongbox back in the armoire.

"What I am going to tell you is for your ears only and must not be repeated to anyone except Duncan when he is 32 years old. I received this information from your father when he decided to become an undercover spy for MI6 during the war. If he had not died he would have told you himself what I am about to disclose to you."

"The Stuart-Bruce clan, as you know, traces its roots to before Robert the Bruce but the family before him was of little importance other than Robert the Bruce's father, referred to as Robert the Bruce the Elder and Earl of Carrick. Robert the Elder was a ruthless and clever man and traded his support to King Edward the First for more than a few acres of land, a title, a house in London, and a pretty girl. Robert the Elder made sure that Edward could defeat and capture a Scottish rebel called William Wallace. This allowed Edward and his successor to maintain control over northern England and, eventually, Scotland. But Edward paid dearly for this because Robert the Elder negotiated a deal and got Edward to acknowledge that deal by signing what is possibly the single most important document since the Magna Carta."

Shamus opened the first bulky envelope, and pulled a roll of parchment tied with a faded red ribbon. The parchment was very old and very fragile. With meticulous care, Shamus untied the ribbon and with extreme care unrolled the parchment until Ian could read the barely legible letters in old English script.

> *On this the 23rd day of August in the year of our Lord 1305, the signers of this testament witnessed Edward, the rightful King of England, sign and the Duke of York press the King's Royal Seal on a yellow parchment document presented to the King by Robert the Bruce the Younger of Scotland.*
>
> *After the document was signed and sealed, Sir Robert rolled the yellow parchment, tied it with a green and purple ribbon and placed the rolled document in his cloak. None of the signers read the document signed and sealed by King Edward and they do not know what the document contains.*
>
> *This is sworn before God and the witnesses.*

There were several signatures at the bottom of the document.

Ian looked at Shamus. "What did they witness the King sign and seal and what does it mean to us?"

Shamus smiled and held up a hand to quiet Ian. "I am sure you have known that our family has always had significant holdings. Land, companies, shipping lines, railroads, banks, even an airline and other areas of influence here and abroad. But I don't think you knew how much we have."

"What I am going to tell you is hard to fully comprehend so ask questions, but keep in mind that to put your arms around all of it will take more that a few minutes in this room. It will take you years to appreciate what Robert the Bruce the Elder and his son, Robert the Younger were able to get the King of England to agree to, put into writing, sign and seal in front of witnesses."

Now Ian's interest was really piqued and he could hardly wait to hear what Shamus said. Instead, Shamus opened the second bulky envelope and removed a dirty yellowish parchment held in a roll with a ribbon that looked like it was green and blue or purple but very faded and, like the first document, very old.

He untied the ribbon again with meticulous care and barely unrolled the parchment. Shamus held it up to the light and let Ian read the message written on it.

To all who read this document, be it known that I, Edward King of England, being of sound mind award to Robert the Bruce, Earl of Carrick and his son, Robert the Bruce the Younger, the following for their faithful service and unwavering loyalty as they performed missions for England, secret only to them and me -

From this day forward, the 23rd of August in the year of our Lord 1305, I bequeath 1/100 th share of all the land, property, and other holdings owned by England now and those that England will receive in the future to Robert the Bruce Earl of Carrick and his son Robert the Bruce the Younger and their heirs with the following provision.

This bequest shall pass from generation to generation to direct descendants of Robert the Bruce Earl of Carrick into perpetuity but must go to one and only one male heir designated by the previous holder of this bequest and shall not be diluted by multiple claims by heirs other than the sole male heir designated to receive this bequest by the previous holder.

As long as there is a sovereign England, this bequest shall be honored by all future monarchs with no exceptions until the end of time.

Barely visible to Ian was a signature and traces of what looked like a wax seal at the bottom of the document. He looked up, stared at the first document now tied with the red ribbon and back to the second. He looked at Shamus, trying to understand what he had read. He knew he was a direct descendant of Robert the Bruce the Elder and Robert the Bruce the Younger. Now he put the pieces together and realized that his family had received 1% of all that England had colonized, conquered, traded, possessed and otherwise owned for the last 700 years.

His mind flooded with questions. Does this mean 1% of England's treasury? 1% of the Royal Jewels? And Buckingham Palace? Ian stood and walked around the table as his mind raced on. My God, 1% of all the British colonies? Does that include Canada and the U.S.? One percent of Australia? One percent of the colonies in Africa and South America and Asia? One percent of India? What else did England actually own or more specifically, what did the Stuart-Bruces own 1% of? Shamus was right. It was too much to try to cram into his head.

He looked at Shamus puzzled but excited and Shamus nodded a confirmation.

"Now, stop letting your mind roam the Earth. Think now instead about the immense responsibility we have and what this legacy means to the family, particularly to you and Duncan."

"Who takes care of all that we own?" asked Ian slowly. "The holdings must be immense, there must be thousands of people involved."

"Ian," Shamus said seriously, "I take care of everything and when you are 32, you will take over and I will retire. A very well-deserved retirement, I must say."

"And, yes, there are thousands of people, but I have been fortunate. My brother, your grandfather, was brilliant at organizational management. He set up a simple but very effective way to keep track of things with only six executives and a staff of ten administrators. Of course, there are about fifteen legal and accounting firms but, all in all, it is a pretty smooth operation. The Stuart-Bruce family business may be the pinnacle of what our military and naval brothers call delegation of responsibility and authority.

"As to the question you asked about what we own, a better question is what we do not own. I'm not trying to be flip but the Bruces, initially, then later the Stuart-Bruces have been involved in almost every major industrial, political, economic, scientific, or intellectual advancement during the last 500 years. Mostly, we own land and have huge agricultural operations on six continents. Of course, when you own land, there are other things that can happen on that land. Like oil wells, many, many oil wells. Then there are the natural gas fields. And, of course, there are gold mines, silver mines, platinum mines, diamond mines, titanium mines, copper mines and coal mines. There are the cities that grew on the land we owned. Edinburgh, New York, Cape Town, Hong Kong, Shanghai, Bombay, Delhi, Toronto, Vancouver, Nairobi, and Sydney. If you have all that money, the best place to put it is your own bank, so we have two major international banks and several top-rated regional banks.

"Get the idea? The list goes on and on and on. At times, I get bored seeing the lists of all we own. But there are times when I cannot believe what we are doing. All the responsibility gives us tremendous power and we must be very careful not to abuse it. That is the hardest thing. Learning how to reasonably and responsibly use the power."

Shamus stopped talking, looked at Ian and let all of what had been said sink in.

"Let's go for a walk, I need some fresh air. I am not going to tell you anything else right now, but I will answer your questions," Shamus said as he led the way out of the secret room. He closed the bookcase door and locked it.

They walked in silence. The sky was dark and there was a cold, drizzling rain falling. They both wore slickers and they walked slowly, taking in the spring morning smell. Small white flowers were blooming on the hillside and the river was rushing its way to the loch. The more they walked the more they liked not talking. Each had his own thoughts and each one had to sort out those thoughts. They walked for the better part of an hour before Ian broke the silence.

"What is in the third envelope that you did not open?" Ian queried as he looked over at Shamus.

Shamus stopped walking then moved a few feet to the stone wall next to the path and sat on the top of the wall. "It contains the microfilmed records of all of England's monarchs since Edward I to our new queen, Elizabeth II, acknowledging the validity of Edward's bequest. It is really not necessary but my advisors say that continuing to get the reigning monarch's acknowledgment in writing is a precaution in case someone would ever question the documents," Shamus answered slowly. "The originals are kept in a sealed box in a vault at our solicitor's office in Edinburgh."

"Is it difficult to get England to continue to share its holdings with us? It seems that someone would like to make sure that we stop receiving 1% of everything from the Royal Treasury." Ian asked. . "Hasn't Parliament tried to stop the payments? Those tightwads wouldn't pay if Jesus Christ had ordered them to."

Shamus chuckled a little, then became serious quickly. "You're right, the Prime Minister and Parliament secretly ordered payments and transfers stop in 1916 during the First Great War and there has been no money or other holdings received from the modern day equivalent to King Edward's 'sovereign England' to our family since." Shamus spoke without any bitterness. "It was the best thing, because frankly the Empire started shrinking and England has not regained and most likely will never return to its Victorian glory. If 20th century British people ever became aware of England sharing her wealth with the Stuart-Bruce family, well, you can imagine the way your grandfather would have been chastised and many of the U.K. holdings would not have remained in the family's portfolio."

Ian looked at Shamus under the hood of his slicker and saw his eyes twinkle. "You don't seem to be very upset about all of this," Ian said, exploring Shamus's mood. "Wouldn't our family have gotten something from the First and Second World Wars since England won both?"

"We did. We financed much of the cost of the First War for England, France and other European allies. Repayment was on very favorable terms and increased our holdings significantly. And we financed the British war effort from about 1938 through the end of World War II and for a couple of the post-war years while England got back on its feet. It took a lot of our cash for about 10 years but, as with the First War, repayment was under very favorable terms, especially with the Americans making most of the payments for England early on," said Shamus with a light voice. "In a lot of ways, the Stuart-Bruce family provided the economic wherewithal for England to not only stand up to Hitler but to eventually defeat him.

Much of the remaining debt that England has left from the war will be paid back to us by transferring large blocks of oil-producing property in the Middle East, particularly in Saudi Arabia and Persia. It is very valuable and may prove to be worth a whole lot more than the original amount we loaned to England." Shamus added very quietly.

"But you cannot talk about this with anyone. Negotiations are ongoing and very tricky. The Arabs are a paranoid group and will change or stop a deal because they smell a camel passing gas at the next oasis." Shamus chuckled.

"Let's walk back to the house and get lunch ready for Duncan and Isabella when they return from shopping," said Shamus. They walked back to the house the way the walked out — in silence.

As they were removing their slickers, Shamus said, "Let's meet in the study at 9:00 tonight after you have put Duncan to bed."

Ian spent the afternoon with Duncan fishing at the loch. The sun was out and a fresh breeze was blowing from the sea. Even with the startling revelations of the morning, he actually felt better than he had for a long time.

Dinner was at 7:00 and country formal, the men in sports jackets and turtleneck sweaters and Isabella in a red velvet gown with long sleeves. She wore a simple, but stunning necklace of diamonds that seemed to frame her face in sparkling lights. The dinner was wonderful and everyone enjoyed the conversation and the food. Finally, at 8:30, Ian and Duncan excused themselves and went to Duncan's room for some bedtime reading from *Treasure Island*. Duncan promised to shut off the light at 9:30 and Ian went downstairs to Shamus's study justifiably late for their 9:00 o'clock meeting.

Shamus poured two glasses of cognac and joined Ian in front of the fire.

"Let's get back to your submarine salvage project for a moment. You haven't told me exactly where the sub is located," Shamus said, somewhat impatiently. "Its location can be the key to the success of the salvage operation."

Ian went to Shamus's desk and wrote something on a piece of paper and handed it to Shamus as he sat down. "This is the exact latitude and longitude. I checked it three times to make sure and haven't told anyone else. The salvage ship is about 1/4 mile away and no one got close enough to the Sea Rover control panel to see where the Sea Rover was working."

Shamus took a sip of his cognac and said, "I made a few calls this afternoon and this is what is going to happen. Tomorrow morning an airplane is going to crash about a mile from the salvage ship. The pilot will eject and parachute into the sea and be rescued by the Coast Guard," Shamus said. "The captain of our salvage ship will reluctantly volunteer to assist the Coast Guard in searching for the plane and trying to recover its cargo. The cargo is a load of antibiotics destined for the United Nations' hospital in Rotterdam and our salvage ship is trying to save the drugs for the children in the hospital."

Ian was absolutely fascinated by the whole thing. How did Shamus come up with these wild ideas?

"Under the guise of a humanitarian effort to save the drugs, you will be able to recover the submarine's secret, valuable cargo. Do you like this so far?" asked Shamus.

"Sure, sounds great. But where am I going to put all the cargo that I recover?" Ian challenged.

"Try this on for size. During the war, Allied submarines refueled from large bags of diesel fuel stored 50 feet or more below the ocean's surface. The fuel is lighter than water and would be weighted to remain submerged at 50 feet or so and out of sight." Shamus said with a little trepidation, "We, or I should say you, will do the same thing with your cargo. The first bag is on its way by tanker from Le Havre."

"When you have recovered all the cargo you can tow the bags to a remote harbor in the north of Scotland, load the cargo on a ship and pump the fuel out of the bags." Shamus was smiling at this point.

"You are a very clever Scotsman and I only wish I had thought of it myself," Ian said with admiration.

"To carry out the plan, you must leave for the salvage ship by noon tomorrow. So have fun with Duncan in the morning and I will have John drive you to the harbor at noon. After you recover the sub's cargo, we can talk about the rest of business and start the transition process so I can retire and spend more time in Italy. You know how I love the sunshine, pretty women, and beautiful scenery down there," Shamus said with a hearty laugh and twinkle in his eyes.

"I will call you on the radio every day with a progress report," Ian said with new-found energy. "You know, with the sub salvage on top of the family responsibility business, I won't sleep for a month. Too many things to think about."

"Now, go get some sleep and take care of your son in the morning. I have a lady to entertain," Shamus said as he left the study.

Contrary to Ian's prediction, he fell asleep the second his head hit the pillow. He woke when he heard a very soft tapping on his door. "Come in, I'm awake," said Ian with a big yawn.

Duncan poked his head around the door, smiled at his dad and hit the bed at a full run. They wrestled in the bed for a few minutes and then Ian chased Duncan to his room where Duncan got dressed and headed for the kitchen and breakfast. Ian joined Duncan ten minutes later after a quick shower.

"Let's go riding this morning. I want you to show me where you have caught all those fish," said Ian with real enthusiasm. "I'll bet I can catch a pretty big fish if you show me your secret spot."

"Sure, Dad," Duncan said, smiling, but he got serious and said in a whisper, "but you can't tell Uncle Shamus because it will be our secret. Okay?'

"You got it," Ian beamed, "let's get going."

Ian was pleased that the man-to-man talk yesterday did not come up again and did not seem to affect Duncan in any way. He thought, *I sure hope I handled that situation yesterday so that it helps Duncan in the future.*

Instead of horses, they took the jeep and drove off singing a song about a dog named Bingo. The morning went too quickly and Ian had to drive faster than normal to get back to the castle by noon. He and Duncan had had a great adventure and, sure enough, Duncan's secret fishing spot proved to be as good for Ian as for Duncan.

They had an early lunch and as he was headed out to the Daimler saloon, he stopped briefly in Shamus's study. Shamus was not there, so he left a note, asking Shamus to look after Duncan until he returned. He also asked Shamus to put Liddy's ring and the watch Liddy gave him in a safe place so he could retrieve it when Duncan was old enough to understand how much his mother loved him.

He was having a grand time and his life was free of the gloom that had draped around him after Liddy's death. The only thing that would make everything even more perfect would be if Liddy had not died. But he was not going to dwell on that and get depressed.

He did not want it. Duncan did not need it.

And he was sure that Liddy would not stand for it.

So he would make the very best of the life he had with Duncan and Shamus.

Thank God they were there for him.

CHAPTER 14

Aberdeen Harbor, Scotland
June 1953

....

The harbor was buzzing with activity because a plane had crashed out beyond Storm Island this morning and the Coast Guard had rescued the pilot. Lucky man, that pilot.

Ian paid little attention to the activities along the pier as he walked to the supply trawler for his journey back to the salvage ship. As he was about to step over the gunwales and onto the deck, he heard someone calling.

"Ian Stuart-Bruce, I presume," said the Coast Guard Commandant, "I'm Vice-Admiral Hathaway, I spoke to your uncle a half-hour ago and he suggested I contact you before you made your way back to the salvage ship."

"Yes, Admiral, how can I assist you?" said Ian respectfully. "Won't you come aboard and join me for some tea?"

"Why, yes, very good of you to ask," the Admiral said appreciatively.

The meeting lasted about 30 minutes and Ian agreed to help the Coast Guard raise the plane and its cargo of antibiotics for the U.N. hospital. As the Admiral departed, he looked at the sky and said, "Mr. Stuart-Bruce, you might want to wait until tomorrow morning to go to the salvage ship. It looks like a storm is brewing and, this time of year, these quick storms can test the resolve of even very experienced sailors."

"Thank you, Admiral, but our crew is the best and I trust their ability to get us to the salvage ship safely," Ian said with confidence.

The Admiral saluted and left. Ian asked the supply boat's captain if the weather was going to be a problem and he was assured that this supply boat could handle anything. Anyway, they would have him at the salvage ship in less than 90 minutes and the storm wouldn't really start kicking up until after sunset.

By the time the supply trawler was approaching the salvage ship, Ian knew that the storm was not going to be a little wind and some salt spray. He transferred to the salvage ship quickly and sent the trawler back to Aberdeen harbor, hopefully before things got really rough.

Ian made sure that the Sea Rover was lashed down to the deck and the control panel was in a watertight compartment. Then he went to the galley and got some coffee and waited in the wardroom with the rest of the crew.

The wind was rising and the rain was getting heavier with every passing minute. The salvage ship was a very stout vessel and it was handling the heavy seas with passing marks. Everything would be fine as long as the anchors held and the ship could keep its bow directly into the wind.

About 9:00 p.m., the wind changed from a howl to a screech and the ship started to list from side to side. Ian knew the captain was running the engines to keep the ship taut against the anchor chains and headed into the wind.

At 10 minutes before 10:00, the wind shifted abruptly to the east from the north. The captain maneuvered the ship to the east to head into the wind and everything settled back to the routine only with a new wind direction.

Then at 10:45, the wind changed again but as the captain tried to realign the ship, the wind shifted 180 degrees to the SSW. Before the ship could turn, waves started climbing over the starboard side. Each set of waves came higher and higher until they reached the bridge.

The captain sounded the abandon ship alarm at 10:52. Before anyone could reach the lifeboats, the ship was covered by a giant rogue wave. The ship floundered and rolled over to port. It continued to roll until it was inverted and had capsized.

The salvage ship stayed afloat inverted only 30 seconds before it slipped below the surface. Ten seconds after it disappeared, there was no sign of its existence on the ocean.

Ian and twenty-nine others struggled to get out to the lifeboats but they didn't even get the hatches open before the ship went under.

Ian's last thoughts were of the note he had left on Shamus's desk asking him to care for Duncan.

'Duncan, I love you, never forget how much I love you.' With that thought Ian slipped to the next world where he joined Liddy, his mother and his father for eternity.

Shamus told Duncan about the ship being lost at sea on June 16th, 1953. It was on a Monday he learned his father died when the salvage ship *Sassy Lassy* sank.

At the memorial service, Shamus thought about the secret he shared with Ian, the location of the submarine. Duncan thought about the secret he shared with his dad, the location of the lucky fishing spot at the lake above the castle.

The next day, both Shamus and Duncan threw a single rose into the placid ocean water at the site where the salvage ship went down off the coast of Storm Island. As they watched the roses float away from the boat, Duncan slipped his hand into Shamus's and squeezed it for reassurance.

Shamus remembered what Ian told him about the sunken submarine's valuable cargo and decided not to share the secret coordinates with anyone. Best to let some secrets stay at the bottom of the ocean…at least for now. Sometime in the future Ian's incredible find may serve Duncan and his needs better than serving mine now.

....

PART II

Shamus and Duncan

....

CHAPTER 15

Aberdeen, Scotland
April 1955

....

S hamus took his responsibility of raising Duncan as his own with a degree of seriousness that surprised even himself. He enrolled Duncan at McCloud Academy in Aberdeen as a day student. This gave both of them time to establish a routine that included breakfast each morning, dinner in the evening and Duncan reading to Shamus after he completed his schoolwork.

Shamus kept a notebook with the name of each book Duncan read and the date completed. Duncan's favorite so far was *The Count of Monte Cristo.* Shamus was always amazed at the depth of understanding Duncan had, not only for the plots but also for the characters each author developed. In fact, Duncan seemed at times to bring more from each character than even the author intended. Shamus discovered new things about each book and its characters now that Duncan was reading than he had learned at Oxford. Amazing, truly amazing what Duncan was able to make of their readings. Each evening they journeyed down familiar roads but now Shamus saw new sights through Duncan's eyes and imagination.

Although there was a period of time when Duncan seemed withdrawn, Shamus never saw any signs of depression after Ian's death. In fact, Duncan mourned Ian for about six weeks then on one of their fishing trips to the loch, Duncan told Shamus he was over his father's death. Very adult, very detached and very unlike an 8-year old.

Duncan even started sharing his thoughts about Ian and Liddy being re-united in heaven and how happy he was for them. Shamus listened very carefully to Duncan and asked his staff to do the same. Shamus talked with the

Reverend Hood at St. John's in Aberdeen about Duncan and went to talk with a psychiatrist, Dr. Rosenberg, in Edinburgh.

Both men said that Duncan's response was unusual but not unheard of and that somewhere later in his childhood he would mourn the loss of his mother and father again. Both men wanted to meet Duncan, but Shamus did not want them to pry into Duncan's private thoughts.

One day when Duncan and Shamus were walking in the hills above the castle, Duncan announced quite matter-of-factly that he believed in God. Shamus asked him why he believed in God and Duncan thought for a moment and answered simply, "Because it makes me feel secure knowing I love God and Mom and Dad are with Him."

Who could argue with that logic? The only problem was that you expected to hear that proclamation from a man of at least 30, not from an 8-year old boy. Shamus himself had not found that kind of spiritual security until he was well past his 35th birthday. Shamus was again amazed by Duncan's innate skill to understand not only difficult abstract concepts but also, perhaps more importantly, apply high-level logic to these life problems. Shamus knew that Duncan was a special child; his outlook was refreshing as well as educational.

Everyone at the castle loved Duncan and his cheery disposition. He made them laugh with his fishing or walking stories. At school, the teachers and administrators gave glowing reviews, not only to make Shamus happy, but also because they were enthused that Duncan was a student who wanted to learn everything they had to teach.

However, Duncan did have a problem. He talked too much in class. And nothing that the school tried to stop the talking seemed to work. So Shamus, the uncle/father, had his first disciplinary encounter with Master Duncan.

"I understand that your teachers have tried to get you to stop talking in class," said Shamus seriously while Duncan stood in front of desk in the study. "Is this true?"

"Yes, sir," Duncan said quietly.

"You need to stop talking then and give your teachers the proper respect they deserve," said Shamus, rising from his chair. "I do not understand why this is a problem, Duncan."

Duncan did not say anything because Shamus had not asked a question.

"You have nothing to say?" said Shamus sternly. "That truly is surprising given that you seem to be the boy who talks too much. How should we handle this situation? Do you have any ideas how to keep you from talking?"

"Yes, sir, I do," said Duncan shyly

"Well, what is it?" asked Shamus in his sternest voice.

Duncan hesitated before he spoke then straightened his shoulders and said, "I believe that if I had a dog, I would be less likely to talk in class. Don't you think that a dog would keep me from talking so much, Uncle Shamus?" said Duncan, looking up at Shamus.

Shamus turned away from Duncan so he could not see the smile forming on his face. He almost laughed out loud but swallowed it and turned back to Duncan with a stern face. "What kind of dog would that be, Duncan?" asked Shamus without giving up his stern expression. "I do not know of a dog that will help you stop talking in class."

All of a sudden, Duncan started talking quickly. "But there is, Uncle Shamus, there is a dog that will help me. I read about it when my class went to the library last week."

"What is it Duncan, a non-talking dog from one of your myths and legends books?" asked Shamus without humor.

"You know dogs don't talk," said Duncan with firmness. "They can only bark, all except one kind of dog."

"A dog that does not bark, what kind of dog is that?" Shamus asked with skepticism.

"The breed is a member of the hound family and is called Basenji. They are from the African savannah regions and they're a very old breed dating all the way to ancient Egypt," Duncan continued. "I think, no, I know if I had one of these Basenji dogs that I would not talk in class anymore," said Duncan with confidence.

"Are you bargaining with me for a pet, for a dog?" Shamus walked to Duncan. "You know how to get your way with this old man, don't you? The logic of your proposal appeals to me." Shamus smiled. "Let me make some calls and we will try to find one of these Basenji dogs for you. I think you are right. A non-barking dog for a non-talking boy just might work."

Two weeks later, as Shamus promised, when Duncan came home from school there was a box next to the stove in the kitchen and in it was the most adorable puppy Duncan had ever seen. She was a reddish-brown and white and she had bright eyes and sharp teeth and she licked him all over the face. They instantly fell in love. Duncan would not let the puppy out of his sight the entire weekend.

On Sunday evening after dinner, Shamus asked Duncan if he had decided on a name for the puppy. Duncan looked at Shamus and said, "I would like to call her Mercedes after the lady in *The Count of Monte Cristo* but I don't like the name Mercedes. I think that Christine from *The Phantom of the Opera* is a better name. Do you think Christine would be all right?"

"Duncan that is a perfect name for your puppy. Do you think she will learn her name quickly?"

"She sure will. She is the smartest dog in all of Scotland and she will be the fastest, too. Thank you, Uncle Shamus, for getting me Christine," said Duncan with sincere appreciation.

Sure enough, the pup learned her name in a few days and would come running when anyone called her. She loved running and playing with Duncan, but she also loved to chew on everything: Shamus's shoes, table legs, Persian rugs, and sofa pillows. Her favorite target was the cook's towel. Christine would sneak into the kitchen and steal the towel from Mrs. Kelley and drag it through the kitchen and under the breakfront in the morning room. Christine would destroy the towel, leave all the shredded cloth on the floor and then go in search of another towel.

Duncan kept his side of the bargain and stopped talking in class. In fact, he became a model student and leader at his school. Duncan could not wait to get home each day to play with Christine and to talk with Uncle Shamus. What Shamus did not realize when he had Duncan agree not to talk in class was that he would now talk non-stop when he was at home.

My god can that child ever talk up a storm. He goes on and on and on. About Christine. About school. About our last fishing trip. About the chemistry experiments. About the spelling test. And about the math homework, that of course, he had already completed.

One day while Duncan was talking about Scotland's fight for separation from England, it dawned on Shamus that he loved the boy. He had never thought about it before but now he was sure, he loved Duncan. He could not imagine loving his own son any more than he loved Duncan. He smiled at the thought and turned his attention back to another of Duncan's talks, this one about astronomy.

Will his thirst for knowledge ever be quenched? I hope not, thought Shamus, *I surely hope not.*

CHAPTER 16

London, England
September 1962

. . . .

They left the Saville Row tailor where Duncan had been fitted for his first tuxedo. The final fitting was in three days and the tux would be ready by Friday in time for the reception at Buckingham Palace on Saturday evening. This was also Duncan's first royal reception and he was anxious to meet the Queen and her husband Prince Phillip.

The rest of the week in London was filled with trips to the British Museum of History, the Air and Space Museum, and the Naval History Museum. On Wednesday afternoon they went to the cinema and saw the film of *"To Kill a Mockingbird"* with Gregory Peck. Duncan found himself truly identifying with the little boy, Rory.

On Thursday evening, they saw Gilbert & Sullivan's "H.M.S. Pinafore." Duncan really liked the sailor suits but had some trouble understanding why so much time was spent kissing and crying. At the intermission, Uncle Shamus introduced him to some very old people. One was Lady Butterwick, who kept patting his shoulder and dabbing her eyes with her handkerchief. Uncle Shamus actually pinched him hard when he started to ask Lady Butterwick how old she was.

Uncle Shamus also introduced him to a very distinguished-looking gentleman. At first, Duncan did not hear the man's name, but when he and Shamus started talking he caught the man's name when he was introduced to someone else. Sir Laurence Olivier. He was an actor and Uncle Shamus seemed to be close friends with him.

Friday they went to the National Observatory in Kent and later visited a giant department store called Harrods. They had a lot of food on one floor but they had a great book section and Duncan spent an hour trying to decide how to spend the 10-pound note Uncle Shamus gave him. He settled on one book about World War II warplanes, another about space exploration, and a third about America.

Saturday morning was set aside so Duncan could go to a dog show in Kent. He watched the way each dog was paraded into the arena and the way they were held while being inspected. Halfway through the show, a Basenji was paraded into the arena. It looked exactly like Christine. The regal walk, the super alert ears, the feet barely touching the floor. Duncan was impressed with the whole dog show program but now he was silently rooting for the Basenji as it sat motionless next to her mistress. The Basenji was named Daisy and took second place in the entire show. She lost to an Irish setter that was an incredible color of reddish-brown.

After the British Kennel Club show, they went to the Connaught to change for the reception. The tuxedo fit him perfectly. His white formal shirt was stiff but set off his tanned complexion and his shiny brown hair perfectly. The silk cummerbund was made of the Stuart-Bruce plaid, a striking combination of green and purple. He did not look 15 years old; he looked five, maybe six years older. Very handsome. Very dashing. Very much like his father Ian.

They arrived at Buckingham Palace in a line of limousines that stretched all the way past the gates. Uncle Shamus got out of the Rolls-Royce limo first and Duncan followed dutifully. They made their way into the entrance hall and checked their topcoats in the anteroom. They climbed the stairs to the main ballroom and waited in line to be announced, prior to entering the ballroom.

The man with a funny-looking wig took the card from Shamus, looked at it and announced in the loud, clear voice: "Sir Shamus Stuart-Bruce and his grandnephew, Duncan Stuart-Bruce, of their ancestral Aberdeen, Scotland."

They were escorted to the reception line. Shamus shook hands with a woman in a big hat who looked really old. He guessed she was about 60 years old. Shamus introduced Duncan to her, "Your majesty, Duncan Stuart-Bruce, my grandnephew. Duncan, this is Her Majesty, The Queen Mother."

Duncan promptly bowed and shook hands with the kind-faced older woman. She said, "You are about the same age as my grandson, Charles." She looked at Shamus, "Make sure your grandnephew meets Charles. Maybe they can hunt or fish together next time Charles comes to Balmarol."

Next, Uncle Shamus introduced him to Sir Mountbatten and judging by his uniform and all the medals, Duncan figured he must be a war hero. Shamus asked Mountbatten if he were going to come to Aberdeen for the reunion next year. Sir Mountbatten said that he had scheduled two days in June and looked forward to visiting with Shamus during his stay in Scotland. Shamus invited "Monty" to stay at the castle and Monty accepted.

Next was a lady in her late 20s or early 30s, Princess Margaret, the Queen's younger sister. She was a pretty woman with intense eyes but she seemed to be sad.

Next was Prince Phillip, a very tall, very distinguished looking man who was very pleased to see Shamus. He seemed to break protocol as he held Shamus's hand in both of his as they shook. Shamus took extra care to make sure that Duncan knew that Prince Phillip was a very special person. Duncan bowed and shook his hand. The Prince told Shamus to bring Duncan to Balmarol next month during their visit to Scotland.

Prince Phillip introduced Uncle Shamus and Duncan to a tall, striking, beautifully-dressed woman next to him. Jacqueline Kennedy, the First Lady of the United States. She greeted both of them warmly and said she appreciated Shamus's invitation to join him at his castle in Aberdeen this trip.

Mrs. Kennedy introduced them to President Kennedy. The president turned to Uncle Shamus and gave him a vigorous handshake and warm smile. Shamus introduced Duncan to the President of the United States. Duncan extended his hand and shook the president's hand.

"Duncan, I knew your father and I was sorry to hear that he had died before I got to see him again. You are the spitting image of him. You remind me so much of him when we met in Hawaii in 1944. As I understand it, your father met your mother at a resort in Arizona called Castle Hot Springs. Your father and I had a great time there and I will always cherish those memories."

"Thank you, sir. You are very kind to remember my father and mother. I understand you lost a brother in the war and a sister shortly after the war. My condolences to you and your family for your loss and, again, thank you for your kind words." Duncan said with a steady but firm voice, "and be sure to thank Mrs. Kennedy for honoring us with her presence."

President Kennedy was visibly shaken. This boy, no, this young man had put his own parents' early death aside to honor his brother, his sister and his wife with such eloquence that he could not say a thing for a moment. He regained control instantly, extended his hand to Duncan, again, while he said, "Your condolences are much appreciated. I only wish you could have met Joe and Kick. I am sure that they would be as impressed with you as I am tonight." He looked at Shamus and continued, "This is a very special young man, I hope you will have him come to Washington and visit Jackie and me at the White House very soon."

He then turned to introduce Shamus and Duncan to Queen Elizabeth.

She was not a striking woman like Mrs. Kennedy, but there was a sparkle to her eyes that caught your attention. "Shamus, Shamus, we are so glad to see you. And who is this? This cannot be Duncan. Oh my, he's all grown up, like my Charles. Where does the time go? Will you be able to join us for dinner this evening, Shamus? The President and Mrs. Kennedy are our guests and we are having the whole state dinner thing, you know. Be sure to stay for the private party afterwards, you men do love your cognac and cigars."

"Yes, your Majesty," Shamus said as he bowed. "We would be honored to join you this evening."

"Duncan is coming, too, I hope. Maybe Charles will have someone to play with and stop being angry with me for making him come to a stuffy state dinner."

They exited the reception line and made their way to the ballroom and the refreshments.

"Very impressive, Duncan. Very impressive," Shamus said approvingly, "you are a smashing hit with the royal family, President Kennedy, and the First Lady Jacqueline Bouvier Kennedy. Very impressive.

"To celebrate your success, I'm even going to let you have your first glass of champagne."

CHAPTER 17

The Royal Military Academy Sandhurst
Sandhurst, England
June 1965

....

S hamus enrolled Duncan at Sandhurst when he was 15 with special permission from the headmaster for a cadet under 16 years old. Duncan matured early physically, intellectually and emotionally and everyone including Shamus believed him capable of meeting the rigors of Sandhurst. Now, three years later, he was watching Duncan graduate with honors and 4th in his class. Duncan had been a star pupil in physics and mathematics because of his natural affinity for numbers and logic. But he pursued an even greater curiosity for political science. He received an award from the political science department at Sandhurst and was invited to give a five-minute address at the beginning of the graduation ceremonies.

He chose a rather controversial subject of comparing British socialism to the Soviet Union's communism. After his speech, Sandhurst's senior administrators had deep frowns on their faces. The corollaries Duncan presented were far too accurate for their comfort. They politely applauded Duncan and moved him to the rear of the dais as quickly as possible.

Shamus was sure that he would receive several phone calls from his friends in the government asking why he would let Duncan present such a scandalous paper at Sandhurst on that June afternoon.

A few months earlier during the Christmas holiday break, Duncan asked Shamus if he could attend university in America. He specifically wanted to go to Stanford, the same school his mother attended 20 years before. Shamus wanted Duncan to join the British Army for two years before starting his university training but in the end he agreed to let Duncan attend Stanford University in California if he would serve two years in the British Army after Stanford. Duncan said he would graduate in three years and then go to graduate school for a year before his turn in military service.

Duncan had not spent any significant time in America since he left when he was 6 years old but as he drove through Pacific Heights, the neighborhood came back to him. The parks, the schools, the shopping plaza, and the house he lived in when he was young. They were all there.

He saw that the house had red shutters instead of green and there were four cars in the drive. The rest of the house was as he remembered. He decided not to try and see the inside today but to wait until after classes started at Stanford before coming back.

He drove his yellow Mustang convertible to Carmel along the Coast Highway, through Half Moon Bay, Pescadero, Santa Cruz, Moss Landing, Monterey and then Carmel. He drove down the hill from the Carmel village shops to the line of oceanfront properties. Nestled in the trees was the house his mother and father loved.

Duncan was grateful that Shamus did not sell the beach house and kept it in top-notch condition. When he went into the beach house, everything was precisely as he and his father had left it. Strange feeling being back in this house. Lots of wonderful memories.

Duncan thought he would be sad but instead he was very glad that he had decided to spend a couple of weeks here in Carmel before he had to be back in Palo Alto. The house smelled musty so he opened the French doors leading to the deck and let the house breathe. He loved the views from the deck and sat for a moment. Then he decided to unpack, and take a walk along the water's edge toward Pebble Beach to unwind after the long plane trip from London.

The two weeks passed quickly with trips down Highway 1 to Big Sur to watch the surfers, back to Monterey to buy fresh abalone, and to roadside stands inland to buy fruits and vegetables. When it was time to drive to Stanford, he was relaxed and rested and ready for everything Stanford had to throw at him.

Duncan liked Stanford classes, swam the backstroke on the varsity swim team, and threw the javelin in track and field. He particularly enjoyed his history classes and his physics professor. His first year he had a rather heavy class load with 39 semester hours but he was able to grind out an overall grade point of 3.55.

At the beginning of his second year he joined a fraternity and moved into their house on University Avenue. He became good friends with three of his fraternity brothers. His second year he took a total of 40 semester hours and maintained a steady 3.6 grade point.

To be able to graduate in three years, Duncan needed six hours in the summer between his second and third years. He took a month-long exploration course to the Mayan ruins in Mexico to get three hours in archeology. The other three hours come from an internship in laser physics at Lawrence Livermore Laboratories about 50 miles east of Stanford on the other side of the bay. He aced both classes and started his third year with a 3.65 grade point.

He completed his Stanford studies and received a B.S. in physics with minors in math and computer science.

Shamus kept his word about graduate school but insisted that Duncan concentrate his studies in business. Shamus arranged for Duncan to meet with the Dean of the Thunderbird School in Glendale, Arizona. Shamus told Duncan that it was the premier school in America, maybe in the world, for international business studies.

Duncan was impressed with the Dean, so he flew to Phoenix to visit the campus. What a rude experience after the plush garden-like grounds at Stanford. The Thunderbird School's campus was a desert with a few palm trees and no big buildings, only Quonset huts and aircraft hangers. Not the best first impression.

After meeting the faculty and reviewing the curriculum closer, Duncan decided that Thunderbird would be the best place for graduate school. He could fly to San Francisco every weekend if he still wanted to be close to the hills outside Palo Alto.

Duncan knew his parents met at a resort north of Phoenix shortly after the war so he drove to Castle Hot Springs. He made several inquiries but was told that the resort had closed a few years earlier. There was no one out at the resort except a caretaker and his wife.

After the hellish heat of August and September, the weather moderated and Duncan started to enjoy the beautiful warm days in Arizona. But the class load at the Thunderbird School was demanding and kept Duncan from really getting out to see the area until late November.

Duncan met a lot of interesting people at the Thunderbird School. In his class of 52, there were 26 different countries represented. Two classmates were heirs to the thrones in their respective countries. One of his classmates was being groomed to serve as the head of the treasury for an entire country in South America. Many of his classmates had heard of his Uncle Shamus by reputation but Duncan did not fully grasp how famous, or infamous, his Uncle Shamus was until one day in his international law class.

A classmate from the south of France was talking about his family's manufacturing business and how it worked very closely with Jacques Cousteau in developing new underwater diving gear, particularly the breathing apparatus. Francois explained that one of their biggest investors was from Scotland and had been a great supporter of their efforts to make diving a safer sport and profession. The Scottish investor was Shamus Stuart-Bruce of Aberdeen, Scotland, and he looked at Duncan as he said, "the uncle of our own, Duncan Stuart-Bruce."

Duncan could feel his face redden not because Francois had brought attention to him but because he had to learn about his family's holdings in a classroom in America rather than from Shamus. He vowed to learn more about what Shamus did and how big his holdings were.

Shamus came to Arizona for the graduation ceremony in May, 1969, and seemed to know many of the other people who came to see their sons and daughters graduate from Thunderbird. Shamus introduced Duncan to Senator Goldwater who had given the keynote speech and to Juan Alejandro of Argentina who gave the alumni speech.

Senator Goldwater invited everyone to his home in Paradise Valley for a barbecue. Shamus and Duncan rode with Mr. Allejandro in his car. Shamus and Juan discussed the mining operations in the foothills of the Andes, south of Mendoza. Shamus explained to Duncan that Juan was the founder and president of a mining consortium in Argentina, Chile, Bolivia, Brazil and Columbia that produced more gold, silver and copper than the rest of the mines in the world.

Senator Goldwater's barbecue was a huge success. Shamus, Juan and Duncan were invited to stay for a fireside chat after the other guests departed. Barry Goldwater was a major political force and his conservative approach to America's government was praised by those on the right and considered totally unacceptable by those on the left.

"So Shamus, I have not heard your thoughts on the Vietnam War recently," asked the senator with an arched right eyebrow, "and I would like to get your take on that conflict."

Shamus looked directly into the senator's eyes for a few moments, then took a sip of his drink and started shaking his head. "Barry, I do not have any words of wisdom for you and your country but I would caution everyone, including my own government in London, that the Vietnam experience is not headed for a happy ending for anyone." He paused for moment, took another sip of the drink, and continued, "My advisors recommend that we keep our business interests far away from Vietnam and, for that matter, all of Southeast Asia. I am told that nothing can be done to make that area a reasonable environment for business for many, many years, maybe decades."

Again, Shamus took a sip of his drink and said, "I am going to do just that. I will not get any closer to Vietnam than Hong Kong, Singapore and Shanghai for the foreseeable future. What do your folks tell you, senator?"

"Basically the same thing, only since we are the enemy, we have to stay farther away than you and the U.K.," he said quietly. He turned to Duncan and said, "I read a white paper that you wrote about the U.S. national debt and I agree with you 100%. There is no place in our economic system for extending the national debt. In fact, I believe that it would strengthen the U.S. and our efforts around the world for our government to be debt free and make that a permanent part of our economic policy. If America could pay off the national debt and stop borrowing money to fulfill political promises, do you think America would benefit from that approach?"

There was a tweak of a challenge to Senator Goldwater's question and Duncan gave Shamus a brief glance before answering. Shamus's eyes warned

Duncan not to take the bait too soon and Duncan watched the flames in the fire pit for a moment or two then cleared his throat.

"Senator, I want to say yes but I am also aware that paying off the U.S. national debt, although appealing to the ears, may not be as simple as it sounds. I believe that solving a problem of that scope would take the collective knowledge and wisdom of all your fellow members of Congress, plus many people in the Executive Branch including the president and his staff and those from the private sector both in the U.S. and abroad."

Duncan looked around and everyone was listening to him so he continued by closing with, "but something Shamus has always asked me to do when I came up with my great ideas — Be careful what you wish for, it may come true. So, senator, my concern is that if America did pay off its national debt, would it have the wisdom, discipline and strength to properly manage the economic policies of the country from thereon so that history would not be repeated with the start of a new national debt cycle?"

"Excellent observation and a good place to finish for the evening. Thank you, Duncan. Unfortunately, I believe that your words are closer to the truth than any of us want to admit," said the senator with sincere appreciation and concern.

CHAPTER 18

Mendoza, Argentina
October 1972

....

Duncan arrived in Mendoza in late October to prepare for the climb to the top of Mt. Aconcagua, the highest peak in South America. He had climbed Mt. McKinley, the highest in Alaska and North America, in June and Mt. Elbrus, in Russia and Europe, in August. Both of those climbs were tough but the weather cooperated and each expedition had been completed in near record time. He also benefited from Shamus's insistence that he hire the very best outfitters for all of his climbs and that Scott Bennett from Jackson, Wyoming, do all the advance planning and coordinating.

Not only was Scott in charge of all the preparations and personnel, he also accompanied Duncan to the top of each summit. This personal presence presented a special problem when the expedition tried to enter Russia. Seems that Scott's father, Congressman Bennett of Washington, was the most anti-Communist politician in Congress since Senator McCarthy.

As it turned out, the entire Bennett family was on the Soviet Union's un-desirable list and when entry to Russia was requested, the Soviet border guards were keenly interested in keeping Scott out of their Communist haven. Not only did the Soviet Army guards want to detain Scott, but they wanted to hold onto all of the equipment for the climb.

Duncan knew that this incident could escalate into an international fiasco with a little nudge, so he got to a phone and called Shamus. Shamus called one of his business connections in Moscow who got an appointment with a senior member of the Proletariat within the hour. Two hours later the once surly border guards were falling all over themselves to welcome Duncan, Scott and the entire entourage to the Soviet Union. They even offered to help them find a good restaurant in town.

Duncan returned the favor and invited all the soldiers to join them at dinner and the evening turned into a party to remember and a minor diplomatic coup. Word of the party had gotten to the mayor of the town and he brought his wife who was the sister of a high-ranking Communist party member. Duncan danced with her three or four times during the evening and she was smitten by this handsome young man who paid some attention to her and did not smell of tobacco and onions as all the Soviet men did.

When Mrs. Gorgi called her brother, Victor Ivanovich, the next day in Moscow, she kept raving about this young Scotsman who had danced with her the night before. Her brother liked it when his only sister was happy so he filed the name, Duncan Stuart-Bruce, away in his memory bank for further research. Any westerner who could impress his sister must be a very bright, very handsome and very charming young man. Keep an eye on this one, Victor said to himself as he turned to head out of his office at the Soviet parliament building.

Duncan snapped out of daydreaming as the car turned into a small plaza on the outskirts of Mendoza. *Wonder why I was thinking about that evening in Russia? Maybe the psychological preparation for the climb to the top of South America.* He blinked and looked around the plaza. It appeared to be deserted but then he saw a woman step from under the veranda and wave at them.

She flashed a brilliant smile and walked toward the car. She was tall but not too tall. She wore a white silk blouse and skintight faded blue jeans. She had her raven hair tied in the back with a scarlet ribbon. She took his breath away. Scott raced up to her and gave her a hug.

"Blanca, Blanca. You are even more gorgeous than three years ago," said Scott as he looked at her. "How do you do it? Stay so beautiful."

"Oh, Scott, you are so generous with your praise. I might fall in love with you if you keep talking like that," she said playfully with a slight accent. "You know I'm a sucker for your sweet talk."

"Blanca, I want you to meet everyone," said Scott with a sweep of his hand. "And everyone, this is Blanca Montoya, my Argentine sister and our guide."

Several people went to Blanca to shake hands and make small talk. She motioned everyone into the restaurant for lunch and fussed over getting all of her guests seated around five or six tables. The restaurant, Cielo Royal Grande, had a beautiful terrace that overlooked the foothills and to the left the guests could see the snow-covered peak, Mt. Aconcagua, their destination.

The mountain looked deceptively small in the background. With its broad ridges to the top, it looked like an easy climb. But, mountains, like women, have a way of fooling climbers. Just because they look easy doesn't mean they are easy.

Duncan had seen mountains before but he had never seen anyone like Blanca. He felt his face flush as she started toward him. No, she wasn't coming toward him, she wanted to talk to Scott. And they did talk. All through lunch, they talked about her family, Scott's family, friends they had in high school on Vashon Island, racing to catch the ferry and the terrific times they had at Pike Place or Lake Union. Duncan loved to watch her laugh and he enjoyed the way she kidded Scott about his girlfriends in high school.

The afternoon and evening passed without Duncan really knowing what he ate or drank or said. All that he could remember was Blanca's flashing eyes and inviting smile. He did not want the night to end. He did not want her to go away. He began to fantasize about them together. Walking in the forest, running on the beach, hiking to the top of a mountain. Being together, forever.

This is a first. A beautiful, young woman and my fantasies are not about being in bed together. There must be something wrong. Why am I not thinking about sex? Every 25-year-old man thinks about sex when he sees someone like Blanca. Now I'm more confused than ever. Does this mean I'm not sexually attracted to her? Does it mean that I'm losing my sex drive? What do the books say; a man's sexual peak comes when he is 17 or 18 years old? Am I already over the hill?

He stopped questioning and told himself to 'settle down.' *It's the beer, the heat and the loud music. Nothing more than that. Relax. Enjoy the evening. Maybe you should ask her to dance. Yeah, I want to dance with her. What if she says no? Oh well, better find out now before I imagine myself married to her and having four or five kids.*

He waited for a slow dance, "Unchained Melody," a really good slow dance.

"Would you like to dance?" Duncan asked in a low voice.

Blanca turned and faced him, "That's the nicest thing anyone has said to me this evening. Yes, I would really like that."

They moved to the center of the dance floor. She put her head on Duncan's shoulder and they moved with the rhythm of the music. They did not talk. Both of them had their eyes closed as if they were absorbing the very essence of the music.

Scott watched from across the dance floor. What he saw were two of his favorite people in the world moving like they had been together for years, although they had only been dancing for a few minutes. Whether Duncan or Blanca knew it or not, Scott could see that were going to be more than dance and mountain climbing partners. Scott smiled and silently wished the evening's newest couple the very best.

Duncan closed his eyes as he and Blanca swayed across the dance floor. As he breathed, he could smell her hair. She smelled of sunshine and spices. Like cloves and cinnamon. Her movements were smooth and steady with a natural rhythm that emphasized the beat of the music. It was like she felt the music in her bones and they vibrated with excitement to her skin.

She held his hand lightly and Duncan could feel the warmth of her skin. She squeezed his hand a little tighter, barely noticeable. Duncan was only conscious of the two of them. He didn't even know they were dancing. The only thing he knew was that they were together.

She moved her head and looked up at Duncan. She spoke softly, "Let's go outside on the terrace. I want to see the mountains at sunset." They turned and threaded their way across the dance floor to the French doors and the terrace beyond. They walked to the edge of the terrace arm in arm. Duncan stood behind Blanca and held her around the waist.

They stood watching the sun's rays paint new colors on the mountain peaks, first bright yellow, then a glowing orange, followed quickly by a fiery red. The red lingered for about ten minutes, then changed to purple and on to blue. Finally, the mountains were dark against the light sky, turning them almost black by contrast.

Blanca turned in Duncan's arms but he did not loosen his hold on her waist. She looked at him in the eyes. A deep, penetrating gaze searched for any hint of discomfort or hesitation. She saw all she needed to see in Duncan's eyes. Honesty, sincerity, warmth, pain, courage, intelligence and, best of all, humor. Blanca had inherited her grandmother's talent for reading a person's eyes. She knew she possessed it at an early age, 5 or 6. She was attending her first wedding and she watched her grandmother receive greetings from family and friends. Instantly, Blanca knew. She could see the way her grandmother's own eyes changed as she met a person who was not sincere but merely paying respects for superficial or political reasons.

About a year later, Blanca was invited to a birthday party for a classmate. The party was at a large villa. There were clowns, horses, merry-go-rounds and 20 or so children. Blanca's grandmother was her chaperone that day and her grandmother was able to observe Blanca with people she did not know. When the classmate's older brother greeted Blanca, Grandmother knew instantly. Blanca looked the boy in the eyes and determined that he was not a kind person.

As they rode home in the backseat of the Mercedes, Blanca's grandmother asked her what she thought of her classmate's older brother. Blanca did not have to answer verbally. She only had to turn and look at her grandmother's eyes. Grandmother knows and Grandmother knows I know.

Blanca shook off her memories and returned to Duncan. Without saying anything, Blanca took Duncan's hand and led him to a stairway that descended from the terrace to a covered veranda. They walked along the veranda and Blanca opened a door near the end of the building. She led Duncan into the room. It was dark and cool. Duncan shivered; goose bumps rising on his body.

Blanca turned to Duncan, leaned toward him and kissed him on the lips. A tender, moist kiss. Tentative, yet firm. Duncan pulled her closer and responded to her kiss by moving his tongue between her lips. Blanca tensed a little but yielded to his eager advance.

They pulled apart and Duncan held her by the shoulders and looked into her eyes. "Are you sure this is what you want?" said Duncan in a hoarse whisper.

Blanca looked again with the penetrating gaze but only nodded her head. She took his hand again and led him to the bed against the far wall. Duncan sat on the bed and watched as Blanca lit a candle. The light cast by that single candle gave Blanca a glow that was almost surreal. She was so beautiful he could not believe it.

She reached for Duncan's shirt buttons and undid them one at a time until she pulled his shirttail from the waistband of his slacks. She removed his shirt to find that Duncan had an undershirt on — a V-necked, white cotton T-shirt. She reached down and pulled the undershirt over Duncan's head.

Blanca had seen many men before but Duncan's lean torso and slightly hairy chest appealed to her. She looked in his eyes again. She had missed it earlier. *He is sexy and the best part is that he doesn't even know it. That's why she missed it. He doesn't even know his own sex appeal.* She smiled at the thought and it was enough to make her blush.

Duncan touched her neck and let his fingers slowly move up her neck to her ears. *How did he know I liked to have my ears touched?* Then he moved his hands down to the top button of her blouse. The silk fabric slipped around each of the buttons and let the cups of her bra show. It wasn't much of a bra. Just enough to hold each breast gently. The blouse stayed on her shoulders as Duncan moved his hands to unclasp the bra.

He slid his hands into each of the cups and slowly moved the cups from Blanca's breasts. He undid the cuffs of her blouse and let the blouse fall to the floor. Duncan moved away from Blanca, turned her slowly and her bra fell to the floor. Duncan held her around the waist as he had done on the terrace only this time she could feel his warm chest against her back and his hardness against her buttocks.

She took his left hand and placed it on her right breast and his right hand on her left breast. Like those foolish cross-your-heart commercials on American TV.

Duncan reached down and kissed her on the neck, then he nuzzled her right ear. Blanca felt the flush as it ran through her body and she could not control her response. Her nipples tightened and Duncan squeezed first the left one and then the right one, causing Blanca to gasp.

Duncan turned Blanca to face him. The candlelight sparkled in his eyes and they were full of desire.

He reached for his belt buckle and unfastened the belt, unbuttoned his slacks and slipped them off his hips. Duncan stepped out of his slacks and

Blanca could see that he was fully aroused even through the cotton boxer shorts he wore.

Blanca unbuttoned her jeans and unzipped the zipper and let her them fall to the floor as Duncan had done. Her black bikini briefs were almost sheer and left very little to Duncan's imagination as he looked at her body.

Duncan pulled the bedspread and sheets down and turned away from Blanca as he slipped his boxer shorts off. He turned to her as he climbed into bed. Blanca loved seeing Duncan completely naked. His legs were long, his butt tight and compact, and the sight of his penis sent chills through her body.

Blanca quickly removed her panties and moved to the bed alongside Duncan. She always thought her hips were too big and she did not want to ruin the moment with hips that were too big.

Duncan caressed Blanca and she explored his body. She found a scar on his side she had seen while he had undressed. They kissed and they moved closer together. Duncan touched her breasts, circling each nipple with the very lightest of touch.

Blanca moved and pulled Duncan on top of her and at the same moment opened her thighs. Duncan positioned himself above her and both of them reached down to guide him into her. She was very wet and he slipped into her almost magically. They lay together, feeling each other's heartbeat but all too quickly their bodies betrayed them and, uncontrollably, they started moving together.

Blanca was trying her best to satisfy Duncan and Duncan trying his best to satisfy Blanca. Each not knowing that they were both being satisfied physically and spiritually. Although time did seem to stop, they both climaxed with deep, toe curling orgasms that left both Blanca and Duncan breathless.

Blanca had not said anything to Duncan since they had left the dance floor and Duncan had spoken only to ask if she was sure this was what she wanted. The silence continued and they fell into a deep sleep.

Duncan woke first, his face buried in Blanca's hair and his arm around her waist. He did not move but checked his senses. He was warm and her naked body spooned against his naked body. Her skin felt smooth and her hair was silken. He could smell her. She smelled of cinnamon and clove but Duncan could also smell the scent of their lovemaking. Not strong but a distinctive hint of sweat and sex. He could hear her breathing. But just barely. Slow, even breaths that moved her chest slightly.

The room was dark but he could make out a faint outline of the window across the room. He did not move except to close his eyes and drift into sleep once more.

What woke him the second time was the smell of coffee. Very strong, aromatic coffee. He opened his eyes and saw Blanca sitting on the edge of the bed. She was wearing jeans, hiking boots, a denim shirt and a quilted vest.

"Good morning," Blanca said shyly. "Welcome back from the land of sleep. Take this coffee, I have another cup on the table." She rose to retrieve her cup of coffee.

Duncan sipped the coffee. It was like her. The coffee smelled and tasted lightly of cinnamon and clove. He reached over and set the cup on the nightstand. He threw the bedclothes off him, rose from the bed naked and walked toward the bathroom. "Excuse me but I need to use the bathroom and take a shower. You look great and I know I look like hell in the morning," said Duncan bashfully. "Hope you don't mind?"

"Of course not," said Blanca with a smile on her face. "And thank you for letting me see you this morning with no clothes. You are a handsome man who is very sexy, both late at night and early in the morning. I thought I was dreaming all this until I saw you this morning."

"Here. Take your coffee with you," said Blanca, "and hurry back. We need to talk."

Duncan saw himself in the mirror as he closed the bathroom door. The image showed a man with puffy sleep eyes; sleep creases on his left cheek, and bed hair standing straight up and at right angles at the same time. Handsome? Very sexy? Where did that come from? He reached into the shower to turn on the water. He saw the clean clothes folded on the counter next to his shaving kit. Where did Blanca get his clothes and his kit? She was already proving to be very resourceful both in bed and out of it.

When he came out of the bathroom, Blanca turned to see him. Cleaned up, hair combed, freshly shaved, and wearing nice-fitting clothes, he looked even better than before, although she thought she could look at him naked forever. *Quit that. This is not the time for those thoughts.*

Duncan walked to the window and looked at the mountains. As usual they were glorious in the white light of the early morning. He leaned down and kissed Blanca softly on the lips and spoke with a sly grin. "You said we needed to talk. I thought we were communicating pretty well last night."

"Duncan, don't tease me," Blanca said earnestly. "We must be serious. Please be serious and stop playing."

"Okay, okay," he said with a fake poutiness, "what do we need to talk about that is so important?"

Blanca looked at her hands a moment then directly at Duncan. "What we did last night was incredibly beautiful and I thank the angels for allowing me to make love to you." She stopped and looked at her hands again. "But we cannot ....," Blanca started to talk but could not continue. She looked at Duncan this time with tears welling in her eyes.

Duncan was startled into reality by the look in her eyes. She was pleading with her eyes for him to understand so she would not have to say the rest of the sentence. He reached over and took her hands into his. Now it was his turn to look at her hands. He thought for maybe 30 seconds but it seemed like hours.

He reached over to her face and lifted her chin so he could see her eyes. The tears were now streaming down her cheeks. He wiped one then the other cheek. Her eyes changed from pleading to hopeful. Hopeful he would intuitively understand.

They stared into each other's eyes for the longest moment. Then Duncan said in a soft but firm voice, "You are right. We cannot make love again until we are married."

"So that only leaves three things to do," Duncan said matter-of-factly. "Ask you to marry me, you to say yes, then we find someone who will marry us today. Right now."

Blanca was stunned. How did he know? That was exactly what she was going to say but couldn't finish the sentence. And as she was about to speak, Duncan got down on one knee, looked up at her and said, "Blanca, will you marry me?"

"Yes. Yes. Yes. Yes. A thousand times, yes." Blanca pulled Duncan to her. "But today, how can I get ready for my wedding in less than a day?"

Duncan looked down at her and said with a firm voice, "You said no more sex until we were married, but you did not say we had to have a long engagement." Then a smile formed on his lips and in his eyes.

"You are right," Blanca admitted, "but I want one more stipulation to our agreement. I want two weddings."

Duncan's eyes grew large and he started to protest but before he could say anything Blanca held her finger to his lips. "Not to get excited," she said as she slipped into the Spanish way of saying it, "one wedding today, a civil ceremony, and a church wedding with a priest at the church in six weeks."

Duncan admired her sense of fair play and nodded his head.

Scott, Jorge and Jorge's wife Maria witnessed the civil ceremony held in the office of Mendoza's mayor. They left immediately to visit Blanca's grandmother and then on to an overnight honeymoon at the posh Castille Resort and Spa 25 kilometers from Mendoza.

Like Blanca, Duncan knew the instant he saw her that they were destined to be married. He could not identify why he felt this way. But something told him that this was what his father and mother would have wanted. He could not explain why he had such a strong premonition involving his mother and father approving of his marrying Blanca after knowing her one day, when they had been dead for 20 years. Strange. Duncan thought. *I must talk to Uncle Shamus about this when I see him.*

Oh my god, I almost forgot, I have to call Shamus and give him the good news.

"Shamus, Uncle Shamus?" Duncan almost shouted in the phone. "Are you there?"

"Of course I am. Stop shouting," Shamus said gruffly. "Where are you? Somewhere in South America?"

"I am. We are getting ready to climb Mt. Aconcagua and we are in Mendoza, Argentina," said Duncan excitedly. "This is a beautiful city and the mountains are glorious."

"Duncan, my son, from the sound of your voice, I would swear you are in love or something," said Shamus jokingly.

"How did you know? Oh, never mind. Are you sitting down?" Duncan said with a bit of hesitation.

"Duncan, get to the point," Shamus said, irritated now.

"Shamus, I got married yesterday. Here in Mendoza. Her name is Blanca. And I have never been happier than I am right now." Duncan said so fast that Shamus could barely understand him.

There was silence on the line.

"Shamus, are you there?" Duncan inquired.

"Yes, of course, I am. Isn't this a little abrupt?" Shamus said tentatively. Then his tone changed and he said heartily, "Congratulations, Duncan, and to your wife, Blanca is it?"

"That's right, Blanca," said Duncan, "she is 22 years old, has a master's degree in geology from the university in Santiago and she will be our guide when we make our climb into the Andes."

"Shamus, we are having a church wedding in six weeks. Get Isabella and come to the wedding." Duncan went on, "It would not be complete without both you and Isabella."

"I can't wait to meet Blanca, and I wouldn't miss the wedding for anything," said Shamus enthusiastically. "I wouldn't miss it if you were getting married on the moon."

They both laughed. "Shamus, we are leaving in two days for a climb and we'll be back in five weeks." Duncan said, "I have already reserved a suite at the hotel for a month, so why don't you come down in about four weeks, get to know the area and we can enjoy the time before the wedding."

"That's a great idea," Shamus said, "but I probably will stay in Buenos Aires, Montevideo, Asuncion and Santiago for a few days each before coming to Mendoza. Plan on us being in Mendoza four days before the wedding. We will stay part of the time with Juan Allejandro. You remember him from the graduation at the Thunderbird School?"

"Yes, of course, I remember Mr. Allejandro," Duncan said. "Do I need to call him?"

"No, I will take care of everything from here," said Shamus quickly.

"I can't wait until you and Isabella get here," Duncan said with genuine excitement. "Shamus, I have a favor to ask."

"Ask away," Shamus said.

"Do you remember the ring you said you had that my father gave to my mother when they were married?" Duncan inquired. "Could you bring it with you when you come to Mendoza?"

"Of course I will," Shamus said quietly. "Your mother and father would want you to have the ring for your bride."

"Shamus, I have the strangest feeling that my mother and father were with me when I married Blanca," Duncan said thoughtfully. "They have been dead for so long, how could they be here in South America somehow encouraging me to marry Blanca?"

Shamus said seriously, "We will talk about this more when I see you in Mendoza. But don't let this dampen your spirits. Give my best to Blanca and have a great climb. My love to you always, Duncan, my boy."

"And mine to you, Uncle Shamus," Duncan said. "Give Isabella a hug and peck for me. Can't wait to see her. She is going to love Blanca. So will you. Take care Shamus, see you in a few weeks."

Shamus put down the receiver and looked out the leaded glass window in the study. The wind and rain left streaks on the window and he let his mind wander:

Duncan is more like Ian than I ever thought. Adventuresome, headstrong, and a romantic. Reminds me of the call I got 25 years ago from Ian when he married Liddy. So happy, so much in love, and so much tragedy. Let's hope the Bruce curse will not plague Duncan and Blanca as it did Ian and Liddy.

CHAPTER 19

Andes Mountains, Argentina
October 1972

....

The climb to the summit of Mt. Aconcagua was physically demanding, made more so because the team decided to make the climb without any supplemental oxygen. At almost 23,000 feet the air is so thin that the act of breathing is tough.

Both Blanca and Duncan seemed to thrive on the low oxygen atmosphere. They outpaced everyone on the trip and seemed to be moving in their own cocoon, insulated from the harshness of the blinding sun, high winds, and constant cold. They attacked the mountain with a passion that few had seen before.

Scott watched them carefully but could only detect one flaw in their normally cautious nature. Duncan and Blanca never ventured more than a few yards from one another during the ascent from the base camp at 17,000 feet. Scott had read about this type of love but he had never known it himself and had never known anyone who had possessed it. That is until now.

Duncan and Blanca together created a presence that almost glowed with vitality.

Together they equaled one thousand. But apart, only one hundred each. The romantics and philosophers call that something "synergy," but really it is much simpler than that…it's love.

Scott was in awe and jealous at the same time. Awestruck by the oneness that Duncan and Blanca possessed. Jealous of not having that oneness with someone himself.

Scott watched them every day. Never once did they waiver. Both were rock solid and always eager to start the next day's climb earlier than any of the other members of the team.

When they reached the summit, everyone was exhausted. Everyone except Mr. and Mrs. Pure Energy.

After all the photographs, several of the team members started back down, Scott asked Duncan if he and Blanca were ready to leave.

"You go ahead, Scott," Duncan said quietly, "We have something we want to do while we are here on the summit. Oh, and please leave the camera, I'm going to need it."

"Duncan, you can't stay here too long, you know the wind will pick up any minute and blow all of us off the mountain." Scott said sternly, "Only five minutes. Understand? Only five minutes."

Scott walked about 400 yards down the slope and turned to look back up. What he saw next was the craziest stunt he had ever witnessed.

Duncan and Blanca removed their clothing and were standing naked in front of the camera and tripod. Blanca's hair was blowing straight back from her head and Duncan was kissing her neck.

Absolutely nuts. Bonkers. Just plain stupid. But at the same time, Scott looked again at the couple, one of the sexiest things he had ever seen.

He wondered what National Geographic would pay for that shot? Then he thought: *forget National Geographic, I'm calling Playboy!*

What will they tell their kids when that photo surfaces in 20 years or so?

"Well, kids, it was the 70s and we were still recovering from the 60s so we slipped once in a while and what would you expect? We were in love."

CHAPTER 20

Mendoza, Argentina
November 1972

....

The afternoon heat was warm but not stifling because at 1200 meters the days were warm without a hint of humidity and the nights were cool and crisp. The view of the Andean foothills with the towering snowcap mountains was a constant magnet to the eyes.

Shamus could not remember a more spectacular view. Maybe the Alps? Or the Canadian Rockies? Or New Zealand? No. This was the best. Why had he not been here before? How many times had he been to Buenos Aires? Ten times or more but he had never come to the Andes. How foolish not to know that this jewel on the eastern slopes of the Andes was a true paradise.

Although Isabella was fascinated by the mountains and the city she was preoccupied with getting checked into the hotel. She wanted everything to be perfect. She was giving a bridal shower for Blanca and she had to make sure that the hotel had prepared everything to her instructions. They expected only 15 or 20 of Blanca's friends and family including Blanca's grandmother. But even with a small group, Isabella wanted the shower and the luncheon to set the tone for the upcoming wedding and everything had to be perfect.

Shamus met many stunning women in his life, but he was not prepared for the glowing energy that Blanca possessed. The sun had toasted her skin a rosy pink that made her hair and eyes more radiant. Shamus also noticed that all the other men and women also watched Blanca as she walked through the lobby. Absolutely breathtaking.

And Duncan. Had he gotten more handsome and taller? The sun had darkened his skin to a healthy tan and his hair had red highlights. His walk was, well, springier. His feet seemed to barely touch the ground, like Duncan's Basenji dog, Christine. Maybe everyone was looking at Duncan not Blanca.

Shamus felt Isabella's arm slip into the nook of his right elbow. "Aren't they lovely?" Isabella said with obvious pride. "Look. Everyone is watching them. They must be the best-looking couple in all of Argentina, maybe all of South America."

Shamus snapped out of his stare and looked again. Isabella was right. It was not just Blanca or Duncan, it was the two of them together. She was also right when she said they were the best-looking couple.

Shamus had seen this before but only once. In San Francisco at the Mark Hopkins. Ian and Liddy stopped the crowd when they walked through the lobby. The same confident walk. Synchronized like precision Swiss watch movements. But not stiff. Smooth and natural. As with Ian and Liddy, Shamus knew that Duncan and Blanca learned to move together when they made love. *Silly thought at a time like this. Why am I thinking of Ian? And Liddy?*

Duncan introduced Shamus and Isabella to Blanca, "Señor Stuart-Bruce, a great honor to finally meet you." He turned to Isabella, "Signora Santino, you are even more beautiful than Duncan described. Again, a great honor for me."

Shamus leaned forward and kissed Blanca's hand, straightened and looked Blanca in the eyes. "I cannot put into words just saying your name, Mrs. Stuart-Bruce. I must say that Duncan understated your incredible ability to stop everyone in this grand room. You are lovely and I am very pleased that you have agreed to be part of our family."

Duncan shook hands with Shamus, gave him a big hug, kissed Isabella on both cheeks and gave her a warm hug. "Look at you. Both of you look great. The trip to Mendoza has been good for you," Duncan started rapidly. "We have so much to tell you that I don't know where to begin."

"I will start," Shamus said eagerly. "We are taking you out to dinner tonight. To a restaurant I have been told is truly spectacular – La Luna and La Cielo – The Moon and the Sky. Do you know it, Blanca?"

"Of course, everyone in Mendoza knows it," Blanca said with respect, "but very few locals can afford the ala carte menu and extensive wine list."

"Well, we will splurge a little tonight and have a great time," Shamus said teasingly. "And to show that we are an equal opportunity family, I am letting Isabella pay for dinner this evening."

"Shamus," Isabella said sternly, but with a twinkle in her eye, "Keep acting like a chauvinist and Blanca and I will be dining alone, while you and Duncan find another hotel to stay in."

"Blanca, please excuse this fiery Italian lady," Shamus said laughing. "She has little patience for my brand of humor sometimes. But I love her all the same. I'm sure you understand?"

Blanca smiled and held Duncan's arm tight. They liked her and Duncan could see that they liked her. That was all he wanted from this evening.

* * * *

The days leading up to the wedding were busy for Blanca. The fittings, shopping, more fittings, and arrangements for the wedding gave her little time with Duncan. Isabella took over the wedding planning like it was her profession. Everyone in Mendoza seemed to be speaking Italian because of Signora Isabella.

What pleased Isabella the most was that the wedding was to be held in an old mission chapel in the foothills about 30 miles from Mendoza. Santa Sierra was built about the same time as the missions in California, 1650 to 1700. The courtyard of the mission was paved in ancient cobblestones with a simple fountain in the center. This was not a mission for the wealthy but a mission for the locals who grew to love God through their simple but strong needs.

In dramatic contrast to the unadorned mission walls and the chapel, there was a very beautiful statue of the Madonna in an alcove near the confessionals. Isabella inspected it closely as she toured the mission with Father Angelo and found that the detail this particular Madonna possessed was most extraordinary.

"Where did this Madonna come from?" asked Isabella with quiet reverence. "It is beautiful and it seems to be old but in excellent condition."

"We are very fortunate to have this Madonna," said Father Angelo. "It was a gift from a local family after they made a pilgrimage to the Vatican to visit the

Pope. They bought it from a family in Northern Italy somewhere close to Lake Como. I am not sure of the exact location of the family's estate."

Isabella looked at the priest and back at the Madonna. "Father, I know this Madonna. I was raised in the Lake Como area and still have a home there." She said quietly, "I had heard rumors about the Pignatelli family selling this priceless statue but did not believe the rumors until this very moment. Ricardo Pignatelli was my father's closest friend and I played at the Pignatelli estate as a child."

"Most interesting, Signora Isabella," said the priest with curiosity. "How can you tell it is the same Madonna?"

"See here at the bottom, the paint on the right sandal is chipped. Rosario Pignatelli and I dropped this very statue one day when we were playing and the Madonna fell on the edge of the table but Rosario caught it before it hit the floor. A single chip flew off the statue when it hit the edge of the table," said Isabella excitedly. "I know this is the Madonna, Father."

"You and your friend, eh, Rosario was it?, must have felt very lucky that day." The priest smiled. "Where is she today?"

"I do not know, Father," Isabella said sadly. "I did not see Rosario again after that day. My father said that her family moved to the south of Italy but I never actually knew what happened. I missed her terribly, but thank God the Madonna is still with us. I can hardly believe that I found it here in Argentina."

"I have many things to talk over with you, Father," said Isabella as they walked out of the alcove. "Tell me about the mass you have planned for my Duncan and his wife Blanca."

After viewing the rest of the mission, dining on a light lunch and saying mid-day prayers with Father Angelo, Isabella left for Mendoza to complete the wedding plans.

Shamus met with Juan Allejandro at his mining company offices fifty miles south of Mendoza. The drive down was leisurely and pleasant. The young man driving knew the local geography and kept Shamus amused with his stories about the small towns and villages they drove through on their way to the mines.

The Mercedes sedan turned from the main road and headed toward the mountains. Shamus noticed that they were going toward a canyon and the closer they got to the canyon's entrance, the steeper the canyon walls appeared. At the mouth of the canyon, there was a cluster of buildings hidden among tall poplar and sycamore trees. The car crossed a small bridge and climbed a steep hill in front of a massive stone building.

Juan Allejandro was out front to greet his old friend. "Welcome, welcome, Shamus," said Juan with enthusiasm. "You honor me with your presence. Come join me for some refreshments after your long dusty trip."

Shamus was always surprised by the natural smoothness Juan possessed when he performed these little social graces. He was a master and made Shamus feel welcomed and relaxed at the same time.

"It is my turn to return the compliment," said Shamus with a smile. "You have not aged a day since I saw you last in Paris. What was it? Seven or eight years ago? Juan, what is your secret? You must tell me."

Juan laughed that deep, masculine way that transmitted genuine pleasure. "There is no secret, my good friend. Only sunshine, mountains, wine and, of course, women."

"You are a rascal," said Shamus. "You wouldn't say those things if Margareta was here."

"Well, maybe my good health is a blessing because I have a good loving wife, five healthy children and three grandchildren now," said Juan with obvious pride.

"Now that is a surprise. Grandchildren!" mused Shamus. "Wonder if I should tell them the bedtime story about how Grandpa Juan went sailing in the Virgin Islands one day when he was much younger. What do you think? I must tell them."

"No, no, no, I give up," Juan said with hands held up in surrender. "Keep my past where it belongs, in your memory, not in my grandchildren's ears."

"Enough jokes and teasing," Shamus said earnestly. "How are you? You look great. And Margareta? She's well, I hope."

"Yes, we are all fine," said Juan, "You, my friend, you look more distinguished than ever. How is Isabella? And Duncan and his new wife? I saw their pictures in the newspaper after they climbed The Mountain."

"Fortune is with us, everyone is doing great. We are having a splendid time here in Argentina." Shamus said, with a gesture to the countryside, "and you, my friend, what an incredible view."

"Yes, it is a very relaxing place for me to have my business," said Juan with satisfaction. "Much of this is due to your incredible generosity over the last 30 years. I could not have put this together without your help. Again, many thanks."

"Again, it is I who should thank you," Shamus said as he starred into Juan's eyes. "If all of my investments gave me the 30 to 40% return like your operation, well, I could have retired years ago."

"You old bullshitter," Juan smiled. "You never had to work a day if you didn't want to and we both know it."

Juan motioned with his hand and a waiter appeared with a bottle of wine. He opened the wine and offered a small sample to Señor Juan who tasted the wine. "Excellent, Miguel, excellent. Please pour Señor Stuart-Bruce and me a glass of this very fine Sauvignon Blanc."

They toasted to good health and sipped the wine. "It is excellent," Shamus said, admiring the color. "What is that I taste? A hint of jasmine? How did you do that in a Sauvignon Blanc?"

"Again, trying to pry family secrets from my lips," said Juan with a smile. "Not even I know this secret. Only my wife's uncle Jorge has this secret and he has not shared it with anyone for more than 40 years. I think my youngest son, Alberto, will get the recipe soon but until then we must beg Uncle Jorge to do his magic." They both laughed and this time drank fully of Uncle Jorge's very special wine.

"Margareta and I are very pleased to see that Duncan is marrying into a respected family in Mendoza. The Montoya family has a long history of faithful and honorable service to our country. Tomas Montoya was mayor of Mendoza for 15 years after World War I. Raul Montoya, Tomas's grandson, was Minister of the Interior in the late '40s with the Perons," said Juan. "As with all families there are some who do not honor their heritage."

Juan stopped for a moment as he poured some more wine, then continued with a somber tone.

"About 25 years ago, Raul Montoya's only sister, Juanita, ran away from her family. For two or three years, no one knew where she had disappeared to," said Juan quietly. "Then one day, she appeared on television, representing one of the radical leftists groups in Columbia. They were loosely tied to Noriega's predecessors in Panama.

"She called herself, 'La Caliente Espiritu,' The Hot Spirit. She had been educated in the finest schools here and in Europe including a university degree from one of the colleges in Spain, so she commanded and got a lot of respect, especially from the poor. She led a minor revolution along the Columbian coast but before she could really catch fire, no pun intended, the Columbian government offered to make her Minister of Education.

"Surprising everyone, she accepted and went to work making the system work for the people rather than the people working for the system," Juan said with a bit of pride. "Then all hell broke loose.

"Some soldiers wrecked a school and raped three or four of the teenage girls who were students there. Well, Juanita tried to get the soldiers prosecuted but the military won out and kept the soldiers away from the courts.

"Juanita did not like this type of justice, so she returned to her old ways as La Caliente Espiritu. This time she joined forces with people who had money." Juan went on warily, "even back in the late '40s and early '50s, cocaine was big business in Columbia."

"So now she was with the drug people, this was before they were called cartels, and, yes, you guessed it, she met someone who was her natural soul mate. His name is not important. What is important is that she crossed the line and married outside her place in society. This was an unforgivable sin in her family's eyes and she was more or less excommunicated from the Montoya family.

"Early in 1950, Juanita gave birth to a baby girl. About a month later, her new husband's drug enterprises were taken over by a stronger band of thugs and the new leader wanted Juanita as his. Juanita's husband was killed in front of her and, rather than risk her baby's life, Juanita bargained with El Hombre. She agreed to be his mistress if he would let her give her baby to her mother and father in Argentina. She promised never to cause a problem, if he would grant her this one wish.

"El Hombre's only condition was that if Juanita ever stopped doing what he wanted, he would have the baby killed even if his men had to travel to Argentina." Juan said sadly, "That baby is now Duncan's wife, Blanca."

Shamus sat for a moment. He sipped some more of the wine, stood, and walked to the edge of the terrace. He looked back at Juan. "Who knows this?" asked Shamus. "Who knows all that you have told me?"

"Very few. To my knowledge, only Blanca's grandmother. The only reason I know is that my mother was a very close friend of Señora Montoya. My mother told me several years ago when she was dying. All Blanca knows is that her parents were killed in an accident in Columbia shortly after she was born and her grandparents brought her back to Argentina to live."

"Why are you telling me all of this?" asked Shamus, slightly annoyed. "What can I do to change any of this for Blanca or Duncan?"

"I wanted you to know because you are a very dear friend. I know that your family has amassed one of the world's great fortunes. And I do not want to see you, Duncan, or Blanca threatened by these people in Columbia."

"Why would they threaten Blanca, or Duncan or I?" asked Shamus with a little anger in his voice. "What have you not told me?"

"You recall El Hombre's bargain with Juanita. If she does anything to displease him, El Hombre kills the daughter who is now Blanca," said Juan with caution. "The best information I can get my hands on indicates that El Hombre is still operating in Columbia and Juanita is still part of his harem."

"El Hombre may become displeased with Juanita at any time and unleash his assassins on your family," said Juan bluntly. "So my friend, you must know all of this so you can protect Duncan, Blanca, Isabella and yourself," Juan said with finality.

As an afterthought Juan added, "Never, never underestimate people like El Hombre. He is a very smart and an incredibly ruthless man who has no conscience. As I understand, no one can control him or his band of men. Not even the government wants to tangle with El Hombre."

Shamus raised the glass, saluted Juan and sipped a bit of the wine. "If I forget to tell you later, thank you for sharing all of this with me. You have always been one of my most trusted allies and now you share your mother's deathbed confidence with me." Shamus said with deep respect, "I am in your debt more than you know. Thank you very much."

"Do you believe that we are in any immediate danger?" asked Shamus cautiously. Then his tone became urgent. "My god, that is the reason you are telling me this. There is something going on, isn't there? Juan, tell me every-thing and tell me now."

"Shamus, calm down," Juan said soothingly, "I do not know of anything specifically but word of Blanca's and Duncan's wedding may have reached Juanita and she may want to see Blanca get married. Just a possibility, but you may want to take extra precautions, to be on the safe side."

"Now can we sit and talk of old times and new plans, enjoy our wine and have some lunch, I'm starving," Juan said, changing the subject.

Shamus was attentive during lunch and talked old times but he was dis-tracted. How could this happen to Duncan? Should I tell him? Should I tell Isabella? A million things went through his mind but always it came back to the same question – Should he tell Duncan?

Shamus thanked Juan for a wonderful day. They set a date for dinner with Margareta and Isabella for the Saturday after the wedding, right before Shamus and Isabella were planning to fly back to Scotland.

Shamus barely knew the Mercedes was moving all the way back to the hotel in Mendoza. He absently complimented Juan's driver for skillful driving and thanked him. But Shamus did not go to his room. Instead, he got a cab to the offices of Toledo Steelworks on the outskirts of Mendoza.

Shamus introduced himself to the receptionist and asked to see Hector Verde. Señor Verde rushed from his office and almost collided with Shamus when he ran into the lobby. After introductions, Shamus asked to speak to him in private.

"Yes, Mr. Stuart-Bruce, of course," said Señor Verde anxiously. "Please come into my office."

Once inside, Shamus asked him if he had a secure phone line to the main office in Buenos Aires.

"Yes, of course, we do," said Señor Verde with a hint of curiosity. "It is inside the lower left drawer of my desk. Can I get anyone on the phone for you?"

"That is very kind of you to ask, but I need to make a call on the secure line," said Shamus. "While I am on the phone, you might want to let your staff know that I will be making a tour of your fine factory in about 15 minutes."

"Of course, of course," said Hector understanding that Shamus wanted to be left alone. Taking the phone from the drawer and handing it to Shamus, Verde said, "I will personally see to the details of your tour."

Shamus made the call and asked the head of the Buenos Aires branch of one of the banks he did business with to send five private guards. Very discreet but very good at their job. He told them that he needed some members of his family guarded because they were wearing priceless family jewelry to a wedding in Mendoza. The jewels were arriving from London on Thursday but the couriers were English and would not blend with the locals here in Mendoza.

Señor Rodriquez arranged for five of the top private investigators in Buenos Aires to fly to Mendoza that afternoon and report to Señor Stuart-Bruce's hotel. Shamus took the tour and left the factory. When the special detail arrived, Shamus shook hands with each man and asked them if they had all the equipment (meaning weapons) that they needed for their assignment. The men showed him the "equipment," excused themselves, and manned their posts around the hotel.

He hated taking these kinds of precautions but he must make sure that there was extra security, if Blanca or Duncan were only remotely in danger. He decided not to tell anyone, not Blanca, not Duncan and not Isabella. His secret protective service would remain just that — secret.

CHAPTER 21

Mendoza, Argentina
November 1972

....

Blanca's and Duncan's church wedding was at 6:00 p.m. on November 18th, a Saturday. The evening breeze was smooth and brought a hint of fragrance from the fields below the mission. The music had both energy and elegance that caught the essence of the bride and groom.

They had energy. Oh, did they ever have energy. They sparkled they had so much energy.

And elegance. When Blanca walked down the aisle of the mission chapel, she gave the old walls new splendor. Her dress was, well, it was simply elegant. What else could be said? Lace and satin and ivory and white. Set off by her dark hair and brilliant red roses. She wore Liddy's diamond and emerald ring. Just before Blanca stopped in front of Duncan, she turned and leaned to give a kiss to her grandmother sitting in the front row.

And Duncan. Not since he had dressed for the reception at Buckingham Palace had he looked so charged with an energy that no one understood except Blanca. You couldn't actually see it but you could feel it. Like strong static electricity. And his tuxedo, tailored to fit his lean, muscular body, was made of the finest wool in all of Argentina. The waistcoat showed the deep green and purple of the Stuart-Bruce plaid.

Shamus had attended a lot of important, dignified, solemn and historic events. The crowning of heads of state, inaugurations of presidents, weddings of the royal families of Europe, and signing of treaties. But none could compare to the simple elegance and phenomenal energy he saw that day in Mendoza.

His heart nearly burst with pride. Duncan was marrying an incredibly beautiful and wonderful woman who would be a great partner and a loving wife. Nothing could make him happier than to see Duncan starting his own family.

Shamus bowed his head and said a very sincere and grateful prayer to God and this time he prayed not only for Duncan but also for Ian and Liddy. Without them, Shamus would never have had the chance to be here to watch Duncan grow into a strong, responsible, intelligent and happy man. Thank you, Ian. Thank you, Liddy. Thank you, God.

Isabella fussed over getting the proper photographs and Shamus was grateful Isabella had taken a personal interest in the wedding. She arranged for every detail, missing nothing. Everything was perfect, thanks to Isabella.

The reception and dinner after the ceremony went on until midnight when Duncan and Blanca left for the honeymoon. Somewhere south, in Patagonia. Good for them. They needed the time together before going to Scotland.

Shamus was relieved that there was not a single incident that required his "quiet army." He was still glad he had arranged for them to be in Mendoza. The possible need for the guards troubled Shamus but now that the wedding was over and Duncan and Blanca were heading off on the three-month honeymoon, he relaxed a little.

After a couple of weeks in Patagonia, Duncan was taking Blanca to Rio de Janeiro, Acapulco, Los Angeles, New York, Paris, Rome, London, and then to Aberdeen. But then what? Were they going to stay in Scotland or establish their home somewhere else? He would press Duncan for an answer when he saw him in 90 days.

Blanca and Duncan did everything on their honeymoon. They kayaked in the fjords of Patagonia, sambaed in Rio, parasailed in Acapulco, shopped in Beverly Hills and New York, visited the Louvre and Montmarte, in Paris, admired Michelangelo's incredible Pietà at the Sistine Chapel, went to every theatre in London's West End, and finally, sat before the roaring fire in the castle in Aberdeen.

They were in love and they enjoyed every minute of it.

Duncan was always so surprised at the intensity of Blanca's love. Not only the lovemaking that kept getting better and better. It was the way she looked at him and the way she wanted to be with him every moment. Duncan was not sure that this was the way it was supposed to be but he sure did like it.

At times Duncan had the feeling that Blanca loved him like there would be no tomorrow. These feelings were frightening, like thinking about his Mom and Dad dying. Nothing specific, merely a feeling.

They had been in Aberdeen for two months and were beginning to see the start of spring when it happened. "Duncan," Blanca said softly, "can we go for a walk? I need some fresh air. Walk with me, darling."

Duncan looked out the window. The wind was blowing about 20 mph and the rain was almost horizontal.

"Now?" Duncan said questioningly. "It is blowing like the devil out there and it's raining, too. What a horrible day for walking. Come sit next to me and enjoy the fire."

"Duncan," said Blanca firmly, "we have been through much worse than this, sometimes without even a stitch of clothing. Remember?"

Duncan blushed a little and said quietly, "Not so loud. Shamus and Mrs. Kelley will hear. They think we are a respectable couple. They don't know that we secretly make blue movies for National Geographic."

"Duncan," said Blanca with resolve, "please get our slickers, rain hats and rubbers and let's walk in the rain."

"All right, but no complaining when we get a 100 yards from the house." Duncan said, "I will not have you whining like a wet puppy."

"Get our coats and hats," Blanca repeated.

As they walked out the front door the rain seemed to get heavier but the wind stopped blowing. Blanca moved quickly down the lane toward the orchard. Duncan had to almost run to keep up with her but then he got his stride and they walked without talking.

Water was rushing in the stream next to the lane and threatened to spill over its banks. The rain lessened and by the time they were a mile or so from the castle, it was only a drizzle. Blanca was still keeping up the strong pace but now Duncan was pushing her to go faster as he got his rhythm.

They topped the ridge and saw the loch. Blanca slowed suddenly, taking a big breath and shaking her head and stomping her feet. Duncan slowed and walked next to her.

"Feeling better?" Duncan asked cautiously.

"Yes, I needed to be out in the open, out of the house," said Blanca as she scanned the horizon. "The castle can be pretty overpowering at times." She continued, "Thanks for coming with me. I need to be alone with you."

Duncan studied her face and watched her eyes as she stared at the hills. "Is that all?" Duncan queried, "I get the feeling there is something else you want to tell me."

Blanca continued to scan the hills as though looking for a friend. "Duncan," she started slowly, "I love you and love being here in Scotland. Shamus has been so good to us and treats me like a daughter."

Duncan listened. He did not interrupt or push her faster.

"I feel that I belong with this family more than ever," Blanca said clearly, "but now I need you to believe in me and give me a chance to do what I think is right."

She scanned the hills again, "Duncan, I want to go back to Argentina. I need to visit my grandmother and talk with her. You know she is very important to me. For some reason, I think there is something wrong with her and she has not told me. Don't ask me how I know this, please accept it as a given."

She stopped talking and turned to look at Duncan. She searched his face and his eyes for a reaction. She could tell that he was thinking about what she had said. She watched as he looked across to the loch behind her. Then he looked at her again.

"When do you want to leave for Mendoza?" Duncan said quietly, "I will buy us tickets and make all of the arrangements."

She studied his face again and found that he was not forcing himself to say what he had said. She almost cried with joy. He understood and he wanted to go with her back home to Mendoza.

Duncan put his arms around her and held her close.

"Thank you," Blanca said. She pulled away, "What are we going to tell Shamus?" asked Blanca with apprehension.

"How about the truth?" said Duncan matter-of-factly. "That we are going to visit your grandmother for a few weeks."

"Are you sure he won't be hurt?" Blanca asked.

"Not a chance," Duncan said quickly, "he will want us back as soon as possible but he'll wish us a great trip."

"Duncan," Blanca said tentatively, "I may want to stay for several months. Will that be all right?"

"Well, I may have to come back to Aberdeen a couple of times for business, but I will get back to Mendoza as soon as I can."

"Thanks again," Blanca said gratefully, "you are really the greatest. Not only the greatest husband but also the best friend I could have. Let's get back to the castle. I want to call British Airways tonight. Okay?"

CHAPTER 22

Mendoza, Argentina
June 1973

....

Blanca was right. Her grandmother was very ill when she got to Mendoza. The doctors could not pinpoint the cause but they were preparing for a trip to Buenos Aires where she could receive the very best medical treatment.

Blanca threw herself into caring for her grandmother and Duncan stayed at her side to help. But three weeks after arriving in Buenos Aires, Shamus called and asked him to come to London for meetings with one of the banks. Blanca drove him to the airport and kissed him goodbye.

Blanca paid little attention to herself during the two months she was caring for her grandmother. She was not concerned when she missed her third period in a row. She thought it was the stress of the trip and caring for her grandmother. It was not until she was reading to her grandmother one afternoon that she was startled to even think about herself.

"Blanca," her grandmother said, "You don't look well. Have you been eating well? Are you worried about Duncan?"

Blanca looked up from the book, saw that her grandmother was staring at her with those very dark eyes. Blanca met her gaze and they stay locked like this for a full minute. Finally, Blanca looked away toward the window.

"Blanca, look at me again," came the soft but commanding voice, "Look at me again, my precious."

Blanca turned and looked again. "I do not know what is wrong, but I feel something inside me is not right. Something is upsetting me and causing me to lose my concentration. Help me find out what it is."

"Blanca, think carefully," said Grandmother, "are you pregnant? Have you stopped having your monthly periods?"

A curious, almost startled look came over Blanca. *Yes, yes, that's it. Of course, I'm pregnant. That is the only thing it could be. Oh, my god. Can I really be pregnant?*

"I do not know," said Blanca cautiously. "I can't remember my last period. Maybe when we were in New York. But I can't be pregnant. I must take care of you. There is no time for a baby right now."

Her grandmother held her hand out to her and Blanca sat on the edge of the bed. "When God decides it's time for a baby, what can we do about it but pray for a very healthy baby?"

"You must go see the doctor this afternoon and have him confirm your feelings," said Grandmother with efficiency. "Then we must go to mass and pray. Blanca, get me out of this wretched hospital now. We have many things to do."

"No. You are still very ill," Blanca said quickly. "We cannot move you. Not until your doctor releases you."

"Tell the doctor if he wants to see me to come to my house," Grandmother said with authority. "I am too busy to be bothered by hospitals or doctors or being ill. Now hand me my clothes and help me get dressed."

The doctor confirmed everything. Blanca was about four months pregnant. She and the baby were healthy.

Back in Mendoza, Blanca's grandmother kept her promise. She threw herself into getting the house ready for her great-grandchild. Painting, cleaning, sewing. Fresh vegetables and fresh fruits and one glass of wine each evening with dinner. Blanca had never seen her so obsessed but Grandmother had a new lease on life and no one was going to stand in her way.

Blanca did not want to tell Duncan over the phone, so each time he called, she would talk about her grandmother's health. Duncan's meetings went from London, to Vienna, to Houston, to Sydney, back to London and now he was on his way to New York. After three days in New York, he would be on his way to Buenos Aires and Mendoza.

Blanca went to airport to meet him. They had been apart almost a month but it seemed like a year. When she saw him get off the plane, she started crying. Duncan held her close. Kissed her. And held her again. Everything was going to be fine.

At dinner that evening, Blanca's grandmother started talking about needing a larger house for all of her guests. Duncan looked at Blanca with confusion and Blanca shrugged her shoulders. Grandmother was going to meet with an architect and draw up plans for an addition to the house, on the north side with wide verandas and big rooms.

Duncan was busy staring at Blanca and wanted dinner to be over so they could go to their room. Finally, Blanca made excuses about Duncan's long plane ride and they left the dining room. They almost ran up the stairs and barely got to their room before Duncan had his pants off and was pulling at Blanca's dress. They made love quickly, passionately. They both were so eager that they forgot to close the door.

As they lay together feeling each other's heart beat, Blanca leaned over and kissed Duncan on the forehead, nuzzled his neck and as Duncan was starting to stir, getting ready to roll toward her, Blanca said quietly, "Could you close the door? I'm sure that Grandmother has heard enough of lovemaking noises for one night."

Duncan jumped as he turned. His face got beet red and he ran to the door stark naked. He closed it silently and turned to see Blanca laughing at him. He was humiliated and she was laughing.

"I'm going to get you for this," Duncan said with mock fury in his voice. "You will regret embarrassing me like that."

Blanca squealed as Duncan dove back in the bed and grabbed her. They wrestled and tickled each other and finally in her waning heroine voice she said, "No, no. Not that. I can't take any more. You heathen. You fiend. You bad boy."

And they made love again. This time slowly, touching each other and pleasing each other. Just the way it was supposed to be.

Blanca rose at 6:00 and went downstairs to get coffee and toast. She kissed Duncan awake when she was back in their room. Blanca needed to talk with him and she needed him fully alert so she got two cups of coffee and got back into bed.

"Duncan, we need to talk," said Blanca firmly. "Are you awake and conscious or are you still asleep?"

Duncan knew his wife and the tone in her voice said clearly that this was not a time to joke or play.

"I'm awake and I'm conscious and I'm in love with you," Duncan said playfully, as he reached for her right breast.

"Not now, Duncan. We need to talk."

"Okay, I want to talk to you too," said Duncan, "I have had a very interesting four weeks. But you first."

"All right, Mr. Smarty Pants," said Blanca with a sassy tone. "I will."

But she hesitated, looking straight at Duncan. A long, hard look. The kind of look that saw right through you.

Duncan knew something significant was going to be said because Blanca was taking too long to talk and she was staring at him too intensely. "I'm pregnant," said Blanca softly, "and I'm scared that you won't be happy about it."

Duncan had not seen this one coming. He expected a new boyfriend or we are going to have to live in Argentina forever or my grandmother is living with us. But not this. He had not expected this to be the issue.

All of a sudden, everything except Blanca and the baby became very insignificant. This is exactly what he had wanted ever since he met her. He wanted them to have babies together. More than one, many, five or six. Maybe three boys and three girls. That would be great.

All of these thoughts came and went in a microsecond. He never changed the dumbstruck expression on his face. He did not know what to do. Finally he snapped out of the trance, went to Blanca and pulled her to him.

At first he didn't say anything but then, very slowly, Duncan spoke to Blanca. "I'm thrilled beyond my wildest dreams. I had no idea. Why didn't you tell me on the phone?"

She looked up at him and said simply, "That is not the way to tell you that you are going to be a father. Not on the phone. I wanted to tell you in person." She looked down.

"Duncan, sit with me on the veranda," said Blanca as she walked to the door. They sat on the wicker love seat, holding hands and looking at the mountains. They stayed this way for five or ten minutes, then Blanca spoke.

"When I met you," she started, "I couldn't believe how I felt. I was overwhelmed with the love I felt for you. Then we got married. The love I had for you as your wife and lover became so strong that I could barely contain myself. I wanted to climb to the tallest mountain and yell out that I loved Duncan Stuart-Bruce as no woman had ever loved a man before." She looked at him quickly, then continued, "When I found out I was carrying your baby... our baby, I became afraid. Afraid that no woman should ever feel such joy. And I went to church to confess to the priest about how selfish I was because I had everything anyone could ever ask for and I feared that God would take away something from me to show that I had not prayed enough for his guidance."

With only a quick breath, Blanca went on, "The priest promised me that I only had to worry about taking care of the baby growing inside me and that God was always pleased to see such happiness. The priest promised that I would have God's blessings for the rest of my life and my baby, our baby, would be strong, healthy and beautiful."

She stopped, stood, walked to the railing and turned back to Duncan, "I want to believe this but I am still afraid. I am afraid of something I cannot see." Blanca looked out at the mountains again. "So I asked my grandmother why I felt afraid of something I could not see. And you know what my grandmother did? She looked at me, turned and left the room. My grandmother has never done anything like this before. She has never turned away from me. All of this happened about two weeks ago. She still has not talked to me about my being afraid for our baby. She acts like she never walked away from me. Duncan, I know this sounds strange and confusing but I am more concerned than ever," Blanca said with genuine fear in her voice.

Duncan had never seen Blanca so upset. She was the strong one. The one with the clear vision and the ability to prioritize everything very quickly and logically. Now she was literally falling apart in front of him.

He did not say anything. He stood, walked to her side, put his arm around her shoulder and kissed her gently on the forehead. They stood that way until Duncan felt Blanca relax. He walked them back into the sitting room and they sat down again. "Blanca, I believe you and I want to do anything to help. What do you want me to do?" asked Duncan with a clear firm voice.

Blanca sighed, shook her head and then said, "I know you will think I'm crazy but can we hire someone to watch over us. Like a bodyguard? Maybe two or three? One for you, one for grandmother and one for me."

She was talking quickly now, like she couldn't wait to get this terrific idea out of her head. "Can we afford to do that — hire bodyguards? Someone discreet. Someone with impeccable credentials. Someone who can truly protect us?"

"Slow down a little," said Duncan as he smoothed her hair with his hand. "Yes, yes, we can afford to hire body guards, but doesn't that seem a little extreme? You haven't been threatened by anyone, have you?"

"No, of course not," said Blanca, "but something tells me to do this and to do this very soon."

"All right, I will make some calls tomorrow, and we will see if we can get someone here in a few days," said Duncan with finality, now that his mind was made up.

"Duncan, I don't want to sound unappreciative, but can you make the calls today and have someone here tomorrow?" Blanca said with a firmness that left Duncan with no alternative but to heed her wishes.

That evening over dinner, Blanca asked her grandmother's permission for Duncan to hire some people to watch over the house and the three of them until the baby was born. She explained that it was the foolish wish of a pregnant woman and that she was very lucky to have a husband who would listen to such a request.

Grandmother listened as her granddaughter explained about hiring men to guard them. She studied Blanca's eyes after Blanca had finished talking. Finally she spoke in a very soft voice, "Blanca, you have been blessed with a gift from God. Until you came to live with me, I thought the gift would die with me but nothing makes this old woman happier than knowing that the gift is going to live in you.

"You know the gift I speak of and you know what power it gives you. The power to feel something about the future so strongly that you cannot sleep until you do something to protect yourself and the ones you love."

She looked at Duncan, "You are the grandson I never had. Strong, handsome, virile, intelligent, brave and, for such a young man, wise. You have shown that wisdom by listening to Blanca and taking her words seriously and acting quickly."

Grandmother turned back to Blanca, "I also feel that there is a darkness around us but I cannot pinpoint the feeling. So rather than feed your fear two weeks ago, I left the room and I prayed to the Mother in the garden. God told me that you would know what to do and that I would only create more fear with my doubts."

"That is the reason I have not talked to you about this," Grandmother said calmly. "I did not want to instill more fear. Do you understand, my dear?

They stared at each other in a mesmerizing way. Finally, Blanca answered, "Yes, I do understand and thank you for not allowing more fear to come my way."

Everyone was quiet for a few moments then Duncan said, "I want some ice cream. Some chocolate ice cream with a cherry on top. How about you, Blanca? Grandmother? How about a scoop of ice cream?"

CHAPTER 23

Mendoza, Argentina
November 1973

....

Alonzo, Juan and Victoria were the perfect bodyguards. They appeared to be workers remodeling the house on Via Espiritu so that there would be room for the new baby. Alonzo and Juan acted as the architects and Victoria was a decorator.

At first the local craftsmen resented the new "experts" but as with construction worldwide, their resentment vanished when the very large payments for their services were made — in cash. The carpenters smiled, the painters were grateful, and the bricklayers were glad to have a good job with nice people.

Alonzo watched over Grandmother, Juan stayed close to Duncan, and Victoria went with Blanca everywhere. To pick out fabric for draperies, select carpets, decide about baby furniture, and to the doctor for her checkups.

Duncan made two quick trips to Miami for conferences with Shamus but was only gone two nights for each trip. To make up for the time he was spending with Blanca, he had to sit on the phone for hours each day talking business and arranging for some very interesting acquisitions to the Stuart-Bruce family of companies.

Blanca was growing larger each day but she was busy and having a great time. Her fears of six months ago were still there but with the trio of bodyguards watching over her family, she had relaxed and was actually enjoying the pregnancy.

Duncan loved to sit with his head in her lap feeling the baby kick and move. The doctor gave her and the baby clean bills of health after each visit. She even had time to work with the orphaned children at the mission.

156

The remodeling was complete and they announced to their friends that they were hiring Alonzo, Juan and Victoria to design and build them a vacation retreat near one of the fjords in Patagonia. This would take at least 18 months, maybe more with a new baby in the picture.

All was well. They were making plans for Christmas because the baby was due the first week of December so there would be little time to shop after the baby arrived.

Shamus sent them one of those giant books with every name you could possibly give a baby. Of course, there was a very nice bookmark in the "S" section with a bold box around one specific name, you guessed it — Shamus. With a curious comment about why Shamus was a great choice written in the margin:

"Have there been any girls named Shamus? Sounds quite nice, doesn't it? Shamus Elizabeth or Shamus Ann or Shamus Agatha? Maybe not that one. Signed 'S.'"

Blanca and Duncan laughed when they saw Shamus's thoughts in the book. But Duncan poured over the book until he came up with the name for a boy. Ian Shamus Stuart-Bruce, if it was a boy.

And Blanca thought long and hard but finally settled on Consuela Elena Montoya Stuart-Bruce, if it was a girl.

By mid-November, Blanca was getting uncomfortable. She did not sleep very much because it hurt her back to lie down. She did not want to walk because her legs were swollen. Her breasts were leaking milk and very tender. She was starting to wonder if the joy of pregnancy was now passing into the horror of childbirth. About all she wanted to do was sit in the baby's room and hum lullabies.

The baby was very active, seeming to turn over and over inside Blanca's belly. The baby sensed it was time to be born and get out of the confines of the womb. When the movements in Blanca's belly became almost violent, you could see the sharp bone of an elbow or knee trying to push through her belly.

All the time Duncan marveled at what he was witnessing. He almost could not leave Blanca because he wanted to see every movement, every jerk that showed that their baby was eager to get into the real world and away from the insulated cocoon it had inhabited for the last eight and a half months. Each and every time Duncan saw Blanca's belly jump or roll or jiggle he would smile. His child, no, their child was going to born very soon and he couldn't wait.

On November 29, Shamus called to ask how Blanca and baby were doing and, of course, the answer was fine but both are restless. During that call Shamus asked Duncan to accompany Juan Allejandro to Santiago for a crucial meeting with Chile's Interior Minister. Shamus made arrangements for a private jet to deliver Juan and Duncan to Santiago before 9:00 a.m. and fly them back to Mendoza before 7:00 p.m. That was in two days, on December 1.

Duncan agreed, reluctantly, only after Shamus promised no more meetings until after New Year's so that Duncan could enjoy the baby, Blanca and the holidays.

On the morning of December 1, Duncan left the bedroom where Blanca was sleeping. The doctor prescribed a mild sedative and it worked wonders. Duncan kissed her on the forehead and again on her swollen belly. He silently said goodbye to his wife and his child.

Since Duncan went nowhere out of the house without his bodyguard, Juan was in the car waiting. They drove to the private plane terminal at the airport without talking. They got out of the car and greeted Juan Allejandro and his assistant Ricardo. They all walked to the Learjet and boarded. The jet taxied to the end of the runway and was airborne within minutes. It climbed quickly to get altitude to cross the Andes on its journey to Santiago.

If Duncan had looked closely when he came out of the house on Avenida Espiritu, he would have noticed a lone figure standing near a pine tree about 50 yards from the house's front door. If he had looked even closer, Duncan would have seen three more figures nearly hidden from view. But Duncan did not look around. He got in the car and drove away without glancing back. With Alonzo and Victoria at the house, Duncan was confident that his family was safe.

After Duncan's car was out of sight, the lone figure near the pine tree moved slowly toward the house. The person was cautious but moved quickly and was almost invisible in shadows. The person's movements were compact, efficient and with a definite purpose. As the person neared the side entrance to the garage, the profile showed that it was a woman. Trim, wearing close fitting clothing, a black or dark blue jumpsuit or something similar.

She tried the garage door. Locked. She reached into a pocket and pulled a packet of lock picks. Within two minutes, she was inside.

That was all the other three figures needed to see. They moved very quickly to get back to the tan van with "Telecom" stenciled on both sides that was parked three blocks away. After they got inside the van, each took up their assigned position. One driving, one at console of electronic equipment, and the third sitting in a swivel chair next to a window on the right side of the van.

Without attracting the slightest attention in the pre-dawn gray light, the van moved quietly down the boulevard and turned right onto Avenida Espiritu. They stopped about a block away from the Montoya house. As though they were checking addresses, they moved slowly forward, stopping at every other house or so.

Alonzo woke and lay still for 15 minutes or so. He rose from his bed and went into the bathroom. As he was standing over the toilet, he looked out the eye-level window on the second floor and noticed the slow-moving Telecom van. He thought only that it was early in the morning for them to be working, then made his way back to the bed.

As soon as he settled in, he heard movement in the hall. *Wonder if Blanca's grandmother is up and getting some tea for Blanca?*

Alonzo's mind finally came awake. When there are too many unrelated things happening at once, they are not unrelated. He jumped from his bed, grabbed his robe, and opened the door to the hall. He ran to the master bedroom to check on Blanca.

As he opened the door, Blanca's grandmother came down the hall with the tea. She did not see Alonzo and he slipped into a closet so he would not disturb Grandmother. She could be a terror if she got mad. No reason to upset her.

After Grandmother went into the bedroom, Alonzo silently followed, quietly opened the bedroom door and saw that Blanca was indeed enjoying her tea and all was fine. Although he scanned the entire room he did not see the trim figure in a dark blue jumpsuit hiding behind the draperies.

Grandmother went to the window facing the street and opened the drapes. She wanted Blanca to have the bright morning light. She did not see the person standing behind the drapes. She fussed over Blanca and her tea and asked Blanca how she felt.

"For some odd reason, I wish Duncan had not gone to Santiago today. Maybe today is the day the baby will decide its time to be born and I am having a premonition," said Blanca cautiously. "At the same time, I do not really feel like the baby is coming today."

"Rest my dear," said Grandmother, "rest and enjoy the morning sun."

Grandmother went to her rocking chair and sat. She and Blanca could be in the same room for hours, each with their own private thoughts, never speaking a word. They both were very content to do this now. Think private thoughts and, at the same time, share each other's presence.

The van moved directly in front of Blanca's grandmother's house. They knew that the room on the 2nd floor at the right corner was Blanca's. The man in the swivel seat slid open the window on the side of the van. He lifted the 3-inch diameter tube to the open window, angled it at about 45 degrees.

The man at the electronic console whispered, "Three people in the room, one sitting down, one lying down and one standing near the window."

"Any way to determine who they are?" asked the man in the driver's seat.

"No, can't get a clear enough image. Three people now," said the console operator. "My guess is the woman, her grandmother, and one of the body-guards."

"It does not matter," said the man with the tube, "because we are only concerned with the woman named Blanca."

"I'm convinced she is in the bedroom," said the electronics operator. "Let's get this over with."

"All right, here we go," said the tube operator.

With that, he pulled a trigger mechanism at the back of the tube and a bomb shot through the open van window and crashed into the window on the 2nd floor.

They drove away quickly, and five seconds later the right front side of the house blew out toward the street with a thunderous explosion and a shower of brick, mortar, lumber and glass. They had timed it perfectly. The van did not get hit with even one piece of debris from the incredible blast.

Blanca opened her eyes when she heard the glass break and the sound of the heavy object hitting the floor. Her first thought was, why would someone throw a rock through the window? Then she saw the figure step out from behind the drapes. It was her own image standing in front of her but the person was dressed in a dark blue jumpsuit. Her next thought was I don't own a dark blue jumpsuit. How can it be me? Then she noticed that the woman had old eyes.

Then the woman rushed to her, gave her a hug and said, "I am your mother and I wanted to see your baby. May God bless you."

That was the last thing that Blanca ever heard.

At that moment, Duncan was looking down on Mt. Aconcagua and thinking of Blanca and him together on the top of the mountain. He ached for her so much he actually had tears in his eyes. Why do I feel this way? Is this natural? He passed it off as emotional feelings about having his first baby. All the same, he could not get that ache out of his heart. It physically hurt.

Victoria and Alonzo tried to get into the bedroom but that entire side of the house had collapsed. They could not find any trace of Blanca or Blanca's grandmother. All they could do was call the fire department and contact Duncan.

CHAPTER 24

Mendoza, Argentina
December, 1973

....

This was where they had married. So happy. So beautiful. So much future. Now he stared at four coffins near the altar. Three long and one short.

He knew the priest was saying all the right things but he could not comprehend the words. He could barely remember what had happened during the last three days.

As the Learjet made its final approach to the Santiago airport, the co-pilot buzzed on the intercom saying there was a call for Mr. Allejandro. Duncan watched Juan Allejandro and could see that he did not like what was being said over the phone. He replaced the phone in the receiver and turned to Duncan, "We must return to Mendoza immediately."

He punched the intercom and instructed the pilot to taxi to the executive terminal, refuel and file a flight plan to return to Mendoza as soon as the fueling was done.

Juan Allejandro looked carefully at Duncan before he spoke then said, "Duncan, there has been an accident at your home and we must get back."

Duncan sat very still but said nothing.

"The only thing that is known right now is that the fire department was called to your house about 20 minutes ago." Juan continued, "They do not know anything else."

Duncan looked at Juan's eyes but could only see that he was telling the truth. He was not withholding anything.

Finally, Duncan said, "I want to call Blanca. I want to make sure she is all right. May I have the phone, please?"

He dialed the number. The voice on the line said that the call could not be completed and to try again later.

He dialed the number again. The same voice with the same message.

He dialed the number again. Same results.

He dialed the number 86 times between Santiago and Mendoza.

Duncan could not remember anything else except that they would not let him see the house or Blanca or Baby Ian or Blanca's grandmother.

He remembered that someone told him that Baby Ian was alive when the firemen arrived at the house and pulled the rubble off Blanca. Although protected in Blanca's womb from the initial blast effects, the bomb still managed to cause serious trauma to the baby. The paramedics could see baby Ian moving inside Blanca's dead body, so they performed a Caesarian delivery. But there was too much damage. Duncan's son, Ian Shamus Stuart-Bruce, lived less than an hour.

Duncan rose as the priest led him past the first coffin to Blanca's grandmother's coffin, then Blanca's coffin and finally to the short coffin with little Ian in it.

Duncan touched his fingertips to his lips then placed them on Grandmother's coffin. Next he bent down and kissed Blanca's coffin. Finally, he knelt at his son's coffin, folded his hands and looked to the Madonna in the corner of the mission. He lowered his head and said a silent prayer.

At the graveside services, he said nothing. He placed a single rose on each coffin and walked back to the waiting limousine. Shamus and Isabella got in behind him.

Duncan looked at Shamus and said quietly, "Why four coffins?"

Shamus expected the question. He knew that even in the haze of emotion Duncan's logical mind would want to know about the fourth coffin.

"It contains Blanca's mother," said Shamus. "We believe she came to see her grandchild."

Duncan looked out the window and said almost matter-of-factly, "I didn't know she was alive."

Shamus reached for Duncan's hand, turned it palm up, and placed the diamond and emerald wedding ring in it. Duncan looked at the ring with tears welling in his eyes. His father bought that ring for his mother in Arizona nearly

30 years ago. One of Duncan's first memories was of this ring. He remembered his mother touching his face. He remembered seeing the dancing light from her hand. He remembered laughing each time he saw the dancing light. That same dancing light caught his eye now and, in spite of the overpowering grief of this day's funerals, he managed a small smile. At that moment he felt his mother's presence so strongly that he looked up and found Shamus's eyes.

"I had the ring removed from Blanca's hand before they closed the casket so that you can always remember your incredible marriage to her. You can always remember your mother and father and their unconditional love that continues to survive in your heart."

As the limousine started to move Duncan looked first at Shamus and then at Isabella, then back at Shamus. He said in a calm voice that took Shamus back to when Duncan was 8 years old and he told Shamus he believed in God. "First my mother, then my father. Now Blanca and my baby son Ian. I try to believe in God, Uncle Shamus, but he must not like me very much."

Then he cried. But the crying could not quell the grief. Only time would make the grief less and diminish the hollowness in his life.

When the sobs stopped shaking his body Duncan looked up for a moment, wiped the tears from his face, and asked, "What day is this?"

Isabella looked at Shamus and he nodded for her to answer. She reached over with her hand and said, "It is the 8th day of December, a Saturday."

PART III

Duncan and the Legacy

CHAPTER 25

New York, New York
August 1998

....

It was a brutal day. Meetings from dawn to dusk and two more days of meetings. Duncan knew that these triennial meetings were vital to the success of all his businesses but they were getting more and more difficult to sit through every three years.

He wanted a distraction from the meetings so he closed his eyes and concentrated on relaxing, even if it was only for a few moments, in the limousine as it moved silently down Broadway toward his townhouse.

The car stopped for a red light and Duncan looked at a sign across the street. He never noticed it before, but now that he saw it, he was intrigued. The sign simply said in letters printed on its face, "Our National Debt" and in a string of bright red LED numbers underneath "$5,258,976, ---, ----" with the last 6 digits changing so quickly you could barely make out what they said at any given moment. There was another line of red LED numbers preceded by "Your Family's Share" and at the bottom of the sign the words "National Debt Clock" were printed.

Like everyone else who saw the sign for the first time, Duncan had to do the mental arithmetic to see that the first number on the left was 5 trillion, next was 258 billion, then 976 million, --- thousand, --- dollars and climbing very quickly with an additional ten thousand dollars or so added every second.

The national debt of the United States was more than five and a quarter trillion dollars and getting bigger very fast. Duncan had never really thought of the U.S. financial obligation in those terms, as a debt. Instead he thought of it as treasury bonds that were bought, sold and traded every day by people, companies and countries all over the world.

Duncan thought to himself, why so much debt for an incredibly wealthy country? He did more calculations and came up with interest payments annually of $350 billion plus change. That was some interest payment, he thought to himself, glad I don't have to pay interest like that in my businesses. He considered what he would do if he did pay that much in interest. The instant conclusion he came to was that he would fire a whole lot of people who had kept his enterprises in that much debt.

Maybe that is what the American people should do. Fire the people who got them this deeply into debt and kept them there. Interesting thought. Wonder if they could fire Congress for something like fiscal mismanagement? Or fire the president for continuing to submit budgets that contributed to the debt.

The car pulled away from the light and passed the National Debt sign. Duncan thought about it a moment and fingered the intercom button, "Jason, could you go around the block and come back to the large national debt sign again? I want to look at it for another moment."

"Yes, sir, but it will take a couple of minutes," came the reply from his driver. Four left turns later, the sign re-appeared. Jason positioned the car so Duncan could easily see the numbers ramping up like a digital stop-watch timing an Olympic event.

Based on the reports that were given at today's meeting, the value of the Stuart-Bruce family holdings was between six and eight trillion dollars. He smiled to himself and thought, I can pay off the national debt for the United States of America and have some left over for a rainy day.

He had never really thought of it in that manner. Not a bad idea. Over the years as the family's businesses continued to prosper, he had adjusted to numbers like a trillion dollars so that a trillion dollars or two trillion dollars did not cause him discomfort or concern. But still he reminded himself that a trillion dollars or $5 trillion dollars or $8 trillion dollars was a very, very large amount of money and should not be treated casually, even if you had that much.

Pay off the debt for the U.S. indeed. Still, an intriguing idea. But what would he want in return? He couldn't think of anything he needed or wanted badly enough to justify spending more than five trillion dollars.

Or maybe there was something he wanted. It wasn't something he had ever thought about seriously because it had never seemed realistic or attainable. Maybe he wanted to be what every red-blooded American kid dreamed of becoming — President of the United States.

Yes, of course, that is the least the country could do after he paid off the ridiculous national debt. Become President of the United States. That does not seem like enough though, does it? Being president would have its perks but for five or six trillion dollars there should be more. Like what?

A bus blocked Duncan's view of the sign for a few seconds and he snapped out of his trance. What a stupid, vain idea. Pay off the national debt. Not a chance. But that kind of money would really twist Shamus's kilt, he chuckled to himself.

He shook his head to clear his thoughts and asked Jason to drive to the house. All the way uptown, his thoughts nagged at him, returning to the sign and the idea that the sign triggered. He learned over the years when his private nagging continued to dominate his mind he should not ignore it and the U.S. national debt issue was now about a 6 or 7 on the nag scale. Not a crisis or emergency but definitely more than an item of passing interest.

Duncan showered and changed for his dinner at Charles Arthur's home overlooking Central Park South. Duncan was not particularly fond of Charles but he was an influential money manager and it always paid very good dividends to keep Charles close. Sort of like the old saying, "keep your friends close but your enemies closer."

The dinner was for a few of Charles's associates and friends, twenty-four to be exact. Duncan always wondered if they were all that close. Charles was not an easy personality to get close to. As always, the hors d'oeuvres were excellent but the pre-dinner cocktail party was a bore and Duncan was not looking forward to a two-hour dinner with these people. He was on the verge of making excuses when a late-arriving guest walked into the living room.

It wasn't her beauty that caught his attention; he had seen thousands of beautiful women. It was her energy. She virtually generated her own glow standing next to Charles. She was attentive to the discussions but not the pushy type who needed to dominate conversations or rooms of people or men or even other women. Duncan had an acute sixth sense when it came to judging American women, particularly those calling themselves career women. She was very sure of herself but not arrogant. She knew she was attractive but did not flaunt it. She was in control of her life but did not need to control everyone else's. Nice. Very nice.

Duncan went to the bar, refilled his glass of Diet Pepsi and walked toward Charles. As usual, Charles was holding court and his stuffiness was wearing thin.

Duncan said casually, "Charles, stop bragging about your last deal and introduce me to everyone, you know how I enjoy meeting new people." Duncan flashed a smile to Charles who looked stunned but pleased at the same time.

"Well, Duncan, you old cad," said Charles with a new level of enthusiasm. "You are just the spark we needed to make my dinner a success tonight. You know Maynard Johnson, the notorious basketball player."

They shook hands. Tattoos everywhere, even his eyelids.

"Haven't you met Pooky Alexander? She was with us at the chalet in Gstaad last winter. And Joseph Haas. He started that incredibly successful dot-com company five years ago."

"Oh, my special guest this evening is Teresa Underwood. She is about the smartest person in the world and she has two PhDs to prove it. One from Wharton and one from Oxford," cooed Charles as he pushed Teresa forward.

"Charles, stop giving this poor man my résumé," said Teresa without taking her eyes off Duncan. "I already have a great job." She extended her hand.

"Duncan Stuart-Bruce," said Duncan shaking her hand. "Charles always tries to sneak in some rude comment about me, so I know what you are going through."

"Can I get you something to drink, Miss Underwood, or do you prefer Dr. Underwood?" asked Duncan.

"Call me Teresa. I usually save the Dr. stuff for my students or when I testify in court," said Teresa with a smile. "Yes, I would like a glass of red wine, merlot if they have some open."

Duncan handed her the glass and asked if she had seen the skyline from the terrace. The lights of Manhattan were coming on and dusk was fading to the west. She sipped the wine. It was very good. In fact it was excellent.

"Do you teach?" Duncan asked.

"Yes, I have been teaching at the University of Kansas for about five years." I love working with the best and the brightest this country has to offer. They challenge me to be better each and every day."

Duncan continued his questioning. "That must be rewarding. Have you always taught at the university level?"

"Yes, I have found a niche and the dean likes me, so I get to do pretty much what I want to," Teresa said, without looking at Duncan.

"What courses do you teach?" asked Duncan with a touch of desperation in his voice. He wanted to get to know her better but she seemed preoccupied with other people at the party.

"Insurance and finance mostly, once in a while I teach a math or statistics class to keep my fingers in that pie," came the answer from Teresa as though it was a recorded message.

"Well, since you understand finance well enough to teach it at a respected university, maybe you could help me with a little problem I have?" said Duncan, as he went trolling.

"You have a problem?" asked Teresa, as she looked Duncan up and down, surveying him in a glance. "The only problem I can see that you have is that you came to Charles's party unaccompanied and that does not fit your image. My guess is you usually show up at these shindigs with a trophy on each arm."

"Accurate but my problem is not totally personal, it is more of a business problem that has personal implications," Duncan ignored her little jab and continued with a bit of mystery. "Let me get you another drink and I will explain the business problem a little further."

Teresa caught the keen, mischievous but warm look in his eyes and replied with genuine interest, "I would like that."

He handed her another glass of the excellent California merlot the color of very ripe Bing cherries and started with a question. "This evening when I was coming uptown, I saw a large, bright sign that displayed the ever-increasing U.S. national debt at something like five and a quarter trillion dollars. What is your opinion as to why the U.S. maintains such a large debt when it has assets and income sufficient to retire the debt?" Duncan asked.

When Teresa turned back to look at him, Duncan saw a new look of respect in her eyes, as she said, "That is a question better asked of a political scientist or politician than a simple finance professor."

"I think I understand your statement, but I am not looking for the politically expedient answer, I am looking for the financial justification for the U.S. national debt," said Duncan in a pleasant, requesting tone. "Please continue, if you don't mind. I am really very interested in what you have to say."

Teresa took another sip of the wine, looked up at Duncan and said, "Okay, but you may not like what I have to say."

"Please continue," said Duncan rising to the challenge. "I will risk learning something hard to hear."

"It is very difficult for me to give you a financial justification for the U.S. national debt. The U.S. government is supposed to be a not-for-profit organization and I have not seen a credible financial model for a not-for-profit organization to borrow money. Particularly when the organization has a huge asset base and a very large income stream. That is why I believe, and most of my conscious and responsible colleagues believe, that the U.S. should pay off its national debt at the earliest possible date."

"That's quite a statement considering the size of the debt. What would be the most financially sound way to go about paying off the debt?"

"Well, that in itself is a very interesting question. Again, putting aside the obvious solution like getting a fat, rich kid to give it to the country, the best way would be to either sell assets, increase income, reduce spending, or a combination of all of the above," Teresa said with a clever smile and a twinkle in her eye. She went on, "Know any fat, rich kids looking for a way to become famous?"

Teresa grinned with a brilliant smile that made Duncan lose his concentration for a moment. Wow, what a stunning woman. He shook off his fascination as quickly as it came on.

"A fat, rich kid is a crude slang term to define a person who has a lot of money and invests in projects that lack sound financial foundations but has some kind of intangible reward. Like wanting to be popular, to be famous, to join a winning team, etc." Teresa said with a little humor in her voice, but now more serious.

"I think that the fat, rich kid is the most doable because the other options call for too much politics and you could never get the government, particularly Congress, to agree on a program to sell assets, increase taxes, and reduce spending all at the same time.

"Members of Congress are not that kind of animal. They are money junkies. They cannot get enough of it because that is the only way they believe they can get themselves re-elected." Teresa said with a hardness in her voice, "They are so shortsighted that they can never get beyond the next election and they are the same people who make some of the most far-reaching macroeconomic decisions in the world."

"Do I detect a note of displeasure from our resident finance scholar?" Duncan said to lighten the conversation.

"You bet I'm displeased," Teresa said with a scolding tone. "I want to see the country stronger in every way including financially and I cannot see how we will get there without paying off the national debt. What do you think?"

"Well, to be honest, I have not given the subject too much thought," Duncan said sincerely. "But as a businessman, I have trouble with the U.S. carrying so much debt when there is no solid financial basis for doing so and the country has real assets it can sell to pay off the debt. I don't want to sound naïve about the politics but it seems that there is a time for the people who run the government, both elected officials and career government employees, to put their heads together and come up with a wiser plan than exists today. What's funny is that your first and most feasible idea — the fat, rich kid — has someone paying off the national debt without dealing with all the political compromises. I like the logic and simplicity of the fat, rich kid plan and I believe it would work."

"Thanks," said Teresa softly as she took on a more philosophical tone. "But without our proverbial fat, rich kid who seeks fame and I mean really, really rich, that option doesn't even make it to the qualifying rounds at our own little game of pay-off-the-national-debt."

As Teresa finished talking, Charles called everyone into the dining room where they were seated according to the name placards around the table.

Duncan sat next to Charles at one end; Teresa on the same side of the table at the other end. Duncan could not even see Teresa without standing up or leaning halfway across the table.

After dinner, they saw each other briefly before Teresa left. Teresa said she had to catch a plane back to Kansas City. They traded cards and shook hands as Duncan walked her to the elevator. She did not want him to escort her down to the lobby. So they said goodbye and promised to talk on the phone.

Duncan thanked Charles for inviting him and left the party about 11:00. On the way home, he couldn't get the insightful and bewitching Dr. Underwood out of his mind.

A fat, rich kid was her first choice of how to get the U.S. out of debt. Extraordinarily simple but with a certain, but adolescently cruel, elegance and with enough shock value to make it exciting.

Well, he was rich and according to the beautiful and smart Professor Teresa you had to be really, really rich to make the fat, rich kid plan work.

He didn't think of himself as fat nor a kid but her metaphor was good and if the shoe fit, well, maybe he should wear it.

So, now I would be the fat, rich kid who would pay off the national debt. The thought made him smile.

Fat, rich kid, is it? To be on the safe side he sat up straighter and held in his stomach until he reached his townhouse.

We can't be too realistic, can we?

CHAPTER 26

Washington, D.C.

August 1998

....

Duncan thought about the national debt payoff idea the next day and during a break in the meetings at 3:00 he called Senator Creason. Wayne Creason was the senior senator from Missouri and Duncan rarely called him but asked him to meet that evening and apologized for the short notice. Since this had to be important, the senator agreed to see him that evening and set up a time to meet at small, quiet restaurant in Old Town Alexandria.

Duncan then called his pilot and asked that the Gulfstream be ready to leave Teterboro for Washington Reagan at 5:30. Duncan arrived at the restaurant at 6:45 and the senator was already there. Since both of them had dinners later in the evening, they talked quietly over beers.

"Duncan, you look great. How is your Uncle Shamus? And his lady, Isabella? Good, good," said Senator Creason. "So why the need for a meeting on such short notice?"

"Senator, how is your lovely wife Thelma? Be sure and give her my best regards," replied Duncan, ignoring the urgency in the senator's voice. "I wanted to meet with you and discuss an idea I have been tossing around. Drink your beer and listen for a few minutes and you will know why I called."

Duncan paused only briefly then started, "Although I was raised by Shamus in Scotland and went to elementary and secondary school in Scotland and England, I was born in Carmel, California, and the U.S. is my native country. I still maintain my U.S. passport along with a New York driver's license. I have always wanted to do something for my native country, not only to honor the U.S. and its people but also to honor my mother and the love she had for America. She was a true patriot and believed deeply in the American dream."

"I have been so busy the last 25 years running around the world, buying and selling companies that I haven't had time to think of an appropriate tribute. Well, I have been able to delegate most of my day-to-day responsibilities to others. Now I want to put some time into the project to honor my mother and my birth country."

He stopped to drink deeply from the mug of beer. "I need your help," Duncan said, looking Senator Creason in the eyes, "in deciding if the project I have in mind is worthwhile."

"Well, Duncan, I am honored that you want my help. But what can I do to help you? You seem to have done all right thus far in building the Stuart-Bruce family interests. I'm not sure I can do anything that will be helpful."

With a smile forming on his face, Duncan said, "Always the modest, charming man who tries to convey that he has no influence. You're the third, maybe fourth, most powerful elected official in America and you are trying to be modest."

"My mother and father taught me not to brag about myself and that lesson has served me well," said the senator without a hint of a smile.

"There you go again, modest upbringing by simple, God-fearing folks." Duncan shook his head. "Back to my request, will you help me determine if the project is appropriate?"

"Of course, Duncan. You can always count on me to be fair and give the best advice I can. Have you got any project in mind?"

"As a matter of fact, I have one particular project that I have been thinking about that really appeals to me," Duncan said as he leaned back in his chair and looked around to make sure no one could overhear the conversation.

"I want this project to leave a real impression on everyone in America. No, that is not true. I want everyone in the world to know that Americans love America, like my mother loved America."

"Now Duncan…" the Senator started but Duncan held up his hand to stop the senator and continued, "So I have decided that I want to honor the U.S. and my mother by paying off the U.S. national debt," Duncan said with sincerity as he looked into the senator's eyes.

The senator stared back. He was not sure he heard what Duncan said. Pay off the U.S. national debt? It was so simple to say but the scope of the statement was, well, way beyond anything the senator had every considered. He looked deeply into Duncan's eyes and slowly started shaking his head. "Son, do you know what you are talking about? The national debt is what — $5 ½ trillion and climbing every day. Where in the world would you get that kind of money?"

Duncan smiled and chuckled a bit, then said earnestly, "Senator, my family has been making investments for more than 700 years and I can raise that kind of cash without selling off all of our assets. For the sake of our discussion, assume that I have access to enough cash to pay off the debt. But I think that if I do pay off the U.S. national debt, I should get something substantial in return, don't you?"

"Duncan, I stopped second-guessing you years ago, so I believe you when you say you can get five or six trillion dollars, Lord knows where it will come from, but I do believe you. So for the sake of discussion, what do you want if you pay off the national debt? Do you want to be an ambassador? Do you want to be chairman of one of those art or science foundations? No. No. I know what you want. You want to be President of the United States!" the senator said, looking amused as he took another sip of his beer.

The senator was sort of joking when he asked the last question but then he stopped chuckling when he saw a bemused look on Duncan's face.

"Yes, as a matter of fact, I do want to be President of the United States if I pay off the national debt. Don't you think that paying six trillion dollars for the privilege is enough?"

"Duncan, are you serious?

"Yes, Senator, I am. I will talk it over with Shamus in a couple of days when he gets here from Scotland. Unless he objects, I will put things in motion to gather the cash together. I am not sure how long it will take but I will get the cash. I want to do this with your blessing and the support of the political, media and business establishments. That's why I came here. I'm starting with you. You know me and you know Shamus and you know that you can trust us. I hope we can trust you."

Senator Creason sat for a minute. He thought he had heard it all in his nearly four decades in Washington but this was a real shocker. Pay off the national debt. One person? This person was someone who most likely was telling the truth, he could get his hands on six trillion dollars. It was times like this that he wished he still smoked cigarettes. He needed a cigarette now. They always seemed to make it easier to concentrate on this type of really big bombshell.

"Well, Duncan, I am not sure what to say. This is a pretty big deal, maybe the biggest deal ever. I know I have never been involved in anything this big and I have been involved in some pretty big deals in my day. I need to talk with some people before I can give you an answer." Senator Creason asked with caution, "When do you want an answer to your proposal?"

Duncan answered firmly, "I would like a call back by tomorrow evening, let's say 10 o'clock. There is no need to drag this out. Either you and your people are with me or you are not," Duncan said matter-of-factly.

"Duncan, this is an incredible proposal you are making. It comes with some very complex issues to consider not just here in Washington but all over the world. We must think through this very carefully before we grab at this particular brass ring."

"All right, you can have two weeks to talk to all of your friends and advisors but I would appreciate a call back on the 15th," Duncan said, giving in to the senator's experience and wisdom.

"I will call you the second I have a program that will work for everyone," Senator Creason said with a twinkle in his eye.

They parted with a handshake and pats on the back.

As Senator Creason drove back to his office, his mind was moving faster than it had since he had been offered the opportunity to run as the junior senator from Missouri at a dinner hosted by former President Truman at the Hotel Muehlebach in Kansas City more than thirty years ago.

How was he going to break this news to his close circle of Senate friends? They weren't going to believe that anyone would want to pay off the national debt and they definitely weren't going to believe that Duncan wanted to be president as a reward for this "generous gift" to the United States.

The more he thought about it, the more he couldn't help but smile. With the smile still on his face, Senator Creason pulled the secure cell phone from his jacket pocket, thumbed the index to the number he wanted, and pressed the send button.

"Hello," said the voice at the other end.

"Meet me at my office in 15 minutes," said the Senator. "I have to discuss a new development with you tonight."

"It is really not convenient this evening," said the voice.

"When was the last time I asked you to meet me in my office in 15 minutes?" the senator asked with a touch of irritation command in his voice. "I will see you in 15 minutes. It is important. You won't believe who I had a beer with this evening and what he told me."

"Give me 30 minutes," the voice said as the call ended.

CHAPTER 27

Washington, D.C.
August 1998

. . . .

Wayne Creason greeted his wife of 42 years when he came into the den of their Rock Creek home. They bought the house nearly three decades ago when he first came to Washington as a congressman. It was a stately, comfortable house but not extravagant like the homes owned by some of his more visible colleagues in the Senate.

"Are you home for the evening, dear?' asked Thelma as he stopped to kiss her on the cheek.

"No, I'm afraid not. I have to go to my office and meet the majority leader for about an hour then I will be back." As he headed upstairs the senator asked, "Want to wait dinner until I get back? I will take you to Ruth Chris's for one of those great steaks."

"All right. We haven't been there in months. I'll call and get us a table at 9:00, if that's okay with you?" said Thelma loudly enough to be heard upstairs. "Did you hear me Wayne? 9:00 p.m. reservations."

He is about as deaf as his daddy but you couldn't get him to see a doctor about getting hearing aids. Maybe I will get one of those ear trumpets from the 1800s, wrap it up and send it to him at his office. Maybe he will get the hint.

Louder still, Thelma said, "Wayne, did you hear me? I will make reservations for 9:00."

From the hallway and in a normal voice the senator replied, "Yes, I heard you and 9:00 is fine. But Thelma, I wonder if you need to see the doctor about your hearing. You always seem to be shouting. Can't you hear very well?" The senator chuckled. "You are so stubborn. You won't go see a doctor about your hearing problem, even when I insist."

Thelma came into the hallway, hands on her hips and looked at him sternly. "Wayne, you are not going to switch this around and make me the bad guy. You are as deaf as your father and if you would stop fooling around, we could get you some hearing aids."

"You are such a sucker," the senator said laughing. "I can still get that Missouri temper stirred up if I try a little." He put his arms around her waist and pulled her to him.

"If you stop nagging me about the hearing thing, I won't embarrass you at the restaurant tonight," he said with a challenge.

Loudly he said, "What did that waiter say, Thel...MEE? You always talk so low to those young men. Are you making a date with that boy for later in the evening? I'm only deaf, not dumb." he said in his country voice. He was teasing her and he loved to get her all flustered.

She pushed him away and shook her finger at him. "Don't you dare. The last time you did that was at The Plaza in New York. I thought I was going to have to crawl under the table, I was so embarrassed."

"Now get," she said, "meet with Ellis and get back here before 8:45 so we won't be late."

"Hey. What did you say? You know you gotta talk a lot louder than that, Miss Thelma. You know I'm as deaf as a stone.

Love you," the senator said quietly with real tenderness in his voice this time.

"Love you, too," came the automatic reply from his wife. They had said the same thing every day since their wedding day. "Tell Ellis 'Hi' for me."

Ellis Hoyle was the most powerful senator in Washington and probably the most powerful senator since Lyndon Johnson left to become vice president in 1961. He was not only smart but he was a cautious man who believed what he was told but verified everything. This credo kept him friendly with almost everyone and he almost never was embarrassed by disinformation, rumors and lies.

Senator Creason trusted Ellis. They had served together in the Senate for the last 30 years and had developed a deep personal and professional respect for each other. Ellis's wife, Beulah, and his Thelma were good friends, which made the relationship even easier. They vacationed together at Ellis's and Beulah's ranch overlooking the reservoir at Tuttle Creek and at the Creason hideaway at Table Rock Lake. They had even had Christmas together with their combined families in Jackson Hole five years ago and it was a great four days.

Wayne walked into his office and Ellis was there with his can of Diet Pepsi.

"Why so secretive?" Ellis said crossly. "This is not like you, Wayne."

Wayne did not reply but walked to the phone. He picked up the receiver and punched in a number. "Steve, it's Senator Creason. Did you sweep my office today?" He listened and said, "Good, thank you, and be sure to sweep my office every day until I personally tell you otherwise. Is that understood?"

"Good, I appreciate the extra care you take to make sure that my office remains secure. Keep up the good work. Talk tomorrow. Thanks again, Steve. Give my best to Trudy and the kids." He hung up.

Wayne looked at Ellis and said, "I have been a little concerned about leaks from my office and I do not want to have this discussion without knowing we are bug free. Being cautious like you taught me."

"Okay, Wayne, but I never thought you would be wearing the paranoia label. You've never seemed to be worried about security before, particularly here in your own office. What has triggered your concern?"

Ellis answered in a serious tone, "Nothing specific, but I have a gut feeling about this. Give me a little space and trust my instincts."

"You got it. I have always trusted your instincts and I am not about to change now. So who did you have drinks with this evening and what did this person have to say?"

Wayne began his story. "I got a call this afternoon at about 3:00 from New York and this person wanted to meet me here in Washington for a brief meeting. Just the two of us. At an out-of-the-way place where we could remain unseen and anonymous. We met at that little French café in Arlington that Beulah likes, what is it called, Les Champs?"

"Okay, who was the mystery guest? This suspense is killing me," Ellis said with a touch of sarcasm. "You like to stretch a story just to get me worked up and I fall for it every time."

Wayne feigned surprise and said, "I do not like to draw out stories but if I don't draw them out a bit, you would be disappointed. And you know the saying in the Senate, 'It's not nice to disappoint Mother Nature or the Majority Leader.' Terrible things can happen to the person who does the disappointing."

"Get on with it, you bullshitter."

"Okay, but hold onto your jockey shorts. I met with Duncan Stuart-Bruce this evening for about an hour," Wayne said very quietly.

"Now that is a surprise. What did he want with the senior senator from Missouri or was he merely meeting with an old friend of the family?" asked Ellis with arched eyebrows.

"The latter. You know his Uncle Shamus made a big investment in MoGro in the '60s and has been a campaign contributor for the last 30 years. I'm not sure why, but Duncan always liked coming to our homes in Liberty and here in Washington. I think that Thelma reminds him of his own mother. I have seen pictures and there is more than a passing resemblance," explained Wayne. "Anyway, Duncan wanted to try out an idea he has been tossing around so he pitched the idea to me."

"This must be some kind of idea to warrant a meeting with me this evening and not wait until tomorrow," said Senator Hoyle. "So what does our young man from Scotland have up his sleeve this time?"

"First of all, keep in mind that Duncan was only raised in Scotland by Shamus. He was born in California in 1947 or '48, so he is as American as you and I. Secondly, his idee, as my Uncle Monty would say, may set the world on fire or more specifically, set the world economy on fire."

"You're doing it again, drawing out your story with your famous, Jimmy-cracked-corn, down-home style," Ellis said impatiently.

"Okay, okay, you made your point. No more stalling," Wayne said in surrender. "Duncan wants to pay off the U.S. national debt and for that generous gift, he wants to be President of the United States."

Senator Creason didn't say anything else. He let his friend think about what he heard.

Senator Hoyle was not a man who showed his thoughts on his face so he remained as before, a mix of interest and impatience on his face. Then you could see a change, not in his face but in his eyes. It was like you could almost see past the back of his eyes, into his brain. The neurons were not sparking the messages across the synapses. They were exploding. His mind was working fast, very fast.

Senator Hoyle was well-known for his incredible capacity to see both the immediate and the much larger picture on almost every issue. He could process the information for the larger picture almost instantly. That is why he was Majority Leader. He had a very fast mind and a very large capacity for information processing.

Wayne had watched Ellis process the information and create his big-picture image many times, but this time it was a real treat because Ellis had to think about all the possibilities for a full three or four minutes. Usually he had everything covered in less than one minute, but paying off the national debt was not your everyday issue and the breadth and depth of this one was as big as an issue can get.

Where Senator Creason had a way with people, Senator Hoyle had a way with issues. In spite of the fact that one was a lifelong Democrat from Missouri and the other was a Republican from Kansas, between the two of them, they could tackle any political problem, come up with a reasonable solution and sell it to their colleagues in the Senate, the constituents at home or on the Sunday morning talk shows. The American political system was a better place because of this unheard-of alliance and that same system would suffer when either or both men left the Senate.

Ellis got up from his seat, went to the window closest to the desk and stared at the cars on the street below. He was thinking carefully about what he had heard. Pay off the national debt in one fell swoop and make the national debt payer President of the United States. Now that should be a final test exam question for political science majors. You could fill your Blue Book with some pretty amazing issues to convince the professor that you had a good grasp of the stated and unstated principles of the American political system and world economics.

Wayne had only seen Ellis think this long on one other issue, the Nixon Watergate debacle and whether Congress should force Nixon to resign or impeach him. It took Ellis a full 15 minutes to think that one through.

After 10 minutes, Wayne said, "Ellis, we need to sleep on this one and we can get together tomorrow evening and see if this is a pig-in-a-poke or the real thing."

Ellis looked at his friend and said firmly, "We can't accept his offer. Paying off the national debt would cause too much confusion. Confusion here on The Hill, confusion in the White House, confusion in monetary and stock markets worldwide, confusion with the Federal Reserve, and confusion with the American people. No, no, we can't have one person paying off the national debt with private funds. It would upset the political power structure in this country and around the world and we are not prepared for this."

Senator Creason asked, "Shouldn't we talk to some of the other senators, some of the folks in the House and maybe talk to the president?"

"Let me think about whom we should talk to and how we should tell them," Senator Hoyle said. "I do not want this information leaked to the press yet. Too big of a story and you know the press will jump in with both feet and screw up everything. Let's keep this under our hats for a few days. When does Duncan want an answer?"

"He wanted a call back tomorrow but I got him to give me two weeks." Wayne Creason said with a smile, "I think we can squeeze another two weeks out of it if we ask real nice like."

"Good," Ellis Hoyle said, "we are going to need every hour of every day to come up with an alternate plan to satisfy our benevolent Mr. Stuart-Bruce."

"Let's meet tomorrow evening for dinner at our house. Bring Beulah along and I'll have Thelma get some of those salmon steaks you like," Wayne said. "How about 7:00 p.m.?"

"Sounds good," Ellis said with a cheery voice. "Do you think that Thelma can make some of the special hot water chocolate cake from her mother's recipe?"

"You know she loves to spoil you and Beulah," Wayne said with mock jealousy. "Now get home and take care of your wife. I'm taking mine out to dinner."

"You old devil," Ellis laughed, "just because you spend $100 on dinner for Thelma doesn't mean you will get lucky tonight."

Both Wayne and Ellis did exactly what they said they would do. They sat on the information about Duncan's proposal until they met at the Creason home the next evening. Over dinner, they confided in Thelma and Beulah about the proposal.

"Is it possible that Duncan and Shamus have six trillion dollars?" asked Beulah. "If they do, I'm leaving you, Ellis, and throwing myself at that Shamus Stuart-Bruce. Not only is he the best looking man over 60 in the world, now you tell me he is the richest man in the world. You are history, Ellis Hoyle."

Everyone laughed. "Yes, I believe that they have that much and more. You know the Scots, they never let on that they have any money at all and if they admit they have $100 then they probably have $100,000." Wayne went on, "They rarely overstate the value of anything unless they are trying to sell you something."

"Wouldn't this have an effect on the monetary markets here in the U.S. and abroad?" asked Thelma in a quiet, inquisitive voice.

"You bet it would," Ellis replied. "The U.S. government would not be in the money borrowing business and that would mean a significant reduction in the demand for money, which would drop the cost of money. All this means that interest rates would drop significantly, assuming that the pool of money available to borrow remains constant."

"Ellis you sound like one of those college professors that are always testifying in front of our committees," jibed Senator Creason. "All I understood was that interest rates to borrow money would drop if the U.S. national debt was paid off. How can that be bad for the American people?"

"Wayne, I have a very simple question," Ellis said in a challenging tone. "How many politicians make promises to get elected and never fulfill the promises to their constituents? Before you answer, would Duncan promise to pay off the national debt but follow in the footsteps of his fellow politicians and renege or weasel-word his way out of it?"

"Whew, Ellis, there you go again. I need a translation." Wayne said with a smile, "Beulah, is this the kind of question he used when he asked you to marry him?"

"Oh, Wayne, you know Ellis," said Beulah. "If it can be said in four words, 'Will you marry me?' he will stretch it out to four paragraphs. In fact, the reason my daddy agreed to our marriage is to get Ellis to stop giving him reasons why he would be a good husband and boring my daddy and mama to death."

Everyone laughed, including Ellis. "Enough of the Ellis jokes," he said with a twinkle in his eyes, "but Wayne, you did not answer my question."

"I have been thinking about it. I do believe that Duncan would keep his word and not hide behind a political-promise-just-to-get-elected façade. Duncan is a fierce competitor and can at times be ruthless but he is honest and honorable. No, I think he is serious and he would actually pay off the national debt."

"That is a pretty strong endorsement," said Ellis. "This is a genuine problem. An honest politician who keeps his promises and has a lot of money, more money than anyone ever imagined. I'm not sure that we, as a country, are ready for this type of man in the White House."

"That's pretty cynical, isn't it?" said Beulah. "I, for one, am ready for a candidate who puts personal integrity above political compromise."

Thelma chimed in, "I agree. You two are two of the most influential men in American politics and you are questioning a genuine offer to help our country from someone who can actually help. What have we become?"

"Are we sure that paying off the national debt is helping the country?" asked Ellis as though he was thinking out loud. "I'm not sure everyone would agree that disrupting the economic and political basis of the world is considered helping."

Ellis continued, "Truth be told, our entire power structure in Washington is based on the fact that the American people let the Congress borrow money whenever and wherever possible to finance almost anything that the senate, the house and the president need to get re-elected. This is one of those basal truths we rarely, I might add, talk about because we don't want to know that each one of us is a participant, a very willing participant, in a system that does not promote common sense and sound economic and political judgment.

"We purport to have capitalism as the core of our system but every capitalistic principle says that a not-for-profit organization, like the U.S. government, should not burden itself by paying interest on borrowed money but, at the same time, we cannot and do not stop the outrageous spending that requires us to use borrowed money. We are looking at a financial savior like Duncan Stuart-Bruce as though he is the Anti-Christ," Ellis said with a hard voice.

"After saying all of this, I personally do not think we should support Duncan for the reasons we talked about earlier." Senator Hoyle continued, "The very system we criticize and find fault with is still the best system to ever evolve from any government. As good as it sounds on the surface, I believe that having one person pay off the national debt with a single check would shake our system at its foundation, potentially pulling out its underpinnings and causing it to weaken. The problem is we don't have another system in the wings to fall back on and we don't have enough time to create another workable system."

"Give it a rest Ellis, you'll pop a vein," said Wayne with admiration. "You're getting cranked up like you do on the Senate floor when you want to really sway the Senate to your side. We are your friends and we believe you're right. Now, what are we going to do to stop this proposal in its tracks?"

"Well, I think we should meet with the president, the Speaker of the House, and the chief justice of the United States, privately, and lead them through the mine field to assure that they conclude the same thing we do," said Senator Creason, "and the sooner the better. These little tidbits have a way of sneaking into the press when you don't need to see them on the front page of the *Washington Post* or the *New York Times*."

"Ellis, why don't we suggest a Saturday afternoon meeting at Camp David? The president does like to have these little talks on his turf. He feels like he's in control even when he isn't," said Wayne with a touch of sarcasm.

"I will call and recommend it to the president. Should we have the secretary of the treasury there, too?" asked Ellis. "She sure seems to have a way with the people on Wall Street. And maybe the Federal Reserve chairman? He is about the most knowledgeable man in the world on the monetary consequences of something of this caliber."

"I think you are right about both of them, but I would not go any further with our invitations to others." Wayne cautioned, "Keeping this quiet with that group will be tough."

CHAPTER 20

Camp David, Maryland
September 1998

....

If there is ever a perfect Saturday afternoon for a meeting in the Maryland hills, this was it. Gloomy, windy, rainy and in some freak broadcasting snafu, no football games to watch on television. Catastrophe in the making except for the intrigue of the meeting called last Wednesday by Senators Creason and Hoyle. The "C&H" Senators, as they were affectionately called by their close friends, asked that everyone meet at Andrews AFB at 1:00 p.m. on Saturday afternoon and Marine One, the president's helicopter, would take them to Camp David.

Of course, the president was already on board and shook hands with the others as they came aboard. The helicopter rotated and banked toward the Maryland countryside northwest of Washington. Thirty minutes later it landed at the pad inside the Camp David compound. All the passengers disembarked in a steady rain and ran into the Lodge where a luncheon buffet was waiting.

At 2:30, Senator Creason stood and said, "Mr. President, thank you again for allowing all of us to join you here at Camp David on such short notice and for keeping our meeting away from the press. They would be after us like a bunch of coon dogs on a bright night along the Missouri River."

Everyone chuckled, but everyone was very curious why he or she had been asked to come to Camp David for a "secret meeting."

"I am sorry, Mr. President, Mr. Speaker and all the rest of you for being so secretive but I learned something this week that I need your help with and only the five of you have the knowledge, the expertise and experience to understand what I am about to disclose."

189

"Hell, Wayne, you are not making a campaign speech to the Ladies Aid Society in Liberty, call us by our first names and tell us why you called this meeting," said the president. "I am not aware of you ever making a request for a secret meeting like this."

"Come on, Wayne, stop stalling. You can drag out this kind of thing more than a Missouri mule," said the treasury secretary.

"All right, all right, let me say that I have discussed this with Ellis, my wife, Thelma, and Ellis's wife, Beulah. You all know our wives and know that they will not disclose what I have told them unless we give them permission to do so.

He paused, looked at each person, then began in a quiet, suspenseful voice, "I received a call from New York Tuesday afternoon about 3:00 p.m. from Duncan Stuart-Bruce. You all know him. He is Shamus Stuart-Bruce's grandnephew and heir to their family's vast holdings. I have known Shamus for some 30-plus years and Duncan for 20-some odd years. They have been to our home in Liberty and to our cabin at Table Rock Lake. I consider both of them good friends. Neither of them has ever asked me to do anything illegal, immoral, unethical or unreasonable. You all know that in our business that is as rare as a virgin at a fraternity house."

They laughed with Senator Creason again.

"Duncan asked if we, meaning he and I, could get together for a short meeting late that afternoon. So we arranged to meet at a small restaurant in Alexandria. No, dammit, I didn't have any bourbon and I was in total control of my faculties."

Another laugh for the group.

"In fact, Duncan and I both had dinner plans elsewhere that evening. During that meeting, Duncan explained that he wanted to do something for the good ole U.S. of A., where he was born. He said that his mother was a great patriot and he wanted to honor her memory by doing something for America. What he proposed will take your breath away. It took mine."

Senator Creason paused again and looked at every person in the room for a second time, stopping and looking directly at the president, as he continued. "Duncan Stuart-Bruce wants to pay off the U.S. national debt. All of it. All five and a half trillion dollars."

Senator Creason stopped for a moment. This time he looked at each person sitting in the room to gauge their reaction. Then he stopped at Senator Hoyle.

The Federal Reserve Chairman took his glasses off and rubbed the bridge of his nose and reached for his handkerchief to perform his ritual of cleaning his spectacles.

The Speaker of the House did not move, not even his eyes. He was still looking at Wayne but he was staring into space and did not see anything. You could tell he was processing the information.

The chief justice turned to look out the window at the rain. Sort of like she was distracted by the weather and couldn't concentrate on what she had been told.

The secretary of the treasury uncrossed her legs and reached for a pad of paper and a pen. She started jotting something on the pad like she wouldn't believe what she had heard unless she wrote it down.

The president reached over to a wooden box on the table next to his chair and opened it. He took a cigarette from it, reached for the gold Dunhill lighter next to the box and lit the cigarette. He took a deep drag and slowly let the smoke out his nostrils.

Ellis was watching everyone as Wayne was.

No one spoke for two minutes. Then the president asked, "Can Duncan get his hands on that kind of money?"

"I asked the same question when Duncan told me what he wanted to do," said Wayne. "He assured me that if Shamus agreed with his plan, he could get more than six trillion dollars and still not touch all of their assets."

"My God, it is true then," said Margaret Flood, the secretary of the treasury. "It has been rumored for years that Shamus and Duncan could raise more than $5 trillion dollars if they sold all of their holdings but no one knows exactly what they own. The rumor also has it that they don't even know what they own."

"Then it is the consensus of this group that they can raise $5 ½ trillion dollars if they want to?" said Eberle Faulkner, Speaker of the House. "Well, if that doesn't take the cake. Pay off the national debt. One person. Incredible to think about it. Gutsy. So what does he want in return? No, don't tell me. He wants to be president."

"Bingo," said Ellis. "He wants to be president and he wants the Congress and he wants you Mr. President to endorse the whole thing."

"Sandra, can one individual pay off the national debt? Does that cause any legal problems that you can think of?" asked the president.

Chief Justice Wilkey looked at everyone and said, "As long as the check doesn't bounce, I think that one person can pay off the debt without causing any undue legal consequences. I am pretty sure that if anyone challenges it, the Supreme Court would not have any problems allowing an individual to pay off the national debt."

Everyone laughed for the first time since the pay-off-the-national-debt bomb was dropped on the group.

The chief justice continued, "The question I see as most intriguing is not the legality of it, but do we want the national debt paid off?"

Again, the room was silent and everyone was trying to grasp the breadth and depth of this issue.

"Ellis, what do you think about this?" asked the president. "You have had a couple of days to think about the consequences of paying off the national debt."

"Well, my first thought was that I should have been smart enough to ask that question when I was teaching political science at K-State," Ellis started bashfully. "Then I would have had the benefit of getting the opinion of several of my bright students and I could pick the best."

"My short answer is — I do not believe that one individual, using private funds, should pay off the U.S. national debt," he said in a firm voice. "The consequences have serious implications here and abroad."

"But, Ellis," Eberle Faulkner replied, "You cannot disregard this just because it has serious implications. I, for one, would look forward to working in Congress with a debt-free government. It's a lifelong dream come true. There isn't an honest conservative in politics who wouldn't jump at this opportunity. Can you imagine how this would strengthen the U.S. dollar in the world markets? It is almost incomprehensible. I'm sure that somewhere in the lower regions of our government there is someone who has developed an econometric model where the U.S. is debt-free. But I haven't heard anyone talk publicly about it other in the most general terms. We all toss around the concept but we haven't really looked at the issues — be they negative or positive."

"Eb, you are by far the most informed, best equipped Speaker we have ever had and everything you say is true," said Blake Boone, the Federal Reserve Board Chairman, "but I want you to stop and think about this for a minute. The United States is the largest borrower of money in the world. As a result, the U.S. can set worldwide interest rates through the Federal Reserve Board. Without the debt, the U.S. government is no longer the largest borrower and the Federal Reserve Board no longer controls interest rates. Someone else will be the biggest borrower, maybe the U.K. or Germany or Japan or, God forbid, China or Russia. The point is that the U.S. loses its control on interest rates and that makes the U.S. economy very vulnerable. So I have to agree with Ellis, too many unknowns and the risks override the benefits."

"You are ganging up on me without fully examining the positives," said Eb, his tone getting aggressive, "All I have heard is 'serious implications,' and 'too many unknowns,' and 'risks overriding benefits,' and, worst of all, 'losing control.' Are you serious? You are the leaders of the free world and the capitalistic economy and you are worried about unknowns? Give me a break. You're a bunch of worrywarts."

Eb was really getting cranked up. "You want to talk about unknowns, I'll give you unknowns that will keep you awake all night, every night. Try this on for size. If we continue to let the national debt increase the way it has for the last two decades, we are looking at an annual interest payment of $4 to 5 trillion on a national debt of $65 to 70 trillion. Not possible. Well, this is your wake-up call. Not only is it possible, it is probable unless we stop Medicare, foreign aid, and every other give-away program that got us elected and we will have to raise taxes to meet the interest obligation alone. Do the arithmetic and you will see that we cannot continue with our dollars-for-votes program very much longer. Then what? That's the unknown, I fear.

"Here is a legitimate proposal to change the course of American political and economic history and make the U.S., and most likely the world, a stronger place and all we have to do is let Duncan Stuart-Bruce pay off the national debt. Oh sure, he wants some things in return, like being president. Well, what did the country do for General Eisenhower after World War II? For his extraordinary skill in leading the Allies to a victory, we made him president. This is no different."

"Slow down, Eb, you always talk too fast when you are trying to sell a program that you know won't make it through the House," said the president. "I don't want to be the one to throw a wet blanket on your speech, but you forget one thing. When this is all over, we, meaning all of us, and the positions we hold, want to be in control. No, we must be in control. We did not take these jobs because of the fine pay package and fringe benefits. We took these jobs because of one thing — the power. I know it. You know it. We all know it. So don't fool yourself into believing that there are higher platitudes at stake here.

"None of you will disagree with me when I say that Ellis and Wayne are two of the most impressive minds we have in Washington and when they come to me with a recommendation like the one they have made today, I tend to give them the benefit of the doubt." The president said with authority, "Eb, I'm sure that you will agree with me on this point."

"Yes, Mr. President, I do agree that Senators Creason and Hoyle are the very best but I want us to think outside the box for a minute." Eb went on in a friendlier tone, "Not everything is about control and power, not this time. There is the good of the country to think about."

"I agree 100%," said Senator Hoyle, "but the part you are not concentrating on is when I say 'too many unknowns' I mean that I do not know who will emerge in control and in power when the dust settles. What if Duncan Stuart-Bruce has ulterior motives and some other agenda than honoring his native country and his patriotic mother? I don't want to get too paranoid here but I think we should, no, we must consider this type of scenario.

"The second point I want to reiterate is this — who but the people in this room are better equipped to serve the needs of the country? That's another unknown that worries me and it goes hand-in-hand with the paranoia about Duncan.

"My daddy taught me not look too hard at a gift horse but at the same time don't forget that what goes into that horse's mouth must come out the other end. Moral: Don't spend all your time looking at the horse's mouth, spend some time looking at the horse's ass, you might learn something."

Everyone chuckled and the group broke to get drinks, go to the bathroom, stretch, walk around and have idle conversation. About 20 minutes later, Senator Creason asked everyone to gather around the fireplace again and continue the discussion.

"Although I do not personally agree with what is being said here at Camp David today," opened Eb, "I can see that as a group, we are not going to support Duncan Stuart-Bruce's proposal. I am saddened that the leaders of this country can't seem to muster more imagination and chutzpah than was shown here today. But I think that maintaining a unified position from this meeting is more important than individual beliefs and desires. So after my parting shots, I will go along with Ellis, Wayne, and the rest of you in turning down Mr. Stuart-Bruce."

"Right when we need it, the 'mom and apple pie' speech from none other than our own Eberle Faulkner," said the president with amusement and sarcasm in voice.

"You are truly an S.O.B, aren't you, Mr. President?" said Eb in a mock tone of indignation.

Everyone laughed but settled back as soon as Chief Justice Wilkey said,

"Here's a point you might want to consider before you pat yourselves on the back too much. What if our Mr. Stuart-Bruce decides to go forward and present this idea to the American people through the media? He can do that, you know. It is a free country and he can start his own third party, make a deal with the people and get himself elected. With several trillion dollars behind him, he might pull it off. Have you thought about the consequences of that scenario?"

No one said a thing. They couldn't think of anything that would lift the shroud of doubt that Sandra Wilkey had thrown on their little conference. It was true. Duncan Stuart-Bruce could go to the people and get himself elected. Then what? Back to the unknowns again, they never seem to go away.

This was pure speculation on Sandra's part, wasn't it? There had not been a serious third party since Ross Perot in 1992 and his threat only divided the vote. But Perot had only three or four billion dollars. Not a thousand times that much. Well, smart politics meant that they had to plan on the off chance that Duncan Stuart-Bruce would do exactly what Chief Justice Wilkey had suggested, no matter how remote the chance of that was.

"We had better start working on some contingency plans," said Secretary of Treasury Margaret Flood. "I will send drafts to each of you by the end of next week."

"In the meantime, Wayne, are you going to talk with Duncan and give him the bad news?" asked Federal Reserve Chairman Boone. "I think he should be told as soon as possible."

"Yes, Blake, I will tell Duncan but I want to wait a little, maybe as long as two weeks until I talk with Duncan," Senator Creason said. "I think I would like to see some of the contingency plans that Margaret is going to prepare before I have that discussion."

"Everyone, and I mean everyone, must keep this quiet. No leaks to the press. Not now, not until I'm out of office. Is that agreed?" queried the president. "I hope you don't mind. I have had Maggie prepare a confidentiality agreement for each of us to sign, including Ann and me."

Everyone signed the agreement to keep the day's meeting and its topic confidential until the next president was sworn into office.

Senator Creason did not usually use a driver but tonight on his way home from Andrews Air Force Base he was glad he could sit back and watch the sights of the nation's capital pass before him. Capitol Hill and the Washington Monument, the twins, The Jefferson and Lincoln Memorials, Key Bridge, the Smithsonian and, of course, the White House. *My god, what am I doing here?*

Every day as always the answer was the same. He was doing his job and making history at the same time. He always tried to convey to the voters in Liberty, or St. Joe, or Maryville, or Orrick or Independence or Hannibal or Columbia or St. Louis or Kansas City, that it was truly an honor and a privilege to serve the people of Missouri in the United States Senate. But he always felt that he just couldn't quite express his true feelings with the proper words.

Thelma told him to stop worrying about it because the folks in Missouri were an intuitive bunch, stubborn but intuitive. They sometimes did not show that they understood someone else's emotions but down deep they felt every syllable of every word that he had ever said to them. Why else would they have re-elected him so many times?

Still, it was times like these; they brought him very close all the majesty and grandeur that Washington possessed. He was making history again. Tonight he would call Duncan and tell him that after consulting with several key people that they had decided to decline his offer to pay off the national debt.

Duncan could buy several countries but instead he wanted to make America greater by giving it the largest monetary gift ever: $6,000,000,000,000.

And I'm going to turn him down. Now if that isn't making history, I don't know what is. Enough thinking about legends. I need to get home and make the call. I am not going to wait until I see the contingency plans from Margaret Flood. They won't change the group's mind and postponing the call is not going to help anyone. After the call, there will still be time to take Thelma to that new Italian restaurant on 'K' Street in Georgetown.

CHAPTER 29

New York, New York
September 1998

....

The phone only rang once. "Duncan, this is Wayne Creason. Is this a good time to talk?"

"Yes, of course," Duncan said, "I always make time for your calls, don't I?"

"Yes, you do and I appreciate it," said Wayne. "Hope things are going well in New York."

"Fine, just fine," answered Duncan.

"Duncan, I am not going to beat around the bush," Wayne said quickly. "I have talked to a few of my friends and the group has concluded, and I reluctantly agree, that we are going to turn you down on the offer we talked about a few days ago. I'm sorry, Duncan, but in this case I think that you are trying to upset the power base in Washington and you know how the boys love their power."

"Does that include you Senator?" said Duncan with a little more sarcasm than he wanted.

"Now Duncan, don't take this personally," said Wayne, "because not once during any of the discussions I heard did your personal motives, other than you wanting to be president, become the focus of the group's attention. Trust me on this. The decision was not against Duncan Stuart-Bruce but instead it was for the current political and economic structure."

"I'm sorry, Wayne," Duncan said, backing down, "but the more I think about my proposal the better I like it. I believe that paying off the national debt, particularly paying it off with minimal political baggage, will open a lot of new doors for the U.S. and for the world at large."

"Yes, Duncan, we agree that new doors will be opened but we are very concerned about the unknowns that lurk behind those doors," said the senator earnestly. "In fact, it was the number and size of the unknowns that swayed me to agree with my friends and vote to turn down your offer."

There was silence for a couple of moments then Duncan said, "I'm disappointed in the group's decision and I really am surprised by your decision to agree with them, Wayne."

"You know, Duncan," Wayne said firmly, "I am a little disappointed with myself. But old age has made me a more cautious man and I am not ready to tackle the unknowns in this situation the way I would have 10 years ago."

"Believe it or not," Duncan responded, "I understand what you are saying. Shamus has tried to teach me the difference between the generations and the benefit to society that comes from becoming more cautious with age. But Shamus also taught me that the pursuit of the unknowns, as you call them, by the younger generations is what makes companies and nations great. So with all due respect, I am going to pursue my plan to pay off the national debt and become President of the United States."

For a second time during this call, there were a few moments of silence, but this time Senator Creason broke it with, "Duncan, I wish you the best in your pursuit and if anyone on this earth can actually accomplish such a monumental task, it is you," the senator said firmly. "Keep in mind if you ever need to talk or want to have a place to get one of Thelma's great dinners and a good glass of wine, you are always welcome at our home."

"Thank you, Senator, and the same offer to you and Thelma particularly when I get to the White House. I will talk to you soon. Take care of yourself and, again, my best to Thelma."

"Good bye, Duncan, and good luck to you, son."

Duncan put the phone in its cradle, turned around in the swivel chair and looked out the window. He thought about what Senator Creason had told him.

Not unexpected. Disappointing, but not unexpected. Well, being turned down by the political establishment in Washington was a setback but not a fatal blow. He would ask his staff of advisors what he should do now that the Senate and, obviously, the House had turned down his offer. And, most likely, the president, too.

CHAPTER 30

New York, New York
September 1998

....

Shamus and Duncan were at Duncan's townhouse having breakfast and after the idle chat about things in Scotland, Isabella, and the general business discussion, Duncan motioned for Shamus to join him in the study.

"Duncan, you look like your dog Christine after she tore up Mrs. Kelley's kitchen towel. You're bursting at the seams to tell me something but you are afraid I will be displeased with what you have to say," Shamus said as he sipped a little more coffee.

Duncan smiled broadly, looked at Shamus and said, "I haven't thought of Christine for a long time. She was a great dog and a very good friend to a lonely boy. Thanks again for getting her for me."

He continued, "You haven't lost your touch, not one bit. You are still as perceptive as when we fished for salmon near the castle. And you are right. I am bursting at the seams to tell you something and I don't know how you will react. But we made a pact not to let time or distance keep us from being absolutely honest and candid."

"Duncan, you are doing it again, too much drama for your tottering old Scottish uncle." Shamus looked over his glasses at Duncan. "Let me guess. You have gotten some young lass pregnant and you don't know how to tell me?"

Duncan nearly sprayed the coffee in his mouth across the room when he heard Shamus's joke. But he quickly swallowed it in a gulp and said, "No, no, nothing quite as seedy as that but you would love to give me a lecture about my responsibilities to the girl, wouldn't you?"

"And don't fool yourself. I would give you a very serious talking-to if that ever happened but I'm sure that is not the reason we are talking today, even though I get a quick chuckle thinking about it," Shamus said with a loving but humorous tone. "So what are we going to talk about?"

Duncan leaned against the desk, looked at Shamus and said, "I want to pay off the U.S. national debt and, for that generous deed, I want to be President of the United States."

Shamus stopped in mid-motion, turned his head slightly and looked at Duncan to assure himself that Duncan was not teasing him again. The look in Duncan's eyes showed he was dead serious. He had his jaw set with the same resolve he used when he was a kid determined to catch a salmon from the stream next to the castle.

Shamus had aged in the last 10 years but his mind was still lightning quick. Duncan saw him gathering information from the far reaches of his mind, processing it and drawing conclusions.

"How much is the debt and where are you planning to get the money to pay it off?" Shamus asked cautiously, as though he already knew the answer but needed confirmation.

"The debt is around five and a half trillion dollars," said Duncan firmly, "and I plan to liquidate about two-thirds of the family holdings to pay it off. That is, if you go along with this."

"Interesting proposal. But what is in it for the family?" Shamus said carefully. "That is a lot of money to invest in a project. I am curious what kind of return you plan to get on the investment."

"Always go to core first, never beat around the bush. That's what you taught me and it has worked every time," Duncan said appreciatively. "The return is that a Stuart-Bruce becomes leader of the most powerful nation on earth and gets a chance to make history like no one in the family has before."

"Duncan, if you want to make history you could give something like five million people one million dollars — each. That would make a lot of history books. Or you could probably buy most of Africa and own an entire continent. That surely would make history," Shamus said a bit too quickly and harshly.

Shamus held up his hand to keep Duncan from talking and continued, "I know what you are saying and ..." Shamus stopped for a moment and looked at Duncan, "will you invite Isabella and me to the inauguration?"

Duncan looked up at Shamus. They looked at each other for a few seconds and Duncan broke into a smile that lit up his whole face, "You bet, front row next to me, right where both of you should be," Duncan said as his voice broke with some emotion.

"Shamus, are you sure?" Duncan walked to him and put a hand on Shamus's shoulder.

"Yes, I am very sure," Shamus replied as he looked up at Duncan. "I raised you to be an independent thinker and to examine all sides of an issue before you take action. I also taught you to make sure that you confer with your closest friends early in a project to find out if they have any concerns." Shamus stood and walked to the fireplace.

"You know you would not have even proposed something as colossal as paying off the U.S. debt unless you reviewed all the issues and you have talked to a couple of your friends before you talked to me," Shamus said quietly, "So why would I object, I trust you, as I have trusted you for the last 45 years."

"I know you better than you know yourself and I know that you are committed to this project and that you will make history like no other U.S. president has before. So let's make this happen and have a great time getting you elected president."

Duncan gave him a hug and said with quiet respect, "Thank you."

CHAPTER 31

New York, New York
September 1998

....

Duncan was a good listener, a very good listener. He learned how to listen from someone who listened better than anyone else he knew — Shamus.

Duncan always hired the very best people in any given field and he allowed them to talk and, of course, he listened. He not only listened to the words but he listened to the tones and he listened for what was not said. He listened with his eyes and nose as well as with his ears. Sometimes the best listening was non-verbal.

It was no different when it came to selecting his political consultants. He interviewed five of the very best minds in politics; each with a very promising career as a political futurist. However, after the first rounds of interviews, he was not satisfied with any of the candidates in spite of their great credentials.

They were too slick and too biased and too packaged to really take on the job of making Duncan Stuart-Bruce President of the United States. Rather than focus on how to make him president, they wanted to focus on making him change to an image they had concocted for him. He knew that the American people and the media would see through this type of campaign within a few days.

So he asked his staff to bring in some more people. He listened some more. He still didn't find what he liked so he asked for more candidates. His staff was starting to panic. They were running out of top-level candidates and they definitely didn't want to go to Duncan explaining that there were no more A-list political consultants.

As though he was reading their minds, Duncan asked them to stop bringing political consultants. He wanted the smartest and most revered retired politicians they could find and he wanted three of them to talk to within 48 hours.

Duncan's staff was very resourceful and very persuasive so two days later, there were five, not three, of the best, retired politicians scheduled to talk with Duncan. The first was the former congressman and Speaker of the House, Virgil Robertson. It was no wonder he was re-elected to 20 consecutive terms in the House. His smile, his eyes, everything about him made you stop and look. He was bigger than life but he had a way of making even the meekest constituent become the most important voter in his district. He was a master. Probably the best that had ever been in the House. Better than Sam Rayburn. Better than Jim Wright. Better than Tip O'Neil. Duncan found himself actually staring at Speaker Robertson. He was mesmerizing.

But behind this seeming made-in-Hollywood façade was a very smart and very honest man whose personal sacrifice and compassion were unsurpassed in Washington. He had retired from the House after forty years as he had promised his wife, Becky, he would do.

Before Speaker Virgil retired, Miss Becky had been the reigning hostess of Washington for more than 20 years. Everyone who met her found that she was even smarter and more honest than her husband was, if that was possible. The Speaker and Miss Becky were legends. There was even a movie in the works about their life together in Idaho and Washington, D.C. Sort of a modern version of the Jimmy Stewart film titled, "The Man Who Shot Liberty Valance."

"Duncan, the first thing you have to do is decide what kind of president you want to be," said Speaker Robertson. "I'm not talking about the liberal or conservative agenda crap, that is the superficial bullshit that everyone leans on when they don't want to talk about the real part of the job.

"For discussion's sake, let's say you want to be an honest president. How are you going to prove it to the people, to the Congress, to the media, to our allies, to yourself?" The Speaker said with a challenge, "Having the American people trust you is the single most difficult part of the job. Never underestimate the importance of it."

"I know you are very wealthy, maybe the richest man in the world, and that your family's money goes back centuries. But ask yourself, do you want to be known as the man who bought the presidency or do you want to be known as the man who brought honesty and integrity back to the White House? I can tell by looking at you that you are a very bright man who took advantage of his wealth and learned from it. So it should not surprise you when I say that getting the American people to trust you is not something you can buy with money. Even if it is a very large sum of money.

"The Clinton thing led a lot of the cynics to conclude that the American people don't care anymore. Well, I'm here to tell you that they care even more today than anytime in history. No president ever publicly flaunted his negative personal or presidential integrity and honesty more than Bill Clinton.

"So, guess what? The people watched and the people listened and they have quietly decided in the privacy of their living room that they do not want that type of politician anymore. They are not on 'Larry King' or 'Good Morning America' or the Sunday news shows trying to get their 15 minutes of fame. But I'm telling you here and now, the core of America is not going to be interested in anything or anyone who does not walk, talk, look or campaign like an honest man or woman. More importantly, they are not going to vote for anyone who does not prove he or she is honest."

Speaker Robertson stopped, took a sip of the Diet Coke and looked at Duncan, who was still listening. "That, Duncan, you can take to your bloody bank and deposit it with the knowledge that you will only earn interest if you are an honest candidate and can prove it literally every day," the Speaker said with finality.

Duncan studied Virgil Robertson. He had rarely seen such intensity in any person. But when someone like Virgil Robertson, former Speaker of the U.S. House of Representatives gave such a speech, you should do more than listen; you should memorize his words and preserve his thoughts for future use. He liked this man, even if he was a tad overbearing and very dogmatic in his principles, but one thing always stood out. He knew politics and politicians and he spoke his mind with an unabashed honesty that no one, not even Shamus, could top. Duncan decided that he needed Virgil on his team and he needed to know more about him.

"I understand you are a fly-fisherman, Mr. Speaker," said Duncan as he stood and walked to the window. "Why do you like to fish?"

"Now that is a strange question; where did that come from?" asked Speaker Virgil.

Duncan explained, "If I'm going to have people helping me with this project, I need to know more about them than their political views. Fly-fishing happens to be a passion of mine that started when I was 7 years old in Scotland. My Uncle Shamus taught me how and I want to know why you pursue that particular sport."

The Speaker looked up at Duncan with a newfound respect, cocked his head to the side and said, "Because both of my grandfathers, both of grandmothers, my father, my mother and everyone in my family taught me to truly respect fishing and the people who fish."

"Because when presenting a fly in the right spot to get the big one, you are trying to make the perfect cast and the perfect cast is unattainable. You may get very close, you may get a part of the cast perfect but a perfect cast and a perfect presentation are like infinite. We talk about them we theorize about how to get to them but no matter how much we try, we will never actually attain either of them. But it is one hell of a good time trying to find the infinite and it is an even better time trying for the perfect cast for the perfect presentation," said Virgil quietly but with spirit.

Duncan sat a couple of minutes, looked around the room and then, with an equally quiet voice, looked at the Speaker, "They told me you were good, but I never knew until this moment, how really incredible you are," said Duncan with admiration. "Have you ever thought about writing a book on fly-fishing? It would be great."

"Why, thank you," said the speaker with humility. "I do not often come across people who understand the sport of fly-fishing as I do, so it is a real pleasure to find that you are one. We will get along fine, son. For the record, everyone told me that there was more to you than a potato warehouse full of money, but they did not tell me you have a gift for truly being able to think like a real person. And that, son, is a compliment I hand out very rarely."

"Thank you, Mr. Speaker," replied Duncan quietly. "I believe that you will be a true asset to me in my quest to pay off the national debt and become President of the United States."

"Since you brought up the subject of fly-fishing, would you like to go with me on a float trip down the South Fork of the Snake River in Eastern Idaho next week?" Virgil said with real warmth in his voice. "There is a group of us who have been going on this float trip for the last 10 years or so and we always like to spark up the group with a few new faces. You know, the old men, teaching the new kids how to tie flies and cast into the wind."

"Mr. Speaker, that would be an honor and this may be the last time I can get away as a private citizen for a while," said Duncan with eagerness. "Once I announce my candidacy, I will no longer have a private life. Where do we meet and what do I need to bring?"

"If you want, you can fly into Boise and we will drive to Idaho Falls with some of the other guys and pick up a couple of the group who fly in from New Hampshire every year. Then up to Swan Valley, down from Palisades Dam, to meet the group that drives down from Montana, northern Idaho, and eastern Washington." Speaker Robertson said, "Why not fly in early like 10:00 next Thursday morning, and we will get you outfitted for the float?"

"Can't wait," said Duncan. "Now back to today's business. I really do need your active support."

"I will think about getting involved and we can talk next week on the river," hedged Speaker Robertson. "Anyway, I don't know if I can support you or not. I haven't even seen you in waders."

Duncan laughed. "Until next week then."

CHAPTER 32

Boise, Idaho
October 1998

....

This was his first trip to Idaho. Everywhere he looked he was pleased with what he saw. It was like walking into a well-proportioned room. You felt comfortable without really knowing why. It felt right.

Boise was a busy metro area with an authentic mix of new and old. Victorian homes on Warm Springs Boulevard east of the downtown and the sprawling modern complexes of Micron, Hewlett-Packard, Albertson's, Simplot and Boise State University scattered throughout the city. The capitol building looked like it belonged in the middle of Boise and again the proportions were right for the town, the river, and the mountains to the north. There was the native beauty that came from the mountains and rivers and farms and ranches and it was a friendly, warm, clean city that made Duncan smile.

He had traveled in America from coast to coast, border to border and he thought to himself, Idaho was America at its best. Modern computer and high-tech businesses next to family farms, with ski resorts and river rafting within minutes of both.

Speaker Robertson's home was on the western hills above downtown Boise in a town called Eagle. It was a sprawling home with a beautiful view and plenty of room to take a walk around the orchard below the house. Duncan's guest room was really part of the garage closest to the pool and had a sitting room with a kitchen, bedroom and bath. A large window overlooked a veranda that had a porch swing and rocking chairs. No wonder Virgil and Miss Becky liked it here, it was like everything else in Idaho, comfortable and scenic.

No one was happier than Becky when she and Virgil returned to Idaho. She had missed the wide open spaces, the majestic peaks but, most of all, she missed being close to her daughters and grandchildren.

The first thing Duncan observed was that when Miss Becky (everyone called her Miss Becky) was in a room, she did not need to dominate the room or the people to be noticed. Miss Becky was not worried about being noticed. She was an observer. She observed everyone and how they interacted. Duncan was struck by the deep serenity that Miss Becky possessed. She had the kind of patience that seemed to endure over time while at the same time had defined limits. Miss Becky projected wisdom and Duncan could see that when partnered with her husband, they together were a formidable pair. Forty years of unquestioned success in Washington spoke volumes to confirm Duncan's observation.

Miss Becky welcomed him into her home and offered him a glass of wine and they went to sit by the pool. They sat in silence for maybe five minutes. Then Miss Becky said, "Watching these mountains is one of the most fascinating things I have ever done in my life. Every minute of every day they are different. They present a new picture for your eyes as the sun rises from the east and sets in the west. Even the moonlight makes these mountains take on a new mystery that day can never duplicate."

"The most incredible part of viewing the phenomenon each day is that it has been going on for thousands of years. Living back east in Washington gave me a chance to truly appreciate our mountains."

She sipped some of her wine and continued, "These mountains are a lot like my husband. You can marvel at their majesty, respect the impact they have on the surrounding area and sometimes curse the obstacle they create, but there is one thing that you do not want to do to these mountains," Miss Becky said as she turned to look straight into Duncan's eyes. "Never, ever underestimate these mountains. They can consume even the most powerful men and women. I have seen that happen more than once."

She turned back to look at the mountains, sipped some more wine and said, "Here in Idaho, we learn very early that the mountains you see are the easy ones. It's the ones that you don't see behind the ones you see that can overwhelm you. Virgil and I taught our daughters that very good lesson."

Miss Becky and Duncan sat some more, then Duncan said, "I have been a fortunate man and I have climbed some of the world's highest mountains but I believe you are right. The most difficult mountains may very well be here in Idaho. I accept your advice not to underestimate them and I will also not underestimate your husband."

Duncan reached over to toast Miss Becky's wine glass when he heard, "There you go again, Duncan. Flirting with the first girl you meet. Pour me some wine and we'll sit and enjoy the mountains together." Virgil Robertson pulled up a chair.

Miss Becky and Duncan looked at each other and smiled a secret smile.

After Duncan got settled in his room, the Speaker asked him to go into town so they could get Duncan some gear for the trip. Duncan brought his own fly rod and reel but the Speaker wanted him to have lightweight waders and the latest wading shoes.

Everywhere they went, to the sporting goods store, to the grocery, to the bookstore, to the gas station, everyone knew Virgil Robertson and the Speaker knew them. He asked about their kids and grandkids, about their parents and brothers and sisters. He seemed to have something to say to everyone. Duncan was introduced to many of the people the Speaker spoke to and they wanted to know where Duncan was from. He always answered that he was born in California but raised in Scotland by his Uncle Shamus. The curious wanted to know about his mom and dad and he would explain that they died when he was a child and leave it alone after sharing a peek at his past.

The Speaker watched the way his friends and neighbors responded to Duncan and how Duncan responded to them. Duncan was a good-looking man who had a quick, genuine smile but the thing that caught people off guard were his eyes. It wasn't only their deep turquoise blue color that caused them to stop and stare. The intense gleam in his eyes drew people to Duncan. This gleam was a combination of warmth and intense concentration. It always made people feel that they could listen to him all day or talk freely with him as an old friend. Sometimes both.

The real test for Duncan was going to be on the float trip down the South Fork of the Snake River. Virgil Robertson's oldest and closest friends came on the annual trip. It was more than a fishing trip — it had grown to be tradition and it was a way to pay homage to the Snake River, fly-fishing, and good friends being together. The guys who met each year to float down the river, were a true cross-section of America. They all had successful careers but each had suffered at least one painful defeat in his life, which gave them a sense of balance that made them careful but aggressive survivors. In short, they were the people Virgil Robertson trusted when he had to make difficult decisions or there were sticky situations to resolve.

Supporting Duncan Stuart-Bruce in his bid for the presidency was going to be a difficult situation that would force many sticky issues to the surface. The Speaker knew that Duncan wanted his support, not only for his politically sound strategies but also for his name, his integrity, and his friendship. These were the things Duncan wanted from the Speaker and Virgil Robertson did not bestow any one of these on people often or without careful scrutiny. He could not think of a time when he had pledged all of them to one person, except for his lovely Miss Becky. In all of his years, she was the only person who had both earned and deserved all of them: his name, his integrity and his friendship.

That evening, Virgil and Duncan went to the Speaker's daughter's home for dinner. She had three very active children and a husband who liked to play with them in the yard. The speaker's other daughter was in Alaska working toward her doctorate. During dinner, the Speaker talked about the up-coming float trip and reminisced about past trips when the weather was bad or the moose had come into the camp.

One of the Speaker's grandchildren, Curtis, a cheerful lad about 3 years old, crawled into Duncan's lap and sat playing with a toy car. Everyone was surprised because Curtis was not usually friendly to strangers but the child seemed to be perfectly content to sit on Duncan's lap and play. The Speaker watched the way Duncan held his grandson. Duncan was talking with Lindsey about the way she had cooked the venison roast and did not notice how naturally he moved with Curtis on his lap. The Speaker was noticing everything about Duncan's actions. His way with his 3-year-old grandson showed how Duncan would react to other children. The baby, Jaycee, watched Duncan from her high chair and was not throwing food and plates on the floor. Jaycee was calmer than Grandpa had seen her in a long time. Maybe Duncan's presence was soothing to her.

At 8:30 Lindsey and her husband rounded up the kids and got them ready for bed. Duncan volunteered to tell them a bedtime story about the castle in Scotland where he grew up.

"Did you really live in a castle?" they asked. That was the only invitation that Duncan needed. He told them stories about his Uncle Shamus, and Isabella, and his dog Christine and about Mrs. Kelley the cook. After an hour, Lindsey wanted the kids to go to sleep but she allowed one more question. Lindsey's oldest, Lia asked, "Why didn't you say anything about your mom and dad in your story about living in the castle?"

Duncan looked at the little girl with two front teeth missing and said, "My mother died when she got sick with cancer when I was five years old and my father died when a ship he was on sank when I was six. My Uncle Shamus raised me in the castle."

Lia had one more question, "Do you miss your mommy and daddy?"

"Of course, I do. Every day, but you know what?" She shook her head back and forth. "Every night I say a prayer asking God to take care of them," said Duncan quietly. "Will you let me say a prayer for them with you tonight?"

"Yes, I would like that," said Lia.

Duncan kneeled beside the bed in the children's bedroom and clasped his hands together. He looked at Lia who was right next him, mimicking his kneeling and prayer hands clasping.

"Dear Lord," Duncan started, "please take care of my mother and my father. I know they have been with you in heaven for a long time but I still miss them every day. Tell them that I love them and that I will never forget them. And take care of all the people who are not as fortunate as I am. And please take special care of my new friend, Lia. Amen."

Lia looked up at Duncan and said, "That was a very nice prayer."

Duncan rose from his knees and moved toward the door. "Sleep tight and don't let the bed bugs bite."

As Duncan thanked Lindsey for the wonderful evening, he hugged her and said quietly, "Your children are living proof that God continues to give us gifts. Thank you for sharing them with me tonight. Take very good care of them."

As they drove back to the Speaker's house, Duncan thought about why he had not had children and quickly concluded the reason why was because he had not found the right woman to marry and mother his children not since Blanca and baby Ian. One thing Duncan knew, is that he liked kids and they seemed to like him. Maybe one day he would have his own children.

As though reading his mind, the Speaker asked Duncan if he had ever considered settling down, marrying and having kids.

"Well, I fell in love once when I was 25 years old and we got married but she died in an accident the following year. Our unborn son died with her in the same accident," Duncan said with a distant tone in his voice. He was silent for a long time then said to no one in particular, "I never found anyone else who interested me since then."

He snapped back to the present and continued, "To be perfectly honest, I was so busy with all the businesses our family owns that I lost myself in my work. But you're right. There is a void in my life that I am feeling more and more every year. Maybe after I become president, there will be time to fall in love, get married and have a family."

"Duncan, I don't want to start sounding like I'm giving you personal advice but falling in love is not something you put on the agenda and expect your staff to accomplish in the time allotted." The Speaker said with a chuckle, "It will hit you like a brick wall like it did when you were 25 years old."

CHAPTER 33

Swan Valley, Idaho
October 1998

....

The next day they drove the Suburban pulling a trailer with the float boats and gear strapped to it. The Speaker explained that they were taking the back roads to Idaho Falls and they would see more diverse scenery than if they took the Interstate. The drive was very interesting. The mountains, valleys, rivers, farms, and towns were constantly changing as they drove east along the edge of the high mountains of Central Idaho.

They stopped outside Boise to pick up another of the guys going on the float trip. His name was Steve Edgerton. Steve was fourth generation Idahoan. His family had homesteaded the area south of Boise in the 1870s when his great-great grandfather came to Idaho from Georgia after the Civil War.

Steve was an avid fly fisherman who knew every stream and river in Idaho. He was a storehouse of knowledge and was eager to share it with Duncan. Steve drove while the Speaker sat in the front passenger seat, which gave Duncan a chance to observe the interactions of the Speaker with a close friend.

The Speaker had a natural way of getting his friend to talk about what was happening in his life. Things about his wife, his children, his work and his parents. As Steve shared details, Duncan began to see the Speaker open up to his old friend. Nothing dramatic but here and there, something would slip into the conversation that showed Duncan that this drive across Idaho with Steve was as important as the float trip down the river.

They did not leave Duncan out of the discussions but they still had private stories that they shared in a way that showed that the respect each had for the other was very deep. Duncan had a feeling Virgil Robertson was one of those

214

rare men who had strong friendships with many people and each one of those friendships he valued equally. It was a personality trait he admired in his Uncle Shamus and now he was seeing it again in this man from Idaho.

When they reached the Idaho Falls airport around noon, a Delta jet was landing and taxied to the terminal. A line of 40 or 50 people walked down the portable stairway and headed for the terminal building. From that group came two more of the float trip group, Jim Blake and Sam Anderson. They flew in from New Hampshire via Cincinnati and Salt Lake City.

It was like a school reunion, everyone talking at the same time and introductions done quickly as bags were loaded into the silver Suburban. The two newcomers were both doctors who had practices in central New Hampshire near Lake Winnipesaukee. Jim Blake was funny in a Saturday Night Live kind of way and Sam Anderson kept talking about the big yella-belly he was going to get this year. As soon as they were in the car and on their way, there were at least three conversations going on at once. Duncan had the feeling he was with a group of fraternity brothers on their way to the favorite bar and strip joint for a fun evening.

Duncan was instantly brought into the little jokes everyone would play on the others when they got the camp set up.

"Remember last year when we moved Chris's tent and he couldn't find it?" asked the Speaker laughing out loud. "I didn't think he was going to talk to us for the rest of the trip." Everyone howled.

"And remember those two-way radios we used the year before?" asked Jim. "If the sheriff had heard what we said on those radios when we were driving to Island Park, we would have been thrown in jail."

They got to the river in about 90 minutes and there was a second Suburban that had come from Spokane to Coeur D'Alene to Missoula and down to the South Fork of the Snake River. More introductions: brothers Chip and Chris Crumley, Brian LaRoche, Don Cable, and Kevin O'Brien. Everyone was talking again and Duncan was treated as an equal from the start.

They started getting the inflatable boats off the trailers. The inflatable float boats were heavier than they looked. It took two men to lift the aluminum-rowing frame. The set-up was faster than Duncan expected, with each person having a specific duty. Duncan got the job of unloading the silver Suburban.

The boats were put in the river and loaded with all the tents, sleeping bags, clothes and food to last four days. There were four float boats for ten guys. That meant two boats with three men each and two with two each. Chris, Jim and Sam shared a boat because they had all gone to medical school together. Chip and Kevin in the second one. Steve and Brian teamed up, and in the fourth boat, Don and Duncan joined the Speaker, who insisted on being called Virgil or Virg on this trip.

Don rowed the boat away from the shore and into the main flow of the river. It seemed like they were out of sight of the launch point within minutes and Virgil had his rod out and expertly tied a fly on the line. As they neared the first pool, the Speaker kneeled on the front tube of the boat and cast the line toward the center of the pool.

The fish struck in a flash but the Speaker was right on top of the line and pulled it tight as he hooked the trout. Don gave a loud hoot saying, "Fish on." Virgil had the first fish and it was a good one. Duncan could hear the guys in the other boat saying that every year it was the same — Virg got the first fish. How did he manage to do that?

They floated for about an hour before Duncan got his first fish. He was casting toward a cliff wall that rose straight up from the river. The cast was a little jerky but the fly landed two or three inches from the rocks, exactly where Duncan wanted it. This time a nice fish grabbed the fly and ran fast and hard with it. Duncan pulled back firmly on the pole and palmed his reel to slow it a tad. He had not set the drag very tightly on the reel and this fish wanted to run. Probably back into a hole he had under the rocks.

Duncan played the fish for three or four minutes until he got it into the net that Speaker Robertson was holding over the side of the boat.

"Nice cutthroat," said Virgil, "it probably measures 15 or 16 inches. That's big for this stretch of the river."

Don got out the camera and snapped a photo of Duncan holding the fish before he released it back to the river. Cutthroat trout were catch-and-release fish on the South Fork; rainbows and whitefish were what everyone kept and cooked.

At about 6:00 in the evening, the four boats pulled into a backwater channel that led up to a campground. The job of unloading almost all of the gear began, with Duncan and others acting as pack mules while Chris and Steve started setting up the kitchen. It amazed Duncan how organized everything seemed when no one was really issuing any instructions. It was like everyone had his job to do and each of them instinctively knew when to do it to keep things flowing smoothly.

After everything was set up and dinner was cooking, some of the guys took off fishing, others stayed around the fire to talk. Speaker Robertson went off to fish with Chip and Steve. Duncan decided to stay at the camp and visit with Don and Kevin.

Kevin asked if Duncan would like a drink. Duncan said, yes, and asked what were the choices.

"Beer, of course," said Kevin, "or you can have a famous South Fork gin and tonic, complete with fresh lime."

Duncan was concerned, but asked, "What is a South Fork gin and tonic?"

"Try it, you'll like it," Kevin said. "You haven't really lived until you have had one."

"All right, you sold me," Duncan said confidently. "Mix up one of those South Fork gin and tonics for me."

Duncan was talking with Don about his business in Spokane and didn't see Kevin walk up behind him with the drink.

"Here you go Duncan," said Kevin.

Duncan turned and saw the largest plastic glass he had ever seen filled to the brim with gin, tonic and ice. There were three slices of lime perched on the edge of the glass. Printed on the side of the plastic glass were the words "Big Gulp."

"My god man," Duncan said, "that is the biggest gin and tonic I have ever seen. How big is that glass?"

"The Big Gulp is 64 ounces or a half gallon," said Kevin with pride, "and I figure I poured at least 8 or 10 ounces of gin over the ice before I added the tonic."

Duncan took the plastic glass with both hands, looked at it and back to Kevin and Don. He shrugged his shoulders and took a sip. It was good. It had the right mix of gin and tonic with a hint of lime to enhance the flavor.

"Come on, Duncan, you can't sip that thing like you're at a ladies' tea party," said Don with a challenge. "Take a real drink and enjoy yourself. You know if you are going to fit in around here you're going to have to get at least a little drunk."

"Well, I guess you're right. I can't think of a better place to get at least a little drunk," said Duncan as he tipped the glass and took a big swig of the South Fork potion.

"That's great, now lean back, look at the sky, listen to the river and let Dr. Gin and Mr. Tonic do their job," said Kevin with a big smile on his face.

Dinner was served about an hour after camp was set up as the sun slowly fell below the ridge to the west. Chip made the fajitas from elk steak that Brian had provided from last fall's hunt. The steak strips were sautéed with onions and peppers, and served with sour cream, guacamole, Chris's homemade salsa, and warm flour tortillas. They smelled great and everyone jumped right in to fill their plate. That is, everyone except Duncan.

Duncan drank his first South Fork gin and tonic, all 64 ounces, in less than 20 minutes. It was so good that he had another. The second one disappeared within 45 minutes. Duncan didn't finish all of the third one because he passed out in his lawn chair.

At about 10:00, Speaker Robertson helped Duncan into his tent and he fell into the sleeping bag. He remembered bits and pieces of the evening but for the life of him he couldn't remember how he got into the tent.

The next morning as he regained consciousness, Duncan smelled bacon frying and all of a sudden he was hungry; even more urgent than the hunger was the need to go to the bathroom. Then he remembered, there was no bathroom. He had to walk into the trees outside of camp to take a leak.

As he threw the sleeping bag off, he noticed that it was cold. Maybe 35 or 40 degrees. He got out of the tent, stumbled into the woods and let his body rid itself of the remnants of the gallon of the South Fork gin and tonic he had consumed.

Feeling alive again, Duncan walked back to the camp and found Sam turning the bacon on the griddle. Sam handed Duncan a cup of coffee and said, "That was a pretty rough way to become a veteran South Fork rafter. How do you feel?"

"Actually, I feel great...and hungry," said Duncan as he took a sip of the coffee. "I hope this isn't some special South Fork coffee concoction?"

Sam smiled, "You're quick. We turn that old phrase, 'Keep your friends close, but keep your enemies closer,' by adding, 'but keep your South Fork buddies the closest because you never know what they put in your drink.' After getting drunk last night and passing out, you are truly one of the South Fork regulars, not a virgin anymore."

Breakfast was the biggest omelet Duncan had ever seen. Fully 24 inches long, 15 inches wide, and 2 inches thick. It was delicious. The best food he had ever tasted. There must be something in the air when you are camping to make the food taste better. After breakfast, they tore down the camp, repacked the gear in the boats and shoved off for a day of fishing and floating. What a life. Maybe I should fish and float and forget about paying off the bloody national debt and becoming president.

The day was glorious, perfect weather with a slight breeze and temperatures in the low 70s. Everyone was catching fish and yelling and whooping and having a great time. Duncan took a turn at rowing while the Speaker and Don fished. He liked to row. He could feel the boat respond to the oars and he had to use all of his strength to keep the boat from bumping into the shore after coming through a couple of mild rapids.

That evening after dinner, everyone was in a more subdued mood. The adrenalin rush of starting the float had worn off. A couple of the guys had drinks before dinner and Irish cream afterwards but not Duncan. He wanted to let his body recover from the previous night's Big Gulp indulgences.

The third day continued with more fishing. Duncan spent more than half the day rowing, getting a better feel for the boat. The group had regained its momentum and that evening everyone was in the mood to talk. Or more correctly, argue.

Speaker Robertson overrode the other conversations when he said loudly, "I have a hypothetical to toss out to the group and I want to hear all of your opinions." Everyone stopped talking to listen to Virgil.

"Last time we had one of these hypotheticals I thought the Hatfields and McCoys lived here on the South Fork," laughed Jim Blake. "Remember that,

Virg? You dragged us into a discussion about the federal government's responsibility to protect the environment." Everyone chuckled a little.

"Yes, you are right, the discussion did get a little heated but I took your thoughts and statements back to Washington and put them into legislation we were working on in the House." The Speaker went on, "and I thank you. Your insights gave me a better approach to use with some of the less enlightened members of Congress."

"Now, I need your help again," said Virgil. "I trust your instincts and I would like to talk about a new situation."

"Is this really a hypothetical or is it a real situation?" said Chip with a bit of sarcasm.

"I think you will all figure that out for yourselves," said Virgil.

Duncan sat in a lawn chair off to the side, on the fringe of the group. He played with the fire by pushing a long stick at the glowing embers and watching the sparks rise out of the flames. He was just going to listen and let the Speaker do his magic.

"Let us say that senior members of the House and the Senate, along with the president and the chief justice of the United States were made aware of an offer to the U.S. government that would change the economic future of the country, possibly change the entire world's economy, for many years." The Speaker continued as he laid out the scenario for those around the campfire, "Let's say that they, as a group, rejected the offer because it would upset the balance of power in Washington."

He let all of this sink in, then added, "And the person making the offer decided to go forward without the backing of the Congress, the president or the Supreme Court."

Everyone around the campfire knew that Virgil Robertson did not throw out this type of discussion for the sport of seeing his friends argue. They knew that some, most, or all of what Virg was saying was probably true. The first to respond was Chip.

"Without knowing what this phenomenal economic offer is, we know that the person making it is prepared to take on the Washington establishment and continue on his quest," Chip said.

"We also know that the person making the offer will want something in return for his generosity," continued Kevin, "but the reason for turning down the offer was because this 'offer' would upset the balance of power in Washington. It was not because of what the generous person wanted in return. Interesting."

"My question is, should the power elite in Washington turn down an offer that potentially can change the economic future of the country because they don't want to risk the balance of power?" asked the Speaker.

Everyone leaned back in his chair; some took a sip of their drinks. They were thinking.

"Nope, they are putting their own personal goals ahead of the country's best interest and that is wrong," came the first response from Don. He usually did not get into the middle of these talks until much later. He usually did a lot of listening before he spoke.

"Don, this must be something you feel strongly about," Virgil said with surprise. "You don't get involved in these talks this early."

"You're damn right," said Don with his voice rising a little. "I'm tired of listening to politicians make promises they will not or cannot keep. Virgil, you are the only politician any of us knows who actually kept your promise to the people who elected you. Now that you are out of Washington, I believe that the snakes have taken over again. I'm not saying this because you are a good friend. What I'm saying is the truth and everyone here and around the country knows it."

Sam Anderson jumped in and said, "Donny is right, we have taken too much bullshit from these politicians and they should at least give us, the voters, the chance to make the choice if it is this big of an offer."

"I agree," said Chris, "this is another example of politicians not being held accountable for their actions and promises. I'm curious, Virg, what kind of an offer could change the economic future of the country?"

"We will get to that in a minute," the Speaker deflected easily. "Brian, what do you think?"

Brian was probably the least talkative of the group, but everyone learned a long time ago that when Brian did speak you should listen and listen carefully. Three years ago Brian had cautioned everyone that the weather was going to change for the worse with rain, snow, and high winds. Everyone thought Brian was letting the liquor do the talking but that night the wind shifted to the north. By morning everyone was nearly frozen with the temperature in the low 20s and wind blowing about 40 miles per hour. Brian had a very finely tuned sixth sense about significant events, be they natural or manmade.

Brian looked at the fire and spoke in slow, quiet voice. "When I look at my kids, I see the future and that's the way it should be. We should see the future in our kids. But when I look to Washington, I do not see the type of government that will make the future secure for my kids and I get worried. I'm a simple man and simple men understand clearly what a promise is and, more importantly, when a promise is broken. I agree with Don, we need to ask more of the people who run the government in Washington. When I hear that the president and top people in the Senate and the House and the Supreme Court are not acting in the best interest of the country, I worry for my kids' future."

As always, Brian had a way of presenting the obvious without all the flowery crap. What was at stake here was the future of the country, not the political ego of a few individuals.

Virgil Robertson started talking again. "The reason I ask these questions is that this is a very real situation. The offer was made earlier this summer. It was rejected by a group that included the president, the current Speaker of the House, the majority and minority leaders of the senate, the chief justice of the United States, and other top officials like the chairman of the Federal Reserve Board and the secretary of the treasury.

"I don't want to turn our annual float down the South Fork into a political forum but I need you all to help me with this." The Speaker continued, "I have been asked to help the person making the offer and I am seriously considering it. What do you think? Chip? Steve?"

Chip got up and walked to the aluminum dry box that held the food. He pulled out the bottle of Irish crème, poured some into his coffee, walked back and stood in front of the fire.

"I need more information." Chip explained, "I need to know what the offer was or is and I need to know what the person wanted in return."

Everyone nodded and looked at Virgil who looked at the whole group, then said, "All right. This person offered to pay off the U.S. national debt which is about five and a half trillion dollars." He stopped to let that sink in. No one spoke, they all looked into the fire.

"In return, he wants to be President of the United States," continued the Speaker. Everyone now looked up at Virgil. They had heard two of the most incredible things they could think of in less than one minute.

Sam stood and said, "Now that is one hell of a deal. Pay off the national debt and become president."

Kevin asked the obvious question, "Virg, how do you know all of this? You have been gone from Washington for three years, you're retired."

"Good question," answered the Speaker. "I have met this man and he told me all of this personally..." Virg held up his hand to hold the comments "... and I confirmed it with not one but two very reliable and trusted people who were part of the inner circle that rejected the offer."

"You have met someone who has five or six trillion dollars and is willing to use it to pay off the national debt?" Jim asked, incredulously. "Sounds like we need to send him to the psych ward, not the White House." Everyone laughed. This broke the spell holding back the conversation and all of a sudden everyone was talking.

"What is the interest on five and a half trillion dollars ($5,500,000,000,000) something like what, 350 billion dollars per year and what part of the national budget is 350 billion? I don't believe that one person has that much money. I have never read about anyone having that kind of private fortune. Even if he has that much net worth, how will he convert it to hard cash without upsetting the stock and money markets?" The comments continued until Virgil raised his hand to get their attention.

"I will ask my question again," said the Speaker in a strong voice. "Should I help this man become President of the United States in return for paying off the national debt?"

All that could be heard was the popping of the wood in the fire and the noises of the river. Sam looked across the fire and said, "We haven't heard a peep from you, Duncan. What do you think about all this?"

Duncan scanned the group and tried to judge their position, then said, "I think I have heard a lot for one night. I am going to have to sleep on this before I can honestly answer. This is a pretty big deal and I need to sort out some of the issues including the most compelling one that Brian presented. Is this right for the future of the country? But I will tell you one thing, my Uncle Shamus taught me early in life that having a large debt over your head can truly hamper your ability to clearly see the future because all you can think about is meeting next month's interest payment."

Everyone nodded agreement and Virgil said, "That is an excellent way to end the evening. We can talk some more later, maybe not tomorrow, but later in the week."

Most of the group made their way to their tents and sleeping bags. A couple of the guys headed to the river for night fishing.

Duncan watched them as they moved around the camp making sure that everything was secure for the night.

Duncan stared into the fire and thought about what he heard this evening. Honest gut reactions to his plan to pay off the U.S. national debt of almost six trillion dollars and probably a fair gauge of what he could expect when the plan went public.

Virgil Robertson brought him to Idaho and on this float so Virg could observe and listen to some of his closest friends as they mulled over Duncan's plan. Virg will bring up the plan later in the week but Duncan had made up his mind yesterday. It would still be interesting to hear the comments from this group because those comments might very well be significant as he created his campaign credo. Sort of a South Fork of the Snake River think tank.

He had Shamus's blessing to move forward and he knew that Virgil Robertson would mentor him through the next year or two until the election. Duncan also had the money to not only keep his promise about paying off the national debt but also finance a campaign to get elected president.

Duncan switched from the hypothetical to the real as he made a mental project outline to accomplish something that had never been done before. The only really unpredictable difficulty is that he is not married and an unmarried president did not sit well with the public. But he had not even considered getting married since Blanca and baby Ian died.

Could I find someone whom I could love and marry? Who is the woman that will love me, be my partner, soul mate, lover, the mother of my children and First Lady, all at the same time?

Did she really exist or was this just the wishful thinking of a lonely man?

Maybe I have already met her. The list is very short with only one real choice. I think I will call her when we get off the river in a couple of days.

Not only must I convince the American people that my offer is real and not some soon forgotten, unfulfilled political promise, but I must also woo the woman I want to marry and get her to accept that spending a large sum of money to become President of the United States is worth it.

Duncan stood and headed to his tent. His thoughts wandered to that day in Mendoza almost twenty-six years ago after burying his wife and son.

He told Shamus and Isabella that God must not like him very much because his mother, his father, his wife and his son had all died before their time.

His brow furrowed with deep thought as he remembered one of Shamus's most quoted prophecies — 'The more things change; the more they remain the same."

Things had changed significantly over the last 25 or so years but contrary to Shamus's prophecy God now liked him. Duncan made his peace with God during the two years of almost unbearable grief he suffered after the loss of Blanca and baby Ian.

Duncan looked at the stars sparkling above the river and he smiled to himself when he visualized the end of the Oath of Office ceremony when he will say in a clear, sincere voice, "And may God continue to bless America." The thought alone made him stand a bit straighter and taller as he felt his chest swell with pride because all of this pay-off-the-national-debt idea started with a dream to honor his mother's fierce patriotic love of America.

His mother taught him when he was a child that God blesses America every day and when he is sworn in as President of the United States on a not-so-distant day in January with his mother Liddy and his father Ian watching from their heavenly angel perch, a particularly special and much-needed blessing will be fulfilled when their son Duncan Logan Stuart-Bruce pays off the U.S. national debt, making him —

The 6,000,000,000,000 Dollar Man.